Plum Upside Down

Plum Upside Down

A Farm Fresh Romance
Book 5

Valerie Comer

Dedication

For my mother-in-law,
Deanna

Thanks for raising
such a wonderful son.
I am so blessed.

Romances by Valerie Comer

Farm Fresh Romance Novels
Raspberries and Vinegar
Wild Mint Tea
Sweetened with Honey
Dandelions for Dinner
Plum Upside Down
Berry on Top (winter 2016)

Riverbend Romance Novellas (ebook only)
Secretly Yours
Pinky Promise
Sweet Serenade
Team Bride
Merry Kisses

Acknowledgements

Thanks to Kathy, who shared her journal with me of the dark days while her son fought Fusobacterium Necroforum in 2007. She took another trip "through the wringer" while reading and commenting on those chapters in this book, helping me to get it right. With Kathy, I'm so thankful to Jehovah Rapha for healing her son... my nephew.

Thanks to Pastor Tom, who persuaded me to cohost Alpha with Jack. I'm so blessed to have been a part of the journey for Liz, Marion, Jackie and Les. Thanks, also, to Nicky Gumbel, visionary of the Alpha program.

Thanks to Marion Ueckermann and her niece Melanie for giving me a taste of Pretoria, South Africa, including an insider peek at Steve Biko Academic Hospital. Any errors in the story I've managed to introduce myself!

Thanks to Sally Shupe, Robin Mason, and Melanie Pike for providing excellent feedback as beta readers for the earliest version of this manuscript. You ladies *rock!*

A huge shout-out to my fellow travelers within the Christian Indie Authors Facebook group and my blogger buddies at www.inspyromance.com. What amazing folks to share the writing journey with.

Thanks to my fans for reviews, emails, encouragement, and prayers. Also, the gals on my Street Team are amazing and right there the moment I need help. I don't know how I managed without you as long as I did.

Thanks to my friend and editor, Nicole O'Dell, for walking many miles through Green Acres' manuscripts and helping me make the Farm Fresh Romance series so much stronger.

Thanks to my husband, Jim, for always loving me, always believing in me, and always supporting my dreams. Thanks also to my kids and grandgirls who show me unconditional love every single day. You all mean more to me than I can express.

I am so very thankful to worship a God who not only heals but loves me deeply and personally. He loves you the same way. I pray you know Him. If you want to talk about it, shoot me an email!

Chapter 1 --

Chelsea Riehl heard the voices before she rounded the corner on her way to the straw bale house across the yard.

"No, it's fine. I'm glad to help." Keanan Welsh? Who was he speaking with? He hadn't been at Green Acres Farm much longer than Chelsea had and was more than a little strange. "It will be good for her to get some use. We've been together in the Andes several times."

Who was *she,* and why had she been to South America? Chelsea frowned, turning toward the voices. Keanan towered over a guy she didn't know as they stood next to a beat-up truck. Both men had hair past their shoulders, only Keanan's was tied back with a strand of leather. The other guy had dreads.

Seriously? Hadn't she left all that behind in Portland?

The shorter guy pumped Keanan's hand. "I'll take good care of it. I can't thank you enough."

"Shoot me an email from time to time. Photos, man. I will enjoy it through you."

Which still didn't explain who *she* was.

The guy tossed a long nylon bag into the back of the truck.

"My prayers go with you, my friend. God will bless you." Keanan clamped a large hand on the other man's shoulder and began to pray.

Chelsea was so out of there. Not that she didn't believe in God or prayer. She absolutely did. But, in the week she'd known him, Keanan repelled her as much as he fascinated her. He might be sort of good-looking underneath that mass of hair. He might be a really nice guy as her sister said. He didn't even smell bad like she'd thought he might. But what made a guy like him tick?

His upbringing was obviously vastly different from hers. Polar opposite from the upper-middle-class Portland home she'd lived in with two parents who loved each other and their three kids. Who took them to church on Sunday and a private Christian school five other days of the week. She couldn't even imagine the hippie commune he must've lived on. He probably had a wardrobe of tie-dye — not that she'd seen any yet — and a best friend named Starshine Harmony.

She slipped into the relative coolness of the straw bale house that served as Green Acres' headquarters. This whole communal farm thing was right up her alley. Chelsea had been trying to get onboard for three years, almost since the beginning. Now she was finally in Idaho, but so was that irritating Keanan Welsh.

Her sister, Sierra, glanced over at her across the peninsula separating the kitchen from the dining area. "Whew, glad you're here. The guys just dropped off four more boxes of Italian plums. They're trying to get them all picked before the starlings beat them to it."

The raucous black birds had descended like a plague of grasshoppers yesterday. Apparently that meant the plums were ripe, and it was now a race to the finish line to see if the humans could get their fair share before the scavengers pecked a hole in each one.

Chelsea rolled her shoulders as she crossed the space and into the kitchen. "Well, I'm ready to start." The words trailed off as the reality of the fruit invasion slammed her brain like a landslide. Boxes of purple fruit covered every horizontal surface. "Whoa."

Her sister grinned, brandishing a knife. "There's more coming, but also more help. You get a choice. Washing or pitting."

"I thought everything was organic. Why do we have to wash them?" Chelsea took a large bite from a crisp plum. Just green enough to balance the juicy sweetness of it. Warm still from the early September sun.

"It's true we haven't sprayed the trees. Plums are amazingly resilient to disease and pests."

"Other than starlings."

"Birds know ripe fruit when they see it." Sierra split a plum, placed both halves cut-side-up on a dehydrator tray, and dropped the pit in a bucket. "But anyway, there's still the possibility of exhaust from the vehicles creating a film on them. And wildlife in the trees. It's better to be safe than sorry."

"I'll start with washing, I guess." Chelsea eyed the deep sink full of dark purple golf balls.

"We can trade off. We'll have more hands soon. It will go quickly, I promise."

Promises wouldn't make it happen. She'd hoped to use her organizational talent more than her knife-wielding skill but, so far, she'd barely cracked open her laptop even to answer emails let alone create any new processes. Of course, it took a lot of work to feed ten adults and several kids a varied, healthy, and mostly homegrown diet. She'd bet it had been a lot easier the first year or so when it had been only her sister and her two girlfriends.

Chelsea sighed and walked over to the sink. "Just rub them and put them in the other sink?"

"Yep. There's a basket there to fill."

Catchy praise music breezed in via the house's wireless sound system. Chelsea caught herself humming along as she turned the faucet to little more than a dribble. She knew the rule. *Don't waste water.*

"Considering you moved in right next door, I hardly see you," Sierra commented from the island behind her. Plink, plink went fruit onto the trays. "Are you settling in okay?"

"Sure, I'm fine. The duplex has lots of room for one person. Well, you know."

Sierra chuckled. "Yes, I felt the same when I moved into the other half. Hard to believe it was a year ago already. For the record, the unit is still plenty big enough for *two* people."

Chelsea wouldn't tease her newlywed sister about how they'd fit when babies came along. Not when Sierra's endometriosis made pregnancy a long shot.

"You can splash some paint in there, you know," Sierra went on. "You don't have to keep it to Allison's rather austere taste."

Allison Hart had lived in Chelsea's unit for the past several months, but now her adorable timber-frame house had been completed on the hillside, and she and her young nephew had moved up there. That'd opened a space for Chelsea.

Too bad for Keanan. He'd lived in his tent since spring. Not that anything seemed to faze him, and he'd welcomed her as warmly as everyone else. No talk about how he'd been here first or anything like that. Last spring the guy had just ridden his bicycle onto the property, pitched his tent, and stayed.

Unfathomable.

What had they been talking about? Right. "The gray walls provide a terrific backdrop, though." That would get a reaction.

"Gray?" sputtered Sierra. "A great backdrop for what? Talk about a depressing color. I'm not even sure it's an improvement over white or beige."

Yep, Chelsea still knew her big sister's buttons. There was strange comfort in that. "For art, silly, though I wouldn't mind having at least one wall of my bedroom pink. And then there's the spare room. I know the farm mural was painted for Allison's nephew, but it's a little much for me." She hesitated. "I hate to hurt anyone's feelings the first week I'm here. I can live with it."

"It's your home now." Sierra plunked a basket beside the sink and began filling it with washed fruit. "Besides, Brent did another mural for Finnley in the new house. I see no reason why you can't cover it. In fact, I'll give you a hand, but it might have to wait until we're finished with the garden."

"Now why does that sound so ominous?" muttered Chelsea.

"Ominous? Girl, if you have the energy to paint after a fourteen-hour day of canning tomatoes or cutting and wrapping meat, you're way ahead of the rest of us. Today is nothing compared to what's coming."

And she was bored after ten minutes of washing plums. Why again had she signed up for this?

o0o

Keanan Welsh pushed open the door to the straw bale house. This building welcomed him as few ever had, following the ideas of a book on pattern language he'd studied in college. Everything from the deep windowsills to the sunlight flowing in from various angles to the nook by the fireplace had been designed to ease the human spirit at a subconscious level. Even knowing how it was done didn't diminish his pleasure in the result.

The two sisters worked in the kitchen, chatting about fashion. Keanan steeled himself and crossed the dining room to enter the space. "I'm here to help."

Whoa. The fruit-pickers hadn't been kidding when they said the kitchen was backlogged.

Sierra glanced up, her face wreathed in a grin. "Grab a knife. We have all three dehydrators to load in the sunroom."

He lifted a paring knife. "It's a welcome change to face plums instead of peaches like last week."

Sierra's sister shot him a strange look from over at the sink. A pink flowered scarf held her curly hair off her face. "So what do we do with all of these?" she asked.

Good question. There had been few plums in the diet since he'd arrived at Green Acres in May. He angled a glance at Sierra across the island as he pitted.

"We have them for breakfast in smoothies or stewed fruit. We eat the dry ones plain as snacks. We layer the frozen ones into desserts like cakes and crumbles. We go through a lot of plum sauce on meat." Sierra set a loaded tray aside and began filling another. "Noel will make a batch of mead with some of them."

"I didn't realize they were so versatile." Keanan nodded. "What happens to any excess plums? Do we process them all no matter what?" He had visions of the boxes Noel and Gabe were filling outside. A truckload of plums seemed excessive, even for this community.

"The chickens and pigs will get any we don't use."

"Ah, I wondered if there were folks in Galena Landing who might like some."

Sierra eyed him. "Possibly. But a lot of them have a tree or two in the backyard. I doubt anyone hankering plums doesn't have access."

"Would it be all right take a few boxes into town with my bike and trailer and ask around? Not to deny the chickens, of course.

But what if there are people who might enjoy them?"

"We can ask what the group thinks." Sierra scooted another tray over. "Want to slide these into the dehydrator?"

"No problem." He balanced several trays on top of each other and rounded the stone fireplace wall to the sunroom doors. A moment later, mission completed, he headed back to the kitchen.

"...weird," said Chelsea.

"Shh," replied Sierra.

Keanan frowned. They'd been talking about him, no doubt, and the farm's newcomer didn't approve of him. Well, he didn't exactly approve of her, either, with her penchant for makeup and fashion. Even now she wore a pink top to match that scarf, below-the-knee beige pants, and sandals with heels. Oh, and a chunky necklace like the kind Mother designed. For working in the kitchen.

He glanced her way as he walked past.

Her head was bent over the sink, curls all but hiding her face. "Who was that guy outside?"

A nice break from talking about plums. "Logan Dermott. I met him just the other day, but he's been in the valley picking fruit much of the summer."

"Oh? Where's he from?"

Keanan sliced open another plum. "I'm not sure."

He heard or sensed Chelsea turning from the sink, but he didn't look at her. "Then what did you give him?"

"Oh, that?" He chuckled. "My tent. He's going on a trip to Argentina, talking with mission groups about helping the indigenous people regain food security."

"You *gave* your tent to some guy you don't even know? Seriously?"

That was strange, how? Keanan met Chelsea's gaze. Not only were the frames of her glasses pink, she apparently looked at life through rose tints as well. "Why not? He needs it. I don't."

"But—" She shook her head hard, and those curls flew out sideways like so many corkscrews.

"Why is that a problem?" Not that it was any of her business. His tent, his decision. End of story.

"Where are you going to sleep?"

"Not to worry. I won't force myself into the spare bedroom in your duplex."

Her eyes grew large. "You better believe you won't."

This was a woman who could get under his skin. Keanan took a deep breath and let it out slowly. Then again. "My grain bins will be arriving on the weekend, and I'll be staying next door in Zach's parents' spare room until my home is insulated and ready for me to move into."

Chelsea took a step closer. "I think I'm not hearing you correctly. You plan to live in a *grain bin*?"

Sierra snickered, but Keanan had no trouble ignoring that. "I do, in fact. It will be quite snug. It will have solar panels for electricity. Even a bathroom so I needn't cross the yard to shower or brush my teeth."

"You're serious."

"Uh... yes?"

"A grain bin. Wait, you said plural."

"Yes. One is fitted inside the other with straw tamped between them for insulation."

Chelsea looked at her sister then back at him. "Okay, joke's over. What are your real plans?"

"To live in a grain bin." Keanan's patience ebbed. "Which, honestly, is no business of yours. You don't need to look at it. You don't need to visit. It will be tucked away on the hillside where my tent was, and you can ignore its very existence. You can ignore *my* very existence. It's all the same to me."

Her eyes grew wide behind those ridiculous glasses, and her painted lips pursed. She whirled back to the sink, her curls flying out sideways.

Perhaps it *wasn't* all the same to him. But it might as well be.

Chapter 2 --

*Y*ou guys need a hand?" Claire Kenzie, one of the farm's original owners, entered the kitchen through the mudroom door.

Wasn't it obvious?

Sierra glanced over at her longtime friend. "We're doing okay, I think."

In what universe? Chelsea rolled her shoulders. She wasn't used to standing in one spot — even on a rubber mat — for the better part of the day. Sitting at her computer, making phone calls, shopping for party decorations were in her skill set.

Sierra glanced at the whiteboard covering the pantry door, where the week's kitchen schedule had been scrawled with a red dry-erase pen. "You're on supper tonight? Are we in your way?"

Claire grinned at Sierra then winked at Chelsea. "I figured this might happen, so we prepped last night. Noel's famous potato salad is in the fridge, and he'll toss burgers on the grill when we're ready."

Chelsea shook her head. "Seriously? You prepped last night? Am I the only one totally exhausted at the end of a workday around here?" And she was on dessert. Groan. What would everyone say to a basket of plums on the table?

She would not look at Keanan, who chopped fruit for sauce. The guy hadn't taken a break all day, unless he'd done so when she'd gone to switch laundry loads.

Claire stepped up behind her and began to massage Chelsea's shoulders. "I guess we're used to it."

"Ow." Chelsea flinched away from Claire's strong fingers. "But don't stop. You found the killer spot."

Claire chuckled. "Listen, why don't I take over here and you can toss a salad for supper? It will use different muscles."

"Really? That would be awesome."

"Shoo, then." Claire hip-checked her away from the sink. "I've got this."

Chelsea wiped her hands on a towel. Should she feel badly that she got out of plums but Keanan didn't? Nah, a big manly guy like him wouldn't want to make a salad anyway, and he probably had muscles to burn. Actually, she knew he did. His thick biceps were unmistakable with his shirtsleeves rolled up. Even his tanned forearms flexed muscle as he chopped.

She averted her gaze. She didn't find him attractive in any way. She was just fascinated by the sheer bulk of him without an ounce of fat. That was all.

"Want to swap, Keanan?" asked Sierra.

He shrugged. "If you like." His gaze flicked past Sierra to Chelsea.

Did Keanan seriously have green eyes? That wasn't just an old wives' tale about redheads? Not that his hair was exactly red. It was darker, more like auburn. The color of autumn leaves.

His eyebrows rose.

She'd been staring. A burn rushed up her cheeks. She grabbed a basket and broke eye contact. "I'll be out in the garden."

Who was she telling? No clue.

oOo

Keanan leaned back in his chair after an amazing meal. He'd visited dozens of cooperatives around the world, even stayed at one or two for the better part of a year before moving on. Never had he even contemplated settling down until arriving in northern Idaho last May. But then, he'd never found a community that matched all his values, including spiritual, before this.

Green Acres filled him with its satisfying physical labor, with the men, women, and families who loved God and valued His creation. Jo Nemesek, one of the original members, bulged with new life. A sign of growth for the future.

From beyond her, Jo's husband, Zach, spoke up. "How did today go for everyone?"

The man was a veterinarian in the nearby town of Galena Landing, yet pitched in solidly on his days off. Keanan could respect a man who just rolled up his sleeves and did what he could.

"I'm plum tuckered out," Sierra replied with a grin.

Keanan laughed.

Sierra's husband, Gabe, chuckled as he slid his arm across the back of her chair. "I think we all are. But Noel and I got the last of the plums picked. You've got Keanan to thank for sorting out the ones the starlings pecked and tossing a few buckets of those to the pigs."

Keanan leaned forward so he could see Gabe better. "How many more boxes outside?"

Gabe tipped his head to the side and glanced at Noel. "There's probably another six boxes in the truck. What do you think, Noel?"

"Two hundred pounds, maybe two fifty."

From across the table, Chelsea groaned.

Had no one told her farming was work? She wore every emotion on her sleeve. Not that her layered pink top had sleeves.

Not that her tanned arms could possibly be natural. Not that he cared.

Keanan yanked his gaze back to Claire. "Are you the one who decides when we've canned, dried, and frozen enough plums for this crew for the winter?" He swept his hand to indicate the twelve people around the table, children included.

"Is food coordinator my new title?" Claire laughed. "I'm sure we have enough. It's not like plums are the only fruit we have around here. It's just that we're not into wasting food, and the good Lord provided plenty of plums this year."

"Hoarding is waste of a different kind." He needed to be careful not to offend anyone. "If the freezer is full of plums, there is no room for meat. If the canning jars are full of plums, where will the tomatoes go?"

After all, as soon as the plums were dealt with, garden tomatoes would once again resume center stage.

"Good point." Claire nodded. "It's a hard habit to break. Any suggestions?"

"Do you think anyone in town who could use them?"

"I could talk to the Smiths," put in Gabe. "See if they'd like to sell some through Nature's Pantry."

Chelsea tipped two manicured thumbs up.

Keanan caught the gesture from the corner of his eye. Not that her opinion mattered. She only wanted to get out of the labor. All that water must be hard on her nails.

"We can give it a try," Zach said. "I can take a box to the clinic and see if I can give them away. Can you use more at the nursing home, love?" he asked Jo.

"I already took some in, but the chef might want to make some desserts as well as serving them as a snack."

"Don't all the old people need prunes to keep them regular?" Noel asked.

Claire glared at him.

"It was a joke." He held up both hands.

"The staff orders prunes by the case from a distributor." Jo pursed her lips. "They don't have the means to dry plums anyway, and I'm not we could meet the demand."

"Did you have any further ideas, Keanan?" asked Claire.

"I thought I'd go door-to-door with my bike and trailer and see if I could give them away." He looked around the table, avoiding Chelsea's gaze. She was new, and didn't understand all the ins and outs. "I do realize it would take time away from work."

"Take a farm truck," suggested Noel. "Less time, more capacity. I'm all for off-loading these plums to other people who might want them."

Gabe leaned forward to look at Keanan past Sierra. "As far as I'm concerned, take what's left in the truck now. I don't think the girls want to see more plums in the kitchen any more than you do."

Chelsea nodded in Keanan's peripheral vision, and he felt a surge of irritation. He really shouldn't let her bug him so much. A city girl like her, she'd be gone in no time. If he were the gambling sort, he'd bet she wouldn't last a month. At the longest, she'd stay through Thanksgiving. What they needed around here were people who knew how to work, not prissy women in scarves, heels, and nail polish.

Definitely not a single woman who was doubtless on the hunt for a husband, not that she'd given him a second glance that way. He ought to grow his hair a little longer, maybe stop shaving if it would repel her further. Make sure everyone around here remembered he was single by choice, that throwing him together with Chelsea onto the same work teams just because they were the only singles on the farm — Allison was engaged to Brent and didn't count — didn't mean they were the slightest bit suited. Just look at her.

No, don't.

She was watching him. As was everyone else.

"Keanan? You must've been a million miles away." Jo's elbow caught his ribs lightly. "Noel asked if you wanted to do it this evening."

He nodded, sharper than he'd intended. "Sounds good. I can head out right away."

Chelsea jumped up. "Have dessert first. Let me get it." A moment later she returned to the table with a large cast iron skillet exuding an aroma of sugar, cinnamon, and… plums?

"Smells great." Noel stood. "I'll get the ice cream."

"When did you whip this up?" Jo turned to Chelsea. "Last I saw you, you looked like you were dragging."

"It didn't take long. There were plenty of sliced plums." Chelsea's gaze caught Keanan's for an instant. "Besides, the schedule said I was on dessert, and I didn't want to disappoint."

It didn't smell disappointing in the least.

Sierra peered across the table. "Is that Auntie Pam's recipe for plum upside-down cake?"

Chelsea nodded. "I asked Mom for it. It's one of the few memories I have of our aunt before she died of cancer."

"Oh, man. I'd forgotten all about that recipe." Sierra's gaze didn't leave the dessert as Chelsea served.

Noel added a scoop of ice cream to each and passed the plates down the long farmhouse table.

"Plum cake?" asked Jo and Zach's two-year-old daughter. "Maddie lub plum cake."

"Here comes a little dish for you, Maddie," said Noel. "And one for Finnley." He handed two smaller servings along.

"Thank you," murmured Allison's five-year-old nephew, Finnley, his eyes fixed on his serving.

"Maddie tank-u." The little girl nodded as Jo offered a bowl to her. "Good."

Noel returned the ice cream to the freezer as they all dug into dessert.

The ice cream melted onto the warm cake, forming milky rivulets. Keanan lifted a forkful, allowing the aroma to fill his nostrils before taking his first bite. Amazing. His eyes widened and he couldn't help the glance he shot at Chelsea.

Why was she watching him, then looking down with a pink face to match the rest of her? Did she actually care what he thought of it? Him, in particular?

"Great stuff!" Claire said. "Might need another box of plums in the freezer if that means we can look forward to more of these all winter."

Chelsea turned to Claire. "Do you really like it?"

"Totally. I hope you'll put the recipe in the file box in the kitchen."

Noel took a bite. "This is great, Chelsea."

"Wow, it sure it." Allison saluted her with her fork.

Chelsea glanced at Keanan.

He cleared his throat. "Very good." He wouldn't be stingy with words of praise. Not over such a delectable dessert.

She picked up her fork. "I'm glad you all like it."

oOo

Why did it matter to her what Keanan Welsh's opinion of her cake was? His opinion of *her*? That was utterly ridiculous.

Chelsea slammed the last plates into the dishwasher and added detergent. Green detergent, of course. Biodegradable and septic tank safe.

Well, okay, it was because he didn't seem to think she could do anything right, not that he'd used words to express his opinion. He didn't need to. The distaste was evident on his face.

The farm truck rumbled out of the yard, the sound of its engine diminishing in the distance.

Finally. Chelsea's shoulders sagged with relief. With him off the farm, she could relax a little. Feel less judged. Maybe enjoy the final kitchen cleanup, even knowing they'd do it all over again tomorrow, only with tomatoes.

She glanced at the schedule on the whiteboard as she turned on the dishwasher. Gabe was on cleanup with her, but her brother-in-law hadn't come in the kitchen yet. Well, there wasn't much left to do besides the baking dishes. She turned toward the sink.

Keanan popped the plug into the deep sink and turned on the hot water.

Chelsea's heart sped up even as her shoulders slumped. "Um, you're not Gabe at all."

Keanan glanced at her. "Excellent observation." He added a squirt of detergent.

Frowning, she looked at the schedule again. No, she hadn't misread it. "Where's Gabe?"

"He phoned the people at Nature's Pantry and they said they'd take all the plums, so he's gone to deliver them."

"Oh. I guess that makes sense. He used to own that health food store."

Keanan's eyebrows went up. "He did?"

Aha. Something she knew that he didn't. "Yes, for years. He sold it around Christmastime last year then went away to school."

"Interesting."

He didn't sound interested. His tone was a conversation stopper if she'd ever heard one. Whatever. "Want me to dry, or shall I sweep and do the rest of the cleanup?"

His jaw twitched. "I should have asked you which you preferred."

"It doesn't matter, really."

He shrugged.

Fine. She'd sweep then do a spot-wash of the floor. A few plums had left sticky splotches. No need to leave those, even though the floor would need attention again tomorrow. She forced her mind out of that direction. From what Sierra had said, they had weeks of daily canning and freezing still to come.

Chelsea applied the broom to the etched concrete floor with perhaps more enthusiasm than necessary. She eyed the rubber pad by the sink and the bits of kitchen debris around Keanan's feet. Those hippie sandals must be at least size twelve.

He shifted out of her way and she quickly ran the broom across the worst of the mat. "Thanks," she murmured and carried on.

This was a huge commercial kitchen. How could one guy fill the space the way Keanan did? He took up so much room it even crowded into her head.

Enough already.

Chapter 3 --

*O*h, come on. You can't convince me you're not curious to see what grain bins look like before they become a house." Sierra leaned against the closed door inside Chelsea's duplex.

Seriously? "I've seen them before." Chelsea rubbed her curls with a towel. "Besides, I just got out of the shower and don't want to catch my death of a cold. Do you know what the temperature is out there this morning?"

"We had a frost last night, but don't worry. The garden coverings kept the produce from freezing. The guys pulled the old quilts off before going over to help set up Keanan's place."

So the topic had come around again. Her sister was nothing if not persistent. "I really don't care about his pet project, okay? I'm not that interested in architecture."

Sierra studied her. "Well, that's a change. You were the one who always wanted to drive around the fancy neighborhoods to look at the houses."

"And that has what to do with grain bins? Aren't you embarrassed what the neighborhood is going to look like?"

"Not at all." Sierra pursed her lips. "The pictures Keanan showed us from the Internet looked pretty cool, actually. Innovative recycling, and a home that will last much longer than this duplex." She snapped her fingers. "Oh, and eventually it will be recyclable in turn."

Chelsea rolled her eyes. "So recycling is more important than beauty? Than charm?"

"I think this is going to have both."

A large truck's backup beeps sounded from the end of the driveway.

"Come on, Chelsea. Don't be a stick in the mud. Come cheer Keanan on. It's a big day for him."

"Go ahead. Enjoy it. I'm making a pot of tea."

Sierra crossed to the range and turned the kettle off. "No, you're not. Get your jacket on."

"Excuse me?" Chelsea dropped her hands to her hips. "Just because you're my big sister doesn't give you the ri—"

"True. This has nothing to do with being part of the Riehl family and everything to do with being part of the Green Acres family." Sierra marched over to the closet, grabbed Chelsea's coat, and held it out. Her expression brooked no argument.

"He is not my family," muttered Chelsea as she shrugged into the jacket.

"That's where you're wrong. Nobody said you had to marry the guy, but you've both officially joined the team here. And that means you make an effort." Sierra paused, her hand on the doorknob. "Don't make me sorry I recommended you to the others."

"Oh, now I'm here only because I'm your sister? Not because I have skills of my own this place badly needs? And not skills at washing plums, I might add."

"Grow up, Chels." Sierra wrenched the door open and stalked outside.

If only she'd walk away so Chelsea could go back in and turn the kettle on. From her sister's glare, she guessed that wasn't happening. Chelsea shoved her feet into her Crocs and followed

Sierra out.

"I really don't know what's gotten into you since you moved here. You used to be fun."

"So did you."

Sierra searched her face. "Okay, really. Something's gotten under your skin. Want to talk about it?"

Chelsea sank her hands into the pockets of her jacket. Her sister was right, but how could she tell Sierra what was wrong when she had no clue herself?

In a few minutes they were close enough to see the crane lift a round corrugated metal object as Keanan watched from beside Brent, their resident contractor. A surge of irritation at the sight of the tall redhead ran through her.

But that was dumb. Why should she let him bother her? No reason at all. Live and let live. She'd ignore him, and he'd ignore her. The work of the farm would carry on, and sooner or later he'd get tired of it and abandon his grain bins and move along, rejoining his tent in some foreign country.

Couldn't come soon enough. They could use the round structures for storing something like grain. Now there was an idea.

The first truck moved out of the building site with grinding gears, and the guys bolted the bin's base to the footings while the second backed into place. The crane lowered the second bin around the first, and Brent climbed up a ladder, probably making sure the space between the two was relatively uniform.

Gabe slid an arm around Sierra. "Now that's the fastest I've ever seen a house go up."

Chelsea shot a look at her brother-in-law. "It doesn't have a roof. Or windows." She snapped her fingers. "Oh, and don't you think a door would be useful?"

"All in good time." Gabe's gaze slid back to Sierra. "I think this is genius. Want to live in a grain bin, honey? Keanan says there are more where those came from."

Sierra tilted her head to one side. "Hmm. I might have to see it finished before I decide one way or the other."

"You're kidding, right?" Chelsea shook her head.

"Not necessarily. I find the idea intriguing."

Whatever. Brent, Keanan, and the driver were engaged in an arm-waving discussion, while the other guys came over to the spectator area.

Chelsea'd had enough. "Excuse me. My morning tea awaits, or I won't be ready for another tomato canning day." She turned and strode away, her sister's protest masked by the semi's engine.

She could be glad of one thing. Keanan would no doubt be too busy playing with his big toys to help in the kitchen. She'd gladly put in a longer day if he were occupied elsewhere. It would be a relief, really.

oOo

Keanan snapped a chalk line then Brent hauled out his electric saw and carved a doorway out of the exterior bin. Minutes later, he cut the matching hole from the interior bin.

Brent examined the edges and nodded. "I'll get the door frame in place before anyone slices a hand on that sharp lip."

Keanan entered the twenty-one-foot diameter circle. At 364 square feet, it wouldn't be a large house, though the square footage would double when he and Brent laid the joists for the second floor. He looked up, imagining the completed building. A clear autumn sky peered back at him, only a few light clouds looming in the west. The ribbed galvanized steel gave an industrial feel, but he could live with that. So many shanties in third world countries used a sheet of a similar product. On rainy days, they were the lucky ones. On hot days, the sun beat mercilessly on them.

He was blessed. So blessed. He had the privilege of insulating this place. The honor of creating a home for himself at little cost. He stood in the center, spread his hands, and bowed his head, murmuring a grateful prayer to the Lord above who'd given him so much more than he deserved. Could ever deserve.

This evening he'd bring his guitar and play some worship songs.

"What do you think, man?"

Keanan blinked and shook his head. He hadn't heard Brent come up beside him. "It overwhelms me. So simple, yet so beautiful."

"It has a charm all its own. I'll always prefer wood, but your solution is certainly cost-effective, to say nothing of unique. I can already imagine all the cars turning around at the end of Thompson Road as folks ogle your house."

Ogle? "That's not my intention."

Brent shrugged. "I know. But Green Acres causes enough curiosity in these parts. You've just added another reason for them to come."

Hard to figure. Sure, he'd seen a few people staring from slow-moving cars as he drove the team of horses while cutting hay. But there was nothing beyond the farm save a rutted forestry road. It was not as though they were on the way to anywhere, which was one of the reasons he loved this place.

"They can't see much from the road. I left a band of trees." He'd only cut down six, in fact. Why should the land be disturbed for his human needs? Yet the trucks had required access to his knoll. More trucks would come and go before the job was completed.

"The trees will offer some privacy." Brent adjusted his tool belt. "Gabe and I looked over the list of available personnel. We'll get everyone including Allison's students over here Monday morning to start pounding straw into the gap. When it's packed to the window line, we'll call a break until we can get those in."

"I hadn't expected help. Don't we need everyone to preserve the garden produce?"

"There are enough hands to go around, and this is just as important as the winter's food supply. You can't very well sleep out here in the snow." Brent indicated the small stack of windows at the far edge of the clearing. "How many of these are going on the main floor, again?"

"Five." Keanan pointed across from the door. "Two above the kitchen sink there." He pivoted to the right. "One in the bathroom." Then to the left. "Two there, on either side of the wood stove." He could see it clearly in his mind, as though it were already complete.

Would a woman ever stamp this place with softer touches?

Where had that thought come from? He was thirty. Women rarely caught his eye long enough for a second glance. He'd worked beside many of them to alleviate suffering in various parts of the world, and never desired a one.

That curly-haired fairy who'd newly arrived at Green Acres was a good example of someone he'd never be interested in. Rude and spiteful. She detested him. Made no sense. She barely knew him. How could she hate someone she didn't even know?

"Lost in thought?"

He blinked, turning toward Brent's voice and waving his hand to encompass the circle. "She is beautiful. I am all but speechless."

Brent hefted a plank destined to fit one side of the door. "She will be even better if she's closed in before we get rain. That's in the ten-day forecast."

The door would shut nature out, but for a time at least, Keanan could still view the sky. Brent, however, was correct. It would be best to have the roof on before the fall rains came.

o0o

Chelsea knelt in the garden with several small crates beside her. The sun had melted away the remains of last night's frost, but the urgency remained. The days of gathering the harvest were coming to an end.

Was it okay to be thankful? She'd never worked so hard in her life.

The sounds of power tools echoed over the garden as she set orange-to-red tomatoes in one bin and yellow-to-orange in another. As soon as one set was filled, Zach exchanged the full ones for empty ones. The garden remained dotted with colored tomatoes. Even with Claire working a few rows over, this was going to take a while.

"That's quite the structure Keanan is building, isn't it?" Claire shifted a bin of tomatoes beside her. "I've never seen anything like it."

What was with everyone's need to discuss Keanan? "Me, either. Hey, I'm sorry if my arrival forced him to do that. Maybe he'd planned to live in the duplex."

Claire chuckled. "Not Keanan. He could have put in a word for it before Allison and Finnley moved into their new house, but he'd already started researching this. One thing about him, once his mind is on track, it's difficult to shift him."

Well, at least those discussions had taken place before Chelsea's arrival, so it wasn't her fault. And Keanan's stubbornness could go right on that list of ways he annoyed her. "So you guys would've preferred not to have grain bins on the property, too?"

Claire shot her a sideways glance. "No, I think it's cool. Sounds like you don't agree."

Oops. "His call, I guess."

"We've got a pretty eclectic set of buildings here now, and I kind of like it. The straw bale big house, Jo and Zach's log cabin, the timber-frame house Brent built for Allison... Why not add to the diversity? Especially with something so environmentally friendly as recycled galvanized steel? It's perfect, really."

Except that everything else looked more or less normal. Whatever. It wasn't like Chelsea had to live in the thing, and she'd arrived too late to vote it down.

"He went to a bunch of building centers in Coeur d'Alene and Spokane until he found one with a kitchen display they wanted dismantled. He got that thing for a song. It's not solid wood, but the off-gassing is complete."

Chelsea frowned. "How do you put square cabinets in a round house?"

"There will be gaps at the back, but a curved countertop will cover them."

"I hate to wonder what kind of surface he'll put in."

Claire burst out laughing. "Oh, you. One would think you didn't approve of our Keanan."

"I didn't know my approval mattered." Chelsea bit her lip. She'd probably said too much.

"Seriously? What's not to like?"

"It doesn't matter. Forget I said anything."

"No, tell me. We're a team, and it's important not to let stuff fester."

What was it about Keanan she didn't like? Nothing she could put a finger on, really. He just irritated her, and had done so since she'd come to visit in June for Sierra and Gabe's wedding. Did everyone have to be best friends around here?

"It's probably just me. The time of month, you know." That might not even be a lie. Maybe that's all it was.

Probably not.

Chapter 4 --

*K*eanan found himself nodding in agreement throughout Pastor Ron's sermon the next day. He loved Galena Gospel Church and the opportunities to serve. Playing guitar with one of the worship teams was a real joy.

He was content. Thankful to God for what he had. He had the opportunity to look to the needs of others rather than hoarding for himself. These were words he'd lived by all his adult life, and before, really. He'd never had a lot since he'd walked out of his father's life, but then he hadn't needed a lot, either. Plane tickets to places he could serve. New shoes every now and again when his wore out.

Yet Pastor Ron challenged him to deeper thought. How could he do even more with his resources? With his time?

Keanan rose with the other members of his worship team at the end of the service.

"Take my life and let it be consecrated, Lord, to Thee. Take my moments and my days; let them flow in endless praise."

Every verse of Frances Havergal's hymn echoed the prayer of his heart. It didn't matter what people thought. What Chelsea Riehl thought, though why his mind went to her was anybody's guess.

She stood beside her sister in the fourth pew, singing along. If she heard the words — believed them and took them to heart — they'd get along a great deal better. But he wasn't responsible for her attitude. Only his own.

I'm sorry, Lord. Fill me with Your love for her.

He certainly had no desire for any other kind of love. Not from anyone. Definitely not from her.

o0o

Chelsea followed her sister into the foyer. One thing about a small church like this was how everyone seemed to know everyone. Several women introduced themselves to her. That was kind of nice. She could only hope she'd remember any of the names by next week.

A glance across the crowded space revealed Keanan Welsh, his red head higher than any other. She shifted slightly to see whom he was talking to with such animation. An old guy in an outdated suit?

The man shook Keanan's hand and nodded with a smile. Keanan turned to someone else, but the old man's gaze landed on hers. He wove toward her. Uh oh.

"You must be Sierra's sister. You look so much alike, and she told us you were coming. I'm Ed Graysen, one of the elders here."

Chelsea dipped her head in acknowledgement. "Pleased to meet you." Should she call him Ed? Mr. Graysen? How formal was this place? "Yes, I'm Chelsea Riehl."

"Well, you folks must be splitting at the seams at Green Acres. God is doing wonderful things for you out there."

"He is." Chelsea smiled. "I'm delighted to be part of it." And she was. Mostly. If only there were events to plan instead of tomatoes to can. Surely that was coming soon.

"Well, if you ever find yourself with time on your hands, we always have volunteer projects on the go here at Galena Gospel. Just let me know, and I'll put you right to work."

Now that was a temptation. They must have events that needed planning, right? She itched to keep her hand in... before tomato stains covered it. "I do have plenty of experience organizing events. I like to think it's one of my spiritual gifts."

"Now that's what I like to hear. A young lady who knows what God's gifted her with then steps forward in faith."

Maybe she'd overdone the spiritual aspect. Still, it was true, right? God had formed her personality and talents.

"We do need someone to coordinate the kitchen volunteers for the upcoming Alpha sessions this fall. They start in early October and run through November. Jean Stedman usually does this, but she's having health issues right now."

"Um..."

"Jean has a good list of who usually helps out and that sort of thing." Ed looked around the foyer then pointed. "There she is. Shall I introduce you?"

Oh, man. How had she gotten into this? But it couldn't possibly take that much time, and she did like to make sure things ran smoothly. She put a smile in place. "Sure, why not?"

Ed tucked her hand behind his elbow and powered through the crowd, Chelsea in his wake. "Jean! Have you met our lovely new friend, Chelsea Riehl, yet? Sierra's sister, newly come from... Portland, isn't it?"

"Yes, Portland." Chelsea nodded and extended her hand to the middle-aged woman. "Nice to meet you."

Jean's face lit up in a friendly smile. "The pleasure is all mine."

Ed shifted from one foot to the other. "Chelsea would like to talk to you about taking over the kitchen for Alpha. Unless you already found someone?"

"Oh, that would be wonderful. I'd love to have someone to help carry the burden. My strength just isn't what it used to be."

Chelsea wondered what kind of health issue the woman had. "I'm happy to help."

"Oh, you sweet thing. Thank you. Let me give you my phone number. Is there a time in the next few days we could get together? Though I imagine things are busy at the farm this time of year."

"Yes, we're busy." Chelsea tugged her glittery pink phone and matching business card case out of her purse. "But never too busy for the Lord's work. Maybe tomorrow evening? I'll need to make sure nothing else is planned, though." She handed a business card to the woman.

"Tomorrow would be perfect. Thank you so much." Jean rattled off her number as Chelsea entered it into her phone.

"I'll confirm later then." Chelsea smiled and backed up a step. Right into something unmoving, but it couldn't be a wall. She'd walked right through there. A glance behind her showed a jeans-and-sweatshirt clad body. One she knew.

Keanan.

Great. But maybe overhearing would give him a better impression of her. Oh, why did that matter?

"Ed, Noel agrees Wednesdays would be best."

Best for what?

Ed gripped Keanan's hand. "Very well. I'll get the final information to the church office so the advertising can go out."

Chelsea perked up. They were having an event?

Ed nodded to Chelsea. "I should have mentioned the commitment is for several hours Wednesday evenings throughout the fall."

The... what?

"Keanan is leading one of the Alpha groups." Ed turned to Keanan. "And Miss Riehl has just volunteered to coordinate the kitchen. Two volunteers for the price of one tank of fuel." He grinned. "I know how much you folks out there value good use of resources."

Great. Not only was she stuck with Mr. Welsh every single day at Green Acres, now she also had to put up with him when she'd volunteered to get away from the farm?

God had a sense of humor.

Chelsea wasn't sure hers was intact.

oOo

"Want to run the tractor?" Brent asked Keanan as the crew gathered around the building site Monday morning. "Zach's at work."

Keanan shook his head. "Let Noel do it. He's probably the next most experienced operator. I don't want to ask these volunteers to pound straw if I'm not willing to do it myself."

He'd planned to do it alone. Sure, he'd hoped some of the others might join him, but he hadn't counted on it. He'd just been thankful to get an experienced contractor in Brent, who knew how to put the whole project together.

Brent grinned and smacked him on the back. "As you wish."

Scaffolding surrounded the two nested metal circles. Keanan's heart warmed to see so many friends climbing up the rungs, carrying long poles for tamping down the insulation. The tractor grumbled to life. Noel drove the front-end loading bucket into the heap of straw and lifted it high in the air before angling toward the structure.

Keanan climbed quickly to join the others. Chelsea stood directly across the circle from him, her hair bound back in another of her many scarves. Had she been watching him? She averted her gaze when he looked her way. Didn't matter. Hopefully the work gloves would keep the blisters off her dainty little hands.

Maybe she was following the song's dictates. *Take my hands and let them move at the impulse of Thy love.* Maybe she wasn't as antagonistic as she'd sometimes seemed. After all, she'd volunteered to help with Alpha. That had to say something about her devotion to Christ. Even the organizational skill everyone raved about could be used for the Lord. *Take my intellect and use every power as Thou shalt choose.*

He'd misjudged her. *My apologies, Lord.*

As if she'd heard him — though it wouldn't have been possible over the roar of the tractor, even if he'd spoken out loud — she looked straight at him. Assessed him, as he assessed her.

The tractor bucket rose between Keanan and Claire. They guided the straw into the gap then began tamping it down as Noel and the tractor went to the nearby pile for the next load. Within a few minutes, everyone had straw in front of them to pack tightly, and Noel was making the rounds again.

The heavy labor was satisfying. This would be Keanan's home. His shelter from the savage weather to come. For all the places he'd lived, he'd never experienced a northern winter with blizzards, ice, and sub-zero temperatures. He stifled a chuckle. He should probably have waited until he'd experienced a full year at Green Acres before deciding to make his permanent home here.

The grind of the tractor's engine ebbed and flowed as it moved around the circle, scooping straw and dropping it between the rings. The thud of poles ramming the straw tightly into place formed an uneven staccato that grated the musician in Keanan. It was tempting to drum out a rhythm as if he were leading a band.

The tractor lifted straw beside Chelsea. She flexed her shoulders then wiped her forehead with her sleeve as she waited.

She normally lived behind a computer, yet she didn't complain. When the crew decided to take on this project together, she'd come, too, even though she was clearly out of her element. How many muscles could she have built typing on a keyboard and making phone calls? Or from washing plums and skinning tomatoes?

This life was one hundred percent new to Chelsea Riehl. He should give her a little time to adjust. Be patient with her.

She bent on the scaffolding and returned into his line of vision with a stainless-steel water bottle. After turning the cap, she took a long drink. Good idea. Her gaze met his across the circle.

Keanan lifted his own water bottle in salute before slaking his own thirst.

She broke eye contact, pounding her pole into the new load of straw.

"Keanan!"

He blinked and glanced down at Brent, who snapped his measuring tape. "Yes?"

"Looks like we have insulation to the bottom of the first row of windows. Time to cut the steel and insert the frames."

Already? Truly many hands made light work. "Do you need my help?"

"I'm calling an hour-long break to get them framed."

Keanan nodded as Brent strode to the tractor. A moment later Noel cut the engine. The silence seemed louder than the machine.

"Time for a break," Brent called out.

"Coffee and muffins at the house," Claire announced.

A cheer went up. The crew climbed down the scaffold.

Keanan rounded the bin just as Chelsea's feet hit the ground clad in hiking boots. That beat heels all to bits. She stumbled just a little, and Keanan's hand snatched forward to steady her.

"You okay?" He let go the instant she regained her balance, lest she read too much into his touch.

She tipped her head and looked up at him from those clear blue eyes. "I'm fine. I'm sure I'll pay for this tomorrow, though." She patted the corrugated steel beside the door where she'd been working. "I guess we have a few more hours of pounding to go."

Keanan nodded. "Look, you don't have to…"

Those eyes narrowed. "You think I'm not capable, just because I've never done something like this before?"

"I didn't say that."

"You didn't have to. It's written all across your face. Pity for the city girl. Or maybe not pity."

Definitely not pity. But what, instead? He searched her face as though the answer might be written there.

"Come on." Sierra nudged her. "Let's get off our feet for a bit."

Chelsea nodded and linked arms with her sister. Then she glanced back. "Aren't you taking a break?"

She'd caught him staring at her feminine curves. He shook his head and jerked his thumb toward the pallet of building materials. "We're putting in window frames."

"Oh." Chelsea hesitated. "We'll bring you a snack when we return."

Keanan felt a grin break across his face. "Thank you, fair lady. Much appreciated."

Chapter 5 --

*N*ow that was a brutal day." Sierra dropped on the floor in front of where Gabe sat on the love seat. He began to massage her shoulders. "Ahhh."

Chelsea leaned against the thick stone wall that served as a thermal mass, storing heat from the fireplace and sun room on the south and the kitchen ovens on the north.

Noel administered a similar massage to Claire's shoulders and, across the room, Brent rubbed Allison's back. Zach and Jo had retreated to their log cabin right after dinner.

Sure looked cozy in the great room. Chelsea's own best hope for loosening her muscles was a long soak in her tub. Why hadn't the duplex's designers decided jetted tubs would be a necessity for every farm worker? All those couples nearly screamed the reason why. No one had been thinking about single people.

Chelsea shoved away and pivoted, slamming straight into a body as unmoving as the rock wall.

"Whoa." Keanan's hands came to her arms to steady her.

Chelsea stepped aside, breaking contact. Just because she craved a massage — okay, maybe the touch of a man who loved her — didn't mean she welcomed this giant's hands on her, even for an instant.

But something in his eyes caught her. He'd seemed to watch her at the building site today, too. Weird. He was so not her type.

"Thank you, Chelsea. I appreciate your help insulating my home today."

"Um, no problem. That's what was on the day's agenda. Can't pretend it's what I'm used to, though."

A smile tilted one side of his face. "I'm certain. The only women for whom that would be a normal day's work live in Africa and pound their own grain into flour."

She pulled her eyebrows together. Did that mean American women were less female than African women? This guy was so hard to understand sometimes. She didn't even want to.

Still, the image he'd presented was valid to a point. "Do they do it for six hours straight?"

Keanan chuckled. "Probably not. But they do it every day. Either way, I'm grateful for the assistance today. I thought I might be working alone in the evenings after the farm work was done. It would have taken weeks."

That was honorable. But still. "I guess it's part of that whole community thing we signed up for. Now it's done."

The workers had taken another break for lunch when the second-story window level had been reached. And later, everyone had cheered when Brent's machine hoisted the conical roof into place.

"That part's done." Keanan nodded. "It's satisfying to see my little home take shape."

"It's very small." *Brilliant thing to say, Chelsea.* He surely knew the square footage.

"I'm only one person." His green eyes pierced hers. "The lower level will have a small kitchen and bath with a sitting area by the wood stove. On the second level, a bedroom. What more do I need?"

She blinked to get rid of those eyes staring at hers. "Someday you'll get married and have kids. What then?" Oh, man. Dumb, dumb, dumb. So long as he didn't get the idea she was volunteering.

A slow smile creased his face.

Her words had done nothing to cut eye contact. If anything, his gaze increased in intensity.

"Then I'll bring in another bin for a bedroom wing and make a corridor between. Not so hard."

Break the mood, Chelsea, break the mood. "Unless you need to send a disobedient child to stand in the corner. You're rather short on those."

This time he laughed out loud. "Good point. I guess we'll have to see what the future holds. How God leads."

Chelsea rubbed her arms, suddenly chilled as exhaustion threatened to topple her. A person couldn't even have a normal conversation with a guy like Keanan. He was just plain weird.

She glanced back into the great room with its dimmed lights and the three couples chatting quietly while five-year-old Finnley played with a wooden train set. "Anyway. I'm glad for you. Really. But right now, a hot bath with bubbles is calling my name. See you tomorrow."

Keanan looked over her head into the other room. "Ah, yes, everyone else has a personal masseuse. It's the least I can offer for your help today." He grasped her shoulders and turned her away from him. "Let me."

Chelsea's knees nearly sagged under his gentle ministrations. Strong, powerful fingers applied the right amount of pressure in just the right places. She could live like this forever.

No, she couldn't. What kind of wanton woman was she, accepting a massage from a man she barely knew and frankly didn't like at all? Still, it took all her resolve to take three steps away and break the contact. "Thanks, that helps." She smiled back at him. "But I really need to get going."

"Good night."

His words lingered in her ears as she crossed the yard to her duplex. The sun hung low in the cool evening sky, causing a chill to run through her body. It had nothing to do with remembering Keanan's hands on her and everything to do with the upcoming bath. She'd start that new novel she'd downloaded, and get her mind off him.

oOo

The straw bale house felt empty — vacant — without Chelsea's presence. That woman was so intense she took up way more space than her small body did. Keanan's hands tingled with the memory of her sagging against them, accepting his touch for that brief instant.

He understood her flight. First from all the coupleness in the great room, but also from him. At this moment, he had no desire to face his friends, but what kind of person did that make him, when they'd unselfishly given him an entire day in the midst of a busy time of year?

Keanan took a few steps into the great room. "Thanks again for all your help."

Sierra opened one eye as she sat between Gabe's feet. "You mentioned that before."

"I'm still grateful."

"Duly noted."

Claire stood and stretched from one side to the other. "Anyone want tea? Hot chocolate?"

"Coffee?" asked Allison.

Claire grinned. "Like you need caffeine at this time of day."

"Nothing could keep me awake." She leaned back against Brent as he wrapped his arms around her.

50

An astonishing sight, really. Keanan well remembered the prickly person Allison had been a few short months before. Brent had brought out all the best in her.

Would he ever find someone who completed him as his friends had? But that was saying he wasn't fulfilled on his own, which wasn't true. He'd had amazing adventures around the world with more to come. He'd helped drill wells and build solar ovens and worked alongside people while sharing Jesus with them. Not having a wife or children meant he could easily move on when a project was complete and something else called.

The kettle whistled in the kitchen, and Keanan blinked. He hadn't even noticed Claire walk past him.

"Want tea, Keanan?"

He turned toward her in the kitchen. On the one hand, he should head next door to the home of his hosts, Steve and Rosemary Nemesek. On the other hand... why not twenty more minutes?

He nodded. "Much appreciated. Let me carry the tray."

"You're one of the good ones, Keanan. One day some lucky girl is going to notice."

Why would she say that? Especially on the heels of his own thoughts? But she couldn't read his mind. "That's unlikely. My life is complete as it is, but I appreciate the sentiment."

She grinned, shook her head, and filled the teapot.

Wisps of fragrant mint soothed his mind. It didn't matter what she or others thought he needed. That was between him, God, and no one else. Well, possibly it was also a matter for the woman in question. If she existed.

Did Chelsea embrace her singlehood as he did? She seemed less comfortable with the couples in the great room. Yet he hadn't gone in and relaxed, either, but planned to retreat until Claire put him on the spot. Had that been subconscious resistance on his part or simply exhaustion? Hard to know.

He carried the tea-laden tray into the great room while Claire followed with a plate of muffins. Sierra stretched and shifted onto the love seat beside Gabe as Keanan approached with the tray. They helped themselves then he moved around the room. He set the tray on the large round coffee table, helped himself to a cup with a liberal dollop of honey, and dropped into an easy chair.

The first sip of mellow mint relaxed him just a little. "What's on tomorrow's agenda?"

He'd focused his gaze on Gabe, but Brent spoke. "You and I will get the windows in and the hangers in place for the second-story joists. I also hope to get the floor ready for poured concrete tomorrow."

Keanan's gaze swung to his friend. "But the farm work—"

"I've got one more full day I can put into your place before Tyrell Burke's footings will be cured enough to start his timber frame house. I'd really rather push through, if that's okay with everyone else." Brent raised both hands. "There's not much the group can do to help over there. It's a two-man job."

"Go for it, guys." Noel reached for a second muffin. "That third cut of hay is light enough I should be able to bale it all tomorrow. Looks like rain in a few days, so there will be plenty of inside days to process that half ton of tomatoes on the deck."

A thousand pounds was likely not an exaggeration. But this many hardworking adults could go through jars of pasta sauce, barbecue sauce, and ketchup like nobody's business.

"When's Zach planning to butcher that steer?" asked Claire.

"Weather needs to cool off a bit more for that," Noel answered. "Probably another month."

"We used to can a lot of soup, but it takes so many quarts to feed this crew anymore that it seems a waste of jars and power."

"We need a soup freezer." Sierra nestled against Gabe.

Claire chuckled. "Not a bad idea. Jo can get more of those square gallon containers from the nursing home kitchen, I bet.

What comes in those?"

"Stewed prunes," murmured Gabe into Sierra's hair.

Everyone laughed.

"I'll ask Jo tomorrow. She is still working up there for a few more weeks, I think."

Jo was part-time nutritionist at Galena Hills Care Facility, but she'd be leaving permanently before the birth of their second child. Green Acres Farm was operating firmly in the black, thanks to Allison's ability to fund the new school Brent's crew had finished building only last week.

"Do we have another deep freeze available?" asked Keanan.

"We'll have to look for one," Claire said. "The only empty one now will be full of meat after butchering."

Keanan drained his cup and rose. "I'd best get over to Steve and Rosemary's. Steve seems to be in a lot of pain these days. I know he likes to go to bed early, but he usually waits up to ask me about my day."

Compassion covered Claire's face. "I'm sorry to hear about his pain level. He's been through a lot in the past few years."

Brent stood to his feet, pulling Allison up with him. "I should go, too. See you in the morning, darling." He kissed Allison.

Keanan turned for the door. Brent and Allison's would be the second wedding since he arrived at Green Acres. Would he truly remain content if his own never arrived?

Chapter 6 --

*A*wkward.

Chelsea watched Keanan fold his large frame into the passenger seat of her car. The guy's head brushed the ceiling, and his knees angled upward as he fumbled with the seat adjustments. Even lowering the seat and pushing it all the way back didn't fully relieve the cramped look.

What was the guy, six foot four? She'd offered him a ride because, hello, she had a car and he didn't.

Keanan snapped his seat belt and glanced over. "Ready."

She'd been staring. She pushed the electronic start button and the diesel engine purred to life. Would he compliment her car? So much nicer than his bicycle. What guy wouldn't want to own a car like this? Or maybe a truck. He'd fit better in a truck.

Chelsea turned the car toward town. Wasn't he going to talk? She shot a sideways glance. Keanan's eyes were shut and his lips moving ever so slightly. Afraid of her driving?

Her lips curved upward. Couldn't be that bad.

His large hands lay on his thighs, palms up.

Oh, man, he was praying. Didn't look like he was panicked

about her skill — good thing, as she wasn't driving like an idiot at all. He must be praying about Alpha. It sounded like he'd be a teacher.

What did you say to a guy who was praying? Um, maybe nothing. It couldn't take much more than five minutes to get to the church. She could handle his silence that long.

Chelsea followed the curves past Elmer's place, eyes on the road.

"Thank you, Chelsea."

She nearly swerved off. "For what, the ride?" She waited a second. No looking at him. "No biggie."

He chuckled. "I do appreciate the lift, but it's not what I meant. More for seeing a need in the church and stepping forward to fill it."

The church elder hadn't made it that easy to say no. "Galena Gospel Church is my new spiritual home." She lifted her shoulder slightly. "I like people and being involved in things."

She slid a glance across the small car. Keanan was watching her. Heat rose in her cheeks. That was dumb. She didn't care what he thought. Him, of all people.

"That's good to know. People around the world need Jesus, whether they are in Idaho or in Africa."

"You've been to Africa?"

Chelsea caught his nod in her periphery.

"I spent a while there providing solar ovens to refugee camps. Another time my team went from village to village drilling wells and telling the people about the living water to be found in Jesus."

"Wow. That sounds interesting." A few pieces of the puzzle in Chelsea's mind clicked together. Keanan Welsh was for real. He might look like an overgrown hippie, but he lived out his faith.

"There's so much need. Everywhere."

Chelsea slowed to cross the bridge into Galena Landing. "Then how did you end up here?"

"That's a long story."

"Well, I'd like to hear it sometime." That was even true. She bit her lip. "I've never done anything half as interesting as you have."

"God leads us all in different paths. I responded to the Spirit's nudging to help when I saw the need. My eyes have been opened in so many ways. We are so blessed."

Did she feel blessed? Of course. She'd grown up in privilege, all her needs fulfilled and most of her wants. Wasn't that blessing? But beyond an occasional missionary presentation in her Portland church, she'd never really thought about needs elsewhere. Certainly never felt a call to cross the world and dig a well. Had God ever tried to elbow her and get her attention? If so, she hadn't noticed.

She parked near the church kitchen's side door. Only two other cars in the lot. "I thought there'd be more people."

"The leadership team arrives early to prepare, and the guests will come a bit later." He reached for his seatbelt release just as she did.

His hand was warm, his fingertips rough where they brushed against hers. A man with a heart to match the size of his hands. No denying Keanan was a little strange, but had she misjudged him completely?

oOo

"This smells awesome," Chelsea said to Rosemary Nemesek. "Thank you for getting this first meal ready."

Zach's mom, Rosemary, and an elderly woman called Mona had been thick in the finishing touches of slicing roast beef when they'd arrived. Chelsea pitched in, heating vegetables and pouring them into serving bowls, slicing rolls and arranging them on platters, and filling pitchers with ice water.

Wow, there had to be thirty people milling around outside the church kitchen, some chatting with each other and some observing. Keanan's red hair popped above everyone else's. She watched him weave through the group and approach a young man who looked like he might bolt at any second.

Of course Keanan would notice. Of course he'd take the extra step to ensure the guy felt welcomed.

"Have you ever participated in Alpha before?"

Chelsea swung back to Rosemary. Had the older woman noticed where her attention had gone? If so, she didn't let on. "No, I never have. This is all new to me."

"We sure appreciate having you here. I'll help when I can as I've done for Jean, but you'll have a rotating staff each week." Rosemary glanced at the clock. "Time to set out the food."

Chelsea did as she was told, setting bowls and platters on the serving table just outside the kitchen pass-through. Against the wall, another table held beverages, including a gurgling coffee urn and a kettle for tea.

Ed Grayson called everyone to attention, prayed a short grace, then invited the group to fill their plates. Several round tables lay beyond the serving area. They looked naked and uninviting, without even a tablecloth. There should be flowers or some kind of centerpiece.

Chelsea nodded to herself. Next week she'd make sure. She'd need to keep them low, but the tables required something. She stood in the kitchen doorway watching the people fill their plates. A few she recognized, besides Mr. Graysen and Keanan. Maybe other church members were also leading discussion groups.

Keanan parked at a table with the young man he'd talked to and a mix of people of various ages. He glanced her way but didn't seem to make eye contact.

"Would you refill the water jugs, dear?" came Mona's voice from behind her.

Chelsea jumped. "Right on it." This was her job. She should be paying better attention. Keanan's job was to get to know people, to make friends, and to guide them to salvation. Hers was to make sure the food didn't run out.

She analyzed the serving table as she went by with more water. No danger of a shortage.

Over the murmur of voices and the clink of cutlery, Keanan laughed. It seemed to catch around his table. The young guy grinned, looking more at ease when Chelsea glanced their way. So did the others at the table. Keanan was good at this. Good with people.

Maybe she was the only person in the world who'd taken one look at him and decided he was a jerk. Reassessment was painful. It had been easy to dismiss him as an overgrown hippie when he didn't have a car and lived in a tent. Or even a grain bin. A little more difficult when his genuine interest in putting others first shone through.

She didn't want to approve of him in any way, but it was hard not to.

oOo

The lights came on in the darkened lounge when the opening video of Alpha ended. Keanan glanced toward Wesley next to him. What had the younger man thought of the presentation?

Wesley shook his head. "Weird. The stuff he talked about, those are my questions. Sometimes you think there has to be more to life than a hamster wheel, right?"

So much more. Keanan's heart expanded. "There are answers to your questions. We'll be discussing them Wednesday evenings for the next couple of months."

Wesley's head jerked in a nod. "I'll be back. Not sure I buy into all this stuff, but maybe that guy can convince me."

It wouldn't be the man in the video who would persuade Wesley, but God Himself working in the young man's heart. At the moment, Wesley wouldn't understand those words.

Keanan nodded toward the now-dark screen. "He presents biblical truth in a down-to-earth way. I think you'll find it interesting. Challenging, perhaps."

Wesley shrugged as he got to his feet. "Life is full of challenge. That's how you know you're alive, right?" He looked around the lounge, where other people talked quietly on their way to the foyer. "Thanks for inviting me, man. See you next week." He jammed a baseball cap on his head and strode for the door.

Keanan watched him disappear. *Thank You, Lord. Your hand is on that one. So many here tonight who need to meet You. To know You. May we be sensitive to minister in Your way.*

Chelsea carried a plate of cookies into the kitchen at the far end of the lounge. Had she watched the video, or been too busy cleaning up after the meal? What would she think? He'd talked to Sierra enough to know the sisters had been raised by believing parents in a rather sheltered environment. How much of Chelsea's faith was her own, and how much a hand-me-down?

No, he had no right to question the depth of her faith. That was between her and the Lord, yet the question stayed in his mind as he followed her progress around the back of the room.

Pastor Ron's hand clasped Keanan's shoulder, and he blinked back to attention. The other leadership team members gathered around.

"How do you think it went tonight?" asked Ron.

Ed Graysen took a seat beside Keanan. "God brought seekers."

Tracy, a bubbly young woman with white-blond hair, nodded. "I was so excited to see the girls from my office here. They said they'd be back. I can hardly wait to see what happens!"

"Same," Keanan put in. "I invited Wesley last week, and he's definitely interested in learning more."

"We had about seven people under about thirty-five here tonight." Pastor Ron looked from Keanan to Tracy. "Are you two comfortable working together with that group? I know the groups don't have to be divided that way, but sometimes it is easier for young folk to feel the gospel is relevant when their group leaders are closer to their own age."

Keanan glanced at Tracy and nodded. "Yes, that works for me."

Tracy grinned. "Sounds great. I've never led before, so I'm not sure what to expect."

"Keanan has. Observe for a while, and you'll soon feel comfortable." Pastor Ron turned to the other leaders as they discussed how to split the remaining guests into groups.

Keanan watched Tracy for a moment as she listened. She seemed to have enthusiasm for the program and for the Lord. When the team bowed together, Tracy's heartfelt prayer resonated with Keanan. She'd be a fine partner.

After prayer, Ed headed for the kitchen. Keanan remembered seeing Ed's wife back there helping with dinner. The two older women drifted away as Pastor Ron strode to the sound booth to shut down the equipment.

"How long have you been in Galena Landing?" asked Tracy. "I've seen you on worship team a few times."

Keanan pulled his attention back to her. "Since spring. I serve however I'm needed. Where the Lord guides me."

"Where do you work?"

Ah, the big question. Hopefully this was mild curiosity and not a personal interest. "I live and work at Green Acres Farm."

Her face registered nothing. "Where's that?"

"Over on Thompson Road, next to the mountain. It's a cooperative where we grow much of our own food."

"Oh, yes, I've heard of it. I went to school with Liz Nemesek. Her brother is part of that group, right?"

"I haven't met Liz, but if you mean Zachary Nemesek, yes. He and his wife live and work on the farm, as do many others."

Lights dimmed in the back of the room, and Keanan looked up to see Chelsea, sweater and purse tossed over her shoulder, striding near, her unfriendly gaze seemingly fixed on Tracy.

He frowned. What was all that about?

Chelsea's eyes didn't waver from Tracy's as she spoke. "Ready to go, Keanan?"

"Yes." He stood, flexing his shoulders. Sitting for so long was more difficult than physical labor. "Good to meet you, Tracy. I'll see you next week."

He didn't miss the speculative gleam as Tracy looked between him and Chelsea. Discomfort sifted through him. Tracy couldn't be interested in him any more than Chelsea could. Neither woman needed to size up the competition. Chelsea had made her dislike of him obvious enough in the few weeks they'd known each other. Besides, it didn't matter. He wasn't looking for romance.

Tracy stretched a hand to Chelsea. "I'm Tracy Grindle. I don't believe we've met?"

Was she offering sincere friendship? That would be good. They must be about the same age.

"Chelsea Riehl. Nice to meet you." She sidled a bit closer to Keanan as she shook Tracy's hand.

Awkward. Keanan took a step back, further from the two women who seemed to analyze each other. He glanced toward the door.

Pastor Ron waited by the light switch, a bemused expression on his face.

Keanan turned to the impasse before him. "Time to go, ladies. Pastor Ron's ready to lock up."

Neither moved.

He grasped both women by their elbows and propelled them toward the door. "We can talk more outside."

Not that either seemed to have anything to say.

Chapter 7 --

*Y*ou're doing just fine, Chelsea."

She sat at the kitchen table next door at the Nemeseks' farmhouse, going over the church phone list with Rosemary, a cup of tea in front of each of them.

"I wish more people would be willing to volunteer." She'd called at least two dozen households and barely had the next couple of weeks of food covered. "Don't they realize what's going on at Alpha? How important it is?"

Rosemary covered Chelsea's hand with her own. "People are busy going to work every day and running their kids to programs when they get home."

"What kind of programs does Galena Landing have?"

The older woman chuckled. "Nothing like Portland, I'm sure. But there are rotating classes at the recreation complex. Some families are into sports like football. Or they just collapse around the television set when they get home."

Chelsea bit her lip. This was the difference from running events as a business to helping in the church. When she'd been hired, she could sub out parts to other businesses that specialized in certain areas. Caterers. Decorators. Entertainers. Everyone got a paycheck, and the clients were delighted with an event that had gone off without a hitch. She'd never had to operate with only volunteers before.

No wonder Mr. Graysen had been so thrilled she'd said *yes*. Now it was her job to get enough people together to actually do it.

That wasn't entirely fair. The Alpha leaders, although volunteers, had been picked by Pastor Ron. She'd thought the man a good judge of people until he'd put that Tracy as co-leader with Keanan. Didn't Pastor Ron know Tracy had a crush on Keanan? That had to be distracting to the group.

Chelsea had watched the interaction from the safety of the kitchen pass-through for two weeks now. Oh, Tracy seemed to remember the purpose of the group, but Chelsea had eyes. She could see, glasses or not. Read between the lines.

She took a sip of tea, pulling her attention back to the list in front of her and the woman around the corner of the table.

"Have you asked the small group leaders if their groups would like to take on a week each?"

Chelsea drew a thick line across the paper. "No. I didn't know there were small groups. I should never have taken this on until I got to know everyone better. I spend half my time explaining who I am and what I do at Green Acres."

Rosemary grinned. "The community is curious, for sure, though many of the church people have been out to visit a time or two."

Chelsea doodled while she thought. Wait. A circle with a conical roof? Hopefully Rosemary hadn't seen that. Chelsea quickly added a few more lines to disguise the shape.

"Ask Pastor Ron about the small group leaders. Let him know you're having difficulties with this."

Chelsea quirked a lopsided grin. "I hate to admit when I can't do something myself."

"But it's not your burden to carry alone."

"No?" Chelsea raised her eyebrows at the older woman. "Mr. Graysen asked me to coordinate this, and I said *yes*. That makes it mine."

"I don't see it that way at all. The body is there to support each other, and when we're not doing a good job of it, it's okay to get a reminder."

"I suppose." Rosemary had a point, but that didn't mean Chelsea had to concede inwardly. She'd wanted to be the best volunteer coordinator ever to help out at Galena Gospel Church. Oh, man. What she wanted was everyone to know what a terrific job she'd done.

What kind of attitude was that? Shame crept up her cheeks as she stared at the blurring paper. She slid a finger behind her glasses to dab the tears before Rosemary could notice.

Rosemary pulled the paper around the corner. "So the Green Acres gang is providing the meal next week? That's great."

Back on solid ground. Chelsea nodded. "They were happy to help. We're doing tacos that night. Everyone is pitching in to prep at the farm, and then Claire and Noel are coming to serve and clean up."

"Other groups will do it, too." Rosemary nudged the paper back. "Give Pastor Ron a call. He can't know how things are if no one tells him. Let him advise you."

Chelsea sighed and picked up the teacup. "I might have to."

"Is this how you are with the Lord, too?" Rosemary asked gently.

"Am I how?" Chelsea's eyebrows pulled together as her eyes narrowed.

"Forgive me if I'm too forward." The older woman closed her eyes a moment. "Do you ask God only when it's something you can't handle alone, or do you live every day in full dependence on Him?"

Chelsea opened her mouth in protest, but the question stabbed deeply. "Why bother Him when I don't need to?"

"I understand where you're coming from. I truly do. Before Steve got sick a few years ago, I was much the same. I read the

Word, prayed, and went to church." Rosemary crinkled a smile. "Even pitched in wherever I could. I didn't really need to depend on God for my day-to-day life. Everything was under control."

Was a response needed? Hopefully not.

"But then Steve contracted Guillain-Barré Syndrome. He went from a vibrant and healthy man to someone who couldn't walk. Could barely feed himself. In the space of a few days, everything changed for him... and for me."

Chelsea was interested in spite of herself. "I knew he'd had some neurological disease. He's much better now, though, isn't he?" Of course he was. He walked, talked, and ate with the family. But she wouldn't have called him vibrant and healthy. More like frail.

"He is much better than he was, but it's taken several years of painful rehabilitation to get here, and he'll never be the same as he was before. The point I'm trying to make is that we never know when things will change. When our carefully-constructed life will come apart at the seams." Rosemary's hand clasped Chelsea's. "Don't wait for that time to dig your roots deeply into God. Practice taking the little things to Him. Share your day with Him as though He were your friend. Your lover."

Whoa, that sounded a bit personal.

A tap sounded at the kitchen door a second before Keanan's large shaggy head appeared around it. His gaze flicked between the two of them. "Sorry if I'm interrupting anything. I'm here to spend time with Steve."

"Come on in." Rosemary beckoned. "Chelsea and I were just going over the need for volunteers to bring food for Alpha."

"We're doing it this week, right?" His disconcerting green eyes latched on Chelsea's.

She nodded, gathering up her things. "Yes, this week is taken care of. I should be going."

"Oh, no need to rush off. Steve and I will be in the other room."

Rosemary thumbed toward the archway to the living room. "He's waiting for you."

Another side of the multi-faceted Keanan Welsh.

o0o

"I thought you'd moved into your grain bin already."

Keanan glanced at Chelsea. She stood across the kitchen peninsula from where he served up breakfast Saturday morning.

"I did. Why?"

"Just curious why you were over at Nemeseks'."

"I was visiting my friends." Most of the farm's inhabitants sat at the table behind Chelsea, chatting about the day's work to come. He lowered his voice. "In the weeks I stayed with them, I learned that Steve has some struggles his wife cannot easily help with. I go over at least twice a week and keep an eye on him while he's getting some exercise on the stationary bike. As he pedals, we talk about the scriptures. Share with each other what we are learning."

She opened her mouth and closed it again before sighing. "Of course."

Irritation shafted through him. "Why does it matter to you?"

"Merely curious." She shrugged.

That woman never said or did anything without a purpose. Simple curiosity? Unlikely.

"Steve and I both value our time together. He mentors me spiritually, and I help him with some of his physical needs. Our relationship works well for both of us."

"That's good." Chelsea's gaze flicked to his then away. "What's for breakfast?"

Had that been vulnerability in her eyes? "I scrambled a griddle-full of eggs, and there's bacon in the warmer. May I serve you?"

"Thank you." She bit her lip. "I'd appreciate it."

Keanan turned to fill a plate then slid it across the counter to her.

She perched on a stool and bent her head, curls obscuring her face and those pink glasses.

Why didn't she join the others at the table? He'd been just about to do so, but it seemed awkward to leave her alone at the peninsula. When she picked up her fork, he came around with his own plate. "Mind if I join you?"

She shrugged. "Sit wherever you like."

Now that was a resounding welcome. He slid onto the counter stool next to her. "I thought you might like some company."

Her shoulder twitched.

Perhaps he'd thought wrong. But he was here now. He might as well try to draw her out in conversation. One thing about Chelsea. She could never stay quiet for long. "What are you up to today?"

She glanced sidelong at him as she swallowed a bite of scrambled eggs. "I'm not sure. We're finally caught up canning tomatoes, so I might paint my spare room today."

"Covering the farm mural?"

Chelsea's eyes narrowed. "Not you, too."

"What did I say?"

"Brent painted a new mural for Finnley at the new house. Why does everyone think I should keep the original? Finnley's not moving back in."

"Uh. Who thinks painting over it is wrong? Has Brent said anything? Or Allison?"

Chelsea focused on the fork shoving eggs around her plate. "No. Not them."

Keanan stared at her. "Then who?" As far as he knew, the topic hadn't come up at a team meeting. Why should it? The apartment was Chelsea's until deemed otherwise. No one else consulted about paint colors. He certainly didn't expect any input on his choices for his new home. Not that he intended to paint the galvanized walls.

"Never mind."

He opened his mouth to challenge her words, but what would it gain? Nothing. She spent too much time wondering what other people thought of her. Reading into what she thought she saw. But it wasn't his place to point that out.

"Are you painting the entire room, or only the one wall?"

She shot him a look. What it meant, he couldn't tell. "The green on the other three walls isn't my favorite, but it will be okay. Allison had extra of her dark gray paint, and that should cover the mural fine."

If it wasn't Allison then who was Chelsea complaining about? He'd never understand women. "I see," he said with a nod.

Sierra rounded the peninsula into the kitchen and stood facing him and Chelsea. She looked from one to the other.

"Did you have enough breakfast, Sierra? There's more if you want it."

"No thanks. I got plenty. It was scrumptious."

"Thank you."

"Yes, it's really good." Chelsea glanced his way.

He studiously avoided meeting her gaze. "What are you up to today, Sierra?"

She grinned and pointed a finger at him. "Sewing window coverings for your grain bin, buddy. Want to help, Chels? I'll help you paint later."

Chelsea picked up her tea and took a sip.

Keanan knew she wouldn't help him if it hadn't been decreed from on high. Sierra had asked him last week about his preferences for his windows. Well, why not? Yes, trees nearly surrounded his new home, but that didn't mean curtains were a bad idea, so long as there were no frills or lace.

He couldn't resist a little dig of his own, though. "For window covering assistance, Chelsea, I might help you paint, too."

She narrowed her gaze at him over the rim of her teacup.

Chapter 8 --

*S*he'd only agreed to help her sister because she was dying of curiosity. It had been three weeks since they'd all tamped straw as insulation into the gap between the two galvanized steel circles that formed Keanan's home, and Chelsea had heard some of the group talking about how well the place was coming along. Her imagination had come up blank.

Chelsea stopped in the middle of the curved path when the round house came into view. Yes, house. Its sea-green door reminded her of Keanan's eyes, and the natural wood that framed it and the windows glistened with a protective finish. Small corrugated overhangs for each — and a longer one over the door — had been fitted into the wall. To keep rain from ruining the frames? Must be.

In her mind's eye, a flower basket hung from the door awning's brace, while a rectangular planter sat along the edge of the concrete pad in front of the door. This place could look downright welcoming. Who knew?

Sierra nudged her. "Told you it looked great. Brent's been working here most evenings, and it turns out Keanan's pretty handy with a hammer himself."

Was there anything he wasn't good at? Chelsea clung to the remnants of her dislike for Keanan, but couldn't even manage to think *overgrown hippie* with venom attached anymore. Okay, fine. He wasn't a hippie; he just had long hair. He was even a nice guy. She hated to admit it, even to herself.

"Have you seen the inside lately?" she asked her sister.

"Are you kidding me?" Sierra linked her arm through Chelsea's. "That's why we're really here. To do some snooping."

Chelsea grinned. "Well, let's do it, then."

"Anyone home?" Sierra nudged the door, which had been left ajar, and stuck her head around.

"Come on in!" Brent called.

If Brent were here working, likely Keanan would be, too. Chelsea followed Sierra onto the smooth concrete floor, etched with warm amber and gold tones much like the floor of the big house. On her left, the underside of an open staircase begged for a coat closet. Straight ahead — when she'd stepped beside her sister — several segments of boxed cabinetry sat in a jumble and, to her right, Brent and Keanan lifted a sliding door to an industrial-looking track. That must be Keanan's bathroom behind it.

"What do you think?" Brent turned toward them, brushing his hands together.

Keanan rolled the door back and forth.

"It's amazing!" gushed Sierra. "Wow, it's come a long way. I can really see the potential here now."

Brent laughed. "We're mostly past potential and on to reality. Install the cabinets and the wood stove, and Keanan is good to go."

Keanan inspected the track.

If Chelsea hadn't been watching him, she'd never have caught the surreptitious glance he sent her way. Something warmed inside her. He cared about her opinion? Since when?

"Looking good." That was about all she could come up with.

He turned slightly. "You think so?"

Actually, it did. She'd thrown an engagement party in an upscale Portland loft. This grain bin seemed to contain the best of that space but in a smaller footprint. Doubtless for a lot less coin, too.

She needed to break eye contact. Badly. Chelsea pointed at the cabinetry boxes. "What type of finish on those?"

Brent crossed the area and slit one of the boxes to reveal a light-toned wood with strong markings. "Hickory," he announced. "Keanan scored these from a display at a hardware store in Spokane. Last year's models."

Chelsea strolled over and ran her hand over the smooth finish. "It's beautiful. That finish will look good in here."

"It passes inspection?"

She turned to Keanan and came out with a genuine smile. "Yeah, I think so."

His green eyes crinkled and his mouth curved slightly. "Glad you like it."

He was definitely focused on her, not Sierra. An uncomfortable, unfamiliar feeling simmered in Chelsea's gut. She pulled her gaze away and caught a smirk on her sister's face. That warranted a glare, for sure, but Sierra's grin only widened.

Whatever.

Chelsea strode toward the bathroom, and Keanan stepped aside, as expected. Straight ahead, a shallow sink cabinet sat under a narrow window. To her left the floor sloped toward a drain. To her right, some sort of giant toilet. She frowned.

"Composting unit." Keanan's voice came from right behind her. "This place is too far from the septic field to hook into the main farm system."

She didn't even want to know what that was. It sounded disgusting. She pointed the other way. "Are you tiling the shower?" There might be other options, but she couldn't think of any.

Keanan was silent so long she glanced back. He loomed right behind her, close enough to touch. Not that she wanted to. His green eyes gazed down at her. "I could use help picking out the tile." Then his mouth clamped shut.

Was he asking her? What had shifted, and when?

"I'm sure you'd have some good ideas. If you wanted."

He *was* asking. Her mind zoomed into a tile shop where they'd pick out tile together as though she lived there. With him. Like a couple.

Too much. Way too much. "That would be fun." Oh, wait. Her mouth hadn't gotten the memo.

His lips curved in a small smile. "Really? Maybe next Saturday we can run down to Wynnton." The smile disappeared and his eyes chilled. "I guess that means I'm asking for transportation." He ran his fingers through his mass of dark red hair and ducked his head.

Of course that's all it was. A hippie with no car needing a ride. But still, he'd asked her, of all the people on the farm. "Yeah, we can do that. Next week is good."

Keanan's head jerked up and the warmth returned to his eyes. "You don't mind? I've never been in this situation before."

What situation? Needing building supplies? Guess his old tent didn't run to tile.

"Hey, Keanan, is this the layout you'd planned?"

His eyes searched hers for a long moment before he turned to Brent's call.

The tiny bathroom seemed much larger without his presence. She needed a moment to compose herself before rejoining the others. What kind of tile would be best? What size of a budget did he have? They wouldn't be able to use large squares on the curving outside wall, already fitted with plywood bolted to the steel, but six-inch tiles would probably work. A band or two of glass mosaics might add some sparkle.

Chelsea inhaled deeply, still smelling Keanan's musk. Then she let out her breath and leaned across the small sink to the view outside. This was crazy. She was not attracted to this guy. She did not like this grain bin house, and she definitely did not like the idea of a composting toilet. What she needed was to get a hold of herself, stop fantasizing, and go measure windows for curtains.

She turned back into the living area. Sierra's eyebrows rose above twinkling eyes. Chelsea shook her head and rolled her own. This was so not happening.

o0o

Keanan tilted his head. The thirty-inch sink base sat beneath the double windows with a twenty-four-inch drawer section to the right and a two-door base flanking each side.

"You sure that's enough kitchen for you?" asked Brent.

Somewhere behind him, Chelsea watched. He could feel her presence. Keanan itched to ask her what she thought, but he didn't dare put her on the spot again. Not with her sister or Brent here, both probably jumping to conclusions.

Keanan measured the gap to the right of the sink base. Brent had left enough room for the bar fridge. He imagined a reclaimed-wood counter curving the length of the space with the two-burner stovetop inset on the left. Open shelves on either side of the windows.

He glanced at Brent. "I think it's good. All I need is a place to fix coffee and toast, really. Make some popcorn."

Sierra ran purple-tipped fingers across a cupboard. "That's my favorite part of communal living, too. I'd rather cook for the gang a few times a week than cook for two people three times a day."

"Do you think it's okay, then?" Keanan flicked a glance at Chelsea, who leaned against the bathroom doorjamb.

"You have as much kitchen as we do in the duplex," Sierra replied. "I've found it to be enough." She turned to her sister. "Don't you think, Chels? You like to cook more than I do."

Keanan's eyes snagged on Chelsea's eyes, the blue of a springtime sky.

She nodded, clearing her throat. "Good layout."

"I have an island coming. With two stools so we can eat at it." Keanan felt a flush creep up his neck. Where had those words come from? Yes, he could envision Chelsea, hair tied back with one of her flowered scarves, puttering around the little kitchen. Sitting at that island while he passed her a cup of tea. Curling up with him on a living room chair.

Maybe a love seat. Was there room for one? He scanned the area over by the curved stairs. He'd make room.

This place had been designed for one. Just for him. He'd never expected a desire to share his home. His life. His heart.

Keanan blinked and glanced back at Chelsea. She watched him, biting her lip. He grinned at her then turned the smile on the others, too. Not that he'd fool anyone.

Brent scooted a cabinet over a smidge, but Sierra winked at Keanan.

Oh, man. All he needed — all Chelsea needed — was her sister smelling blood. He'd seen how avidly this group watched Allison and Brent's relationship last spring. He'd done it himself, wondering if they were ever going to mend their differences or if Brent would finish building Allison's house and the farm school and disappear back to Coeur d'Alene, never to be heard from again.

Now Brent lived in a small apartment in town until his upcoming wedding to Allison. He still worked for his uncle at

Timber Framing Plus with several contracts lined up around Galena Landing. These days he was building a mansion for Tyrell Burke, a neighboring beekeeper, and spending his evenings and weekends helping Keanan create this house out of a pair of grain bins. Brent refused payment, saying his needs were being met and this was his current contribution to the farm community.

"Got a tape measure?" asked Sierra.

"Uh. Yes." Keanan reached into his toolbox and handed one over. "Measuring windows?"

"Yep. Chelsea and I have a lot of sewing to do." She tilted her head at him. "Want to see the fabric I picked?"

He glanced between Sierra and Chelsea. "Certainly."

Sierra lifted swatches from her bag. "These are from Rosemary's stash. She'd planned to make a couple of more quilts for Romania with them, but offered them to me instead." She grinned at Keanan as her hand smoothed the cloth. "Or rather, to you."

The top piece was a solid green, not that different from the green of his door, so that would be okay. A solid blue peeked from beneath it. The color of Chelsea's eyes. More than okay. Beneath that? It was hard to tell. "Let me see."

Sierra arranged the three pieces with the print in the center. It was kind of wild, swirly, with blues and greens and browns. Then she draped a mottled golden brown across them all.

No flowers. No pastels. Nothing too girly. Good. He glanced at Chelsea, who fingered the fabric. Maybe not girly enough? Her presence zapped his confidence.

"I like them." He tried to sound in charge, but heard the question in his own voice. "Where are you putting each color?"

Sierra laughed. "Wherever you want." She met his gaze.

Keanan shook his head. "Surprise me."

o0o

The upstairs was roomier and brighter than Chelsea expected, with windows on every side. There'd even be room for a king-size bed up here. With Keanan's height, that would likely be his choice, unless he preferred to keep sleeping on the mat and sleeping bag that lay on the wooden floor.

Sierra nudged her. "I'm wondering if the fabrics are too bold. Too masculine."

Bold and masculine about summed up Keanan Welsh. His expression had seemed to approve of the fabrics.

Chelsea raised her eyebrows at her sister. "Why would you say that?"

Sierra lowered her voice. "How long do you think our Keanan will stay a bachelor? I'd hate to have to redo all the window coverings in a few months when he decides to get married."

Why couldn't the heat creeping up her face dissipate instead? Chelsea turned away from her sister to look out the nearest window with its view of evergreens up the mountain. "Who knows what goes on in his mind? I don't think you can count on a change in his status any time soon."

"I should probably inject a bit of purple or pink."

Chelsea pivoted. "As if."

"Aw, come on." Sierra glanced down the staircase then stepped closer to Chelsea. "I saw you two staring in each others' eyes."

"You're imagining things. That's the problem with all of you mushy in-love people here at Green Acres. You think no one can be happy without a spouse. That just because Keanan and I are the only single people on the property, we must be destined for each other." Chelsea realized her voice had risen. Hopefully not enough to get the guys' attention downstairs. "Quit trying to be a matchmaker. I'm so done with that."

"Whoa, don't get your knickers in a knot."

"Do you have all the measurements jotted down? I need out of here." She didn't want to think about Keanan Welsh and his cozy little round house. She didn't want to think about the king-size bed he'd undoubtedly put right over there. She didn't want to think about his green eyes and the intense way he looked at her sometimes.

Air. She needed air.

Chapter 9 --

*K*eanan loaded three tacos on his plate and took a seat across the round table from Tracy with his back to the serving area. This put both group leaders relatively equidistant from each guest in their Alpha group, plus he wouldn't be distracted by Chelsea. He had a job to do here.

Wesley slid into the chair next to him then jerked his head toward the serving table. "*She's* here again. Man, I need to introduce myself. She's hot."

No need to wonder whom Wesley meant. Chelsea was the only kitchen staff who'd been here every week and often the only one under fifty. Keanan ought to cheerfully introduce the pair, but what would he do if they hit it off? No. He couldn't do it.

Wesley elbowed him, apparently oblivious. "Who is she? Do you know her name?"

Chelsea definitely could be classified as hot, even adding lettuce to a bowl. Clad tonight in a long-sleeved floral top matching both her intense blue eyes and her pink glasses, she also wore slim jeans that tapered to bright pink heels. Crazy shoes for being on her feet for so long, but she didn't seem to notice as she scurried back and forth to the kitchen.

Memory returned and he glanced at Wesley. "Chelsea. Her name is Chelsea Riehl."

The young guy's eyes narrowed for a second. "Wouldn't want to interfere."

Keanan shook his head. No more looking at Chelsea tonight. At all. "Nothing to interfere with. She's only a friend." Tell that to his dreams. Ever since last weekend when she and Sierra had been in and out of his space hanging bits of fabric, he'd seen her everywhere in his little home. He'd blinked her away so many times that anyone watching him would think he had a nervous condition.

Wesley glanced back. "Cool." He gathered his taco and had a big bite. "So, what are we talking about tonight?"

The training advised the dinner hour to be Alpha-discussion-free. Keanan waggled his eyebrows. "Guess you'll have to wait and see."

One of the young women leaned closer. "I read ahead in the book. It's about having faith."

"Hmm." Wesley polished off his first taco.

Keanan looked at his plate. Better get to work on the food he'd helped prepare earlier today at the farm. It would never do to scrape good organic beef and beans into the bucket, even if it came home to the pigs.

oOo

Claire slid another tray into the church kitchen's commercial dishwasher as Chelsea returned with another load of dirty dishes. Claire jerked her chin toward the auditorium beyond. "Keanan's really in his element here."

"Umhmm." Chelsea picked up a plate and a scraper. "Seems to be."

"Have you ever taken Alpha?"

"Me?" Chelsea glanced up. "No." It had always seemed something for nonbelievers. She already knew all that stuff. Not only had she gone to Sunday school, church, and youth group, but attended a private Christian school. What could Alpha possibly teach her?

"I love how the program breaks everything down into logical chunks that lead into each other. When I attended the course in Seattle, it really filled in some of the gaps in my understanding."

That's right. Claire hadn't been raised in a Christian home. She couldn't be expected to know everything. "That's cool."

Claire leaned back against the counter. "I can't figure out what makes you tick, Chelsea."

"What do you mean?"

"Tell me what God's been teaching you lately in your quiet time."

Chelsea angled a stack of plates into a clean dishwasher tray. Did she have to answer this? But it seemed rude to say it was none of her friend's business. To paraphrase the farm mandate, everything was everyone's business. "Uh, I've been reading through the prophets." At least she had been, last time she cracked her Bible. "There's a lot of doom and gloom in those books."

"But so much promise, too."

Chelsea nodded.

"God always offers redemption to those who repent and call on His name." Claire pulled a tray out of the steaming dishwasher and slid another in. "Sometimes when I get bogged down, I switch up which version I'm reading."

Who said she was bogged down? Well, maybe she'd admitted it herself.

"That's where I like my cell phone, honestly. I've downloaded several versions, and it's easy to flip between them."

Chelsea should probably do that. She glanced at Claire. "Good idea."

Claire's warm brown eyes met hers and held. "It's okay to struggle, girl, so long as the result is that we dig deeper into God's word. There are some great study guides available online, too."

Noel entered the kitchen carrying the coffee urn. "Empty. Want me to start a new batch?"

Good distraction. "They've moved on to the video?"

"Yes."

"Half full with decaf is good then. Some of them will want coffee over their group discussion afterward."

Noel saluted. "I'm on it." He headed for the sink to dump the grounds.

Chelsea reached for the dessert containers Claire had packed at the farm. She opened the first one. "Plum upside-down cake?"

"Thanks for the recipe." Claire chuckled. "We have so many plums in the freezer I figured this was a good chance to get rid of a bunch."

"Right." Plum upside down. That's how Chelsea felt about life. Portland had been so much simpler. She'd known what to expect of her life there. She'd run her event business from her parents' basement, gone for lunch and church on Sundays with her friends. She'd thought the nature of her business kept her in touch with the outside world but, looking back, the truth was that most of her clients had been people from her parents' wealthy neighborhood and church. She hadn't dealt much with folks outside of her social sphere.

Upside down. What would her friends think of Keanan and his grain bin? The same thing she'd thought. Beneath her. Best to ignore and hope it would go away if she paid it no mind. She'd tried that tack on Keanan. It so hadn't worked.

And now Claire questioned her spiritual life. Politely enough, but that seemed upside down, too, without the structure she'd had back home.

It turned out her skills in event coordination weren't even needed at Green Acres Farm. She could've helped Allison plan her wedding from Portland, as she'd done for Sierra. She was doing the reverse right now, planning her Portland church's upcoming Christmas event from Idaho.

It didn't take any great talent to peel, chop, and puree tomatoes. To do all the other mundane chores around the farm, like feeding the chickens and gathering eggs. Soon they'd be butchering pigs and a steer. How much of her talent did trimming and wrapping meat take?

Maybe she shouldn't have moved to the farm. Maybe she'd deluded herself into thinking she could fit here. To make a difference. She wasn't flexible enough. Spiritual enough.

Chelsea arranged pieces of the cake and assorted cookies on platters as she blinked back tears. No letting Claire or Noel see those, for sure. When would she find her purpose in life? Some fulfillment?

She'd watched Keanan with his Alpha group for several weeks now. He was making a difference. Thankfully ignoring Tracy's advances, which might've slowed as a result. Okay, honestly, Tracy mostly seemed to focus on the group discussions, too. Maybe Chelsea had been reading too much into Tracy.

Maybe she was reading too much into Keanan's attention, too. He probably saw her as someone as needy as those in his group. Someone who needed God's salvation.

She had that, but sometimes it seemed so far away.

oOo

Keanan dropped his elbows to the table and cradled his head in his hands. *Oh, God, sometimes this process seems so slow. Let me trust Your Spirit, Lord. I know You're working, even when I can't see it.*

One of Tracy's friends had spent the whole evening flirting with Wesley. Maybe that's even why the woman kept showing up, week after week. Usually Keanan was able to bring the conversation back around to the discussion topics, but this entire evening had seemed a bust.

"How was tonight, son?" Pastor Ron straddled the chair beside him.

Keanan scrubbed his hair with both hands then tried to smooth down the mess he'd likely made. "I just don't know." He met Tracy's gaze across the table. "What do you think?"

"I'm sorry about Diana. She's always pretty focused on the guys."

So he could be thankful he wasn't the one in her line of fire. He'd take the small mercies. Keanan turned to Ron and spread his hands out.

"And yet God keeps bringing them both back every week." The pastor quirked a grin at Keanan. "Our job is to keep praying for each of them and to provide the venue for discussion. Only God can do the work behind the scenes in each life."

Keanan nodded. "Sometimes I forget it isn't up to me to save the souls. I get so invested and take it personally."

"I agree." Tracy leaned forward, meeting his gaze again. "I work with Diana and Rylee every day. I have to bite back my words constantly, that I don't keep asking them what they thought of the videos and discussions all week long."

"Right. We have to let God do the work only He can do." Keanan took a deep breath and released it slowly.

Ed and Mona joined the group around the table as the distant doors clanged shut behind the last guests. "Good questions tonight." Ed's arm rested across the back of his wife's chair. "I'd say most of our group is considering this step of faith."

Mona nodded.

Across the room, Chelsea flipped the kitchen light switch off and shut the door. She slung her gigantic purse over her shoulder and stood, holding her jacket, waiting for him.

Exhaustion overwhelmed Keanan. "I need to go, if that's all right."

Ron rested a hand on Keanan's shoulder and prayed for the group.

Keanan thanked him, rose, and crossed the room. Chelsea looked as tired as he felt. "Ready? Can I carry anything?"

She shook her head. "Claire and Noel took care of everything before they left. Let's go."

He followed her through the dim building and out to the parking lot then folded himself into the passenger seat of her car. "That was intense tonight."

Chelsea started the engine. "Looked like it."

Why the cutting edge to the words? Keanan turned to look at her. "What do you mean?"

She laughed, but not with humor. "Tracy watching you."

So not what he'd expected Chelsea to say. It took his brain a few seconds to catch up. "Tracy? I'm sorry. You lost me."

"It doesn't take much imagination to see what she thinks of you."

The cold slosh her words first evoked warmed considerably at the tone of her voice. "Jealous?" he asked softly.

The word hung in the air between them, all but visible.

Chelsea shifted into gear and drove down the street.

Keanan watched as she bit her lip and avoided eye contact. "If it's any consolation, I'm not attracted to Tracy Grindle."

"Consolation?" She darted a glance his direction. "Why would it be?"

He forced the grin away from his cheeks. "I've made a habit over the years of not noticing women that way. If I assume they're not interested in me, that becomes true sooner or later."

"Uh huh." She flipped the signal light on and turned onto the highway.

"So far, anyway. Things could change."

"With Tracy."

"No, Chelsea. Not with Tracy." Would she look his way? Did he want her to?

"She's pretty. Petite. Bubbly."

Probably all those things, but what did they matter?

When he didn't respond, Chelsea glanced at him. "What's not to like about her?"

Keanan scratched the back of his neck. Women. Why was Chelsea pushing him this way? "I don't know of any reason not to like her."

Chelsea thumped the steering wheel as though for punctuation.

"But that doesn't mean she attracts me. I don't find myself wondering what she's thinking, or what she's doing, or what her favorite music is. I haven't thought about her favorite color, or her perfume, or what her hair might feel like."

In the dim glow of the car's interior, he could see Chelsea swallow hard. "You've given a lot of thought to what you don't wonder."

"Not really."

She shot him a furtive glance, but he wasn't backing down at this stage. Tired before, now he had a second wind. Lord help him.

"Those are the kinds of things I wonder about you."

Her fingers clenched on the steering wheel. "About me?"

"Every day. Many times a day."

"Oh." Her voice all but squeaked.

"There's something else, too." Keanan took a deep breath. "Sometimes I wonder if you feel the same way."

She narrowed her eyes in his direction. "Sometimes. But I fight it."

Chapter 10 --

*T*hanks for trusting me with your car." Keanan glanced her way from behind the wheel.

"No problem." Chelsea had seen him drive so few times that she'd purposefully thought back to remember if he had a license. But it was his shopping trip, and he should be in control. Besides, in her world, guys drove and girls sat in the passenger seat, not the other way around. The car might be small, but there'd be enough room for his purchases in the trunk.

"Any suggestions where we should go in Wynnton? I'm afraid I haven't been often enough to form an opinion."

Chelsea swiped on her phone and tapped in a search. "We can start with the building center on this end of town. There are several additional options."

In her periphery, she saw his nod. Noticed his glance in her direction. No way, buster. Eyes on the road. Why else had she given him control of her vehicle but to keep him too busy to watch her the way he had on the way home the other evening?

She'd hardly slept, and the two nights since hadn't been much better. Trying to figure him out would be easier if she were rested.

Keanan had flat-out admitted he was interested in her. Before that, she'd been able to block her own growing feelings, but now his words lay out in the open, too blatant to ignore. Wouldn't stop her from trying.

"You've been rather quiet the past few days." His words, so conversational, as though he hadn't rocked her world on Wednesday evening.

"Lots to think about."

"I didn't mean to scare you off." His big hands clenched the steering wheel.

Not that she was looking at his long fingers, brown from the sun, with their calluses and trimmed nails. Chelsea turned and stared out the window, where golden autumn leaves fluttered in the breeze, before joining their friends to carpet the ground.

Keanan sighed.

So she was causing him stress? Well, it was mutual. She felt as tight as... as one of his guitar strings. Ready to twang.

"I'm sorry, Chelsea. I spoke too soon. I... I thought you might feel the same, but I was wrong. I've avoided romantic entanglement in the past and never learned how to read women. I blundered. Dreadfully. I've ruined the friendship we might have had. The working relationship on the farm. Even the remaining weeks of Alpha."

When would he ever stop apologizing?

"Dreams I never knew I had have been awakened. Never before have I desired to know someone. Wondered their thoughts. Their hopes. Their—"

"Keanan."

The car filled with an electric silence. A blessed silence.

"Yes?"

Chelsea shot him a quick glance, just enough to notice his twitching jaw as he stared ahead, to see those hands flex and tighten on the steering wheel. Several thoughts assaulted her.

The guy blathered when he was nervous.

He really cared about her, man to woman.

Forget Tracy.

But Chelsea wasn't worthy.

Where to start? Anywhere? Why couldn't he have left well enough alone instead of pushing her more today? What would she have thought if he'd been quiet? That he hadn't meant it. That he regretted his words.

Obviously not the case.

"Chelsea? Speak to me."

Why wasn't silence an option? She could crank some tunes. They could sing along. But no. "I don't know what to say."

"Is it me? Have I offended you in some way?"

"It's not you."

"There's someone else, then. I should have thought to ask. Some man in Portland?" His voice, so vulnerable.

"No, there isn't anyone else." Not since Robert. That'd been a while.

"But... what? I am too big. Too unfashionable. Too unrefined."

Once she might have thought that. Possibly last week. "Keanan. No."

"Then what? Tell me."

"You talk too much."

Nervous laughter boomed through the car like a jet breaking the sound barrier. "Perhaps this is true."

Definitely true. "I need time. I don't know what I think of you. Of us."

He stared at her so long she wanted to point him back at the highway. "There is an us?"

Trust him to latch onto that one word. "We hardly know each other. Where did you grow up? Do you have siblings? What experiences shaped you?" She stopped before adding *into a hippie.* Still, her questions were reasonable. She didn't even know how old he was.

He nodded at the road ahead. "You wish to know me. This is good. Valid. I turned thirty this summer. You?"

Like he'd read her mind. "Twenty-six. In August."

"I'm an only child. My parents are divorced. My father is in film. My mother a jewelry designer." Keanan glanced at her.

"Were you young when your family split up?"

"Twelve. My mother needed to find herself."

Chelsea would be better off finding herself before marriage. Better for everyone.

"Which parent did you live with?"

He sighed. "Back and forth, a month at a time. My father hired a tutor to oversee my education. Ivan accompanied me."

A life of privilege, then. Perhaps not completely unlike her own. "What do they think of you moving here to Idaho?"

A grin poked at his cheek. "My father has long since washed his hands of me. He is busy with a new young wife — his fourth — and two small children." He tipped his head and glanced at Chelsea. "I suppose I do have siblings. Half-brothers. I don't think of them that way."

"Your mother?"

"Many relationships. Free love, you know?" His voice softened. "But she came to know Jesus several years ago."

"Th-that's great."

"Praying with her has been the greatest privilege of my life."

Something stirred inside Chelsea. She'd never had that experience. Never stepped outside her comfort zone enough to get close to someone who didn't share her beliefs. "When did you become a Christian?"

"I was seventeen. My tutor's sister led him to Jesus, and Ivan told me all about it. Hungry for reality, for something to put my faith in. My father's second marriage was on the rocks. My mother—" He shrugged. "She didn't believe in absolutes. There was no truth. No right or wrong. To her, everything was relative and experiential. My soul craved a foundation. Not authoritarian, like my father, where there was no love. Not free-spirited like my mother, where nothing mattered but the feelings of the moment."

Chelsea hungered, too. "I've sometimes wondered what it must be like to hear about Jesus for the first time. I've known Him since I was a little kid. Maybe you could say I've been brainwashed."

"Where there is a great drought, a spring rain fills the cracks and seeps into the soil. The contrast is stark. From dark ugliness to great beauty."

She nodded at the word picture. He had a way of taking simple words and making them sound like poetry.

"But rain falls on the mountains and in the lush meadows, too. It brings new life wherever it comes. So with the Spirit. The old is gone and no longer matters. All is refreshed."

Her soul craved that refreshment, but her spiritual horizon seemed as empty of rainclouds as the bright October sky.

oOo

Keanan tagged behind Chelsea as she perused the tile section of the third store. She was like a hummingbird, zooming here, hovering there. He could discern no pattern, no concept of what caught her eye and what wasn't worthy of a second glance.

What had been wrong with the tiles at the first store? Keanan was smart enough not to put voice to that thought... and a few others, for all he'd blathered in the car on their drive to Wynnton. He was in no hurry to return to Green Acres. Not until he could redeem the day.

Chelsea seemed in her element, snapping photos on her cell phone, bringing up its calculator to tap in numbers, keying search words into the tiny browser tab.

His fingers nailed three letters at once when he tried that. She was so dainty, so feminine. When had he stopped making mental mockery of her floral scarves and high heels?

Keanan shifted closer, smelling the subtle scent of her, bending until his cheek brushed the top of her hair. "Find anything you like?"

"Oh!" She startled, taking a step back and landing one pointy heel on his leather shoe. It would take more than that to bruise him.

His hands balanced her, giant paws on her slender arms. "Sorry."

"Um, the tiles..." She turned, her blue eyes gazing up into his.

"What about them?" He slid his hands down to her elbows then back to her shoulders. An invisible magnetic field kept him from breaking contact. The same pull kept his eyes fixed on hers.

"There are tiles I like." But her voice was breathy, and she seemed equally unable to look away.

His hands slipped from her arms to her waist and settled on the curve of her hips. "Which do you like?" A bold question, with perhaps more than one correct answer.

She bit her lip, dragging his gaze to the soft flesh. Did pink lipstick come off when kissed? This wasn't the moment to find out. His gaze snapped back to her eyes, and he somehow managed to remove one hand from her hip. The other compensated by sliding around her slender waist.

Keanan turned her to face the tile beside him. "Show me."

Her voice caught. "The tile?"

Or how she felt about him. But tile was safer.

"Um, that one." She pointed, her pink fingernail gleaming. "With a band of the glass mosaic from the first store."

"Okay. How much do we need?"

"About one hundred square feet."

Who knew there was a part of his brain still able to function and multiply by cost? Thankfully the math was simple. "Sounds good."

"We can look some more. If you want."

He pulled her tighter against his side. "If you like this one, it's good by me. Let's get it. May I take you for lunch? I hear the Bluebell has great food." The sooner the shopping was out of the way, the sooner they could focus on the important things.

Like how they felt about each other. Surely she wasn't immune.

o0o

Chelsea took a deep, steadying breath as Keanan and the sales clerk stacked boxes of tile on the cart. What had happened there? Two conversations simultaneously. One about tile and one about... what? He'd hinted — more than hinted — at a desired relationship on the drive to Wynnton. When his hands encircled her waist and his green eyes bonded to hers, anything seemed possible.

But it was expected by everyone at Green Acres. Her sister smirked whenever Keanan was present or even mentioned. Claire, Jo, Allison — each of them had wiggled their eyebrows a time or two. It was like it wasn't possible or acceptable to be single.

She remembered speaking flippant words to Brent a few months before, about the farm water causing people to fall in love. It'd been a joke. He'd been in the throes of unrequited love and hadn't found her words funny at the time. Now it was Chelsea who wondered if it were true and not a tale. What other explanation could there be? Not that she hadn't desired marriage and a family, but with Keanan? When had the thought become less repulsive? Or even inviting?

She trailed behind him as he took the tiles, mastic, and grout through checkout. Followed him to the car, where he popped the trunk and loaded the building supplies.

Keanan opened the passenger side for her and held her gaze while she slid inside. He shut the door and trundled across the lot to return the cart.

Chelsea shivered and rubbed her arms briskly. Right where Keanan's warm hands had rested not long before.

He was safe. She could trust him.

But could she trust herself?

Chapter 11 --

*K*eanan leaned back in the booth at the Bluebell, watching Chelsea as she poked a fork in her dessert. He could hardly take his eyes off her. "Thanks for coming with me today."

She flicked him a wry grin. "You've mentioned that before." Chelsea popped a bite of pineapple upside-down cake into her mouth. A moment later she said, "What was your plan B for getting tile?"

"Brent offered to order extra on his next order." He shrugged.

"Which would've depended on his other client's taste?"

Keanan nodded. "Honestly, they're likely to make a better choice than I would have without help. But it's only shower tile."

"But you'll stand in that shower every day for the rest of your life." Her gaze dropped back to her plate. "Or however long you're at Green Acres, I guess."

Ah, was that part of the problem? She saw him as a transient? "Everyone needs a place to come home to."

If she cut that cake into any more pieces, she might as well run it through the blender. Little structure remained as it was. She glanced up. "What do you mean?"

Time to share his dreams. His plans. "There's a mission in Africa that supplies solar panels and teaches people how to use solar cookers. They make a difference in people's lives every day.

I think I've mentioned them before."

"I'm lost. We were talking about your shower tile. How did Africa get into the conversation?"

"Sorry. I only meant that I now have a home base, but I'll be in Africa for several months this winter. I'll be back in Idaho before spring planting."

oOo

Chelsea became aware of her gaping mouth and snapped it shut. "Just like that? Off to Africa?"

Something squeezed her fingers, and she looked down. Keanan's large hands enveloped hers. She pulled away and laid her hands in her lap. "I thought once you signed on at Green Acres, you were committing to the farm."

A flash of something — pain? — crossed his face, gone again in an instant, though the green eyes seemed a bit more wary. "I mentioned this possibility with the group a few times, perhaps before you came. Once the jars and freezers are full of food and the fall work is complete, there's not much to do every day. Meals to prepare, animals to feed, eggs to gather. It doesn't take ten adults each working a twelve-hour day."

She'd seen Green Acres with a blanket of snow when she visited last winter. She could hardly wait for that slower pace, the chance to catch up on reading and enjoy a cup of tea without feeling she was avoiding work.

Still, he made some kind of sense. Chores through the winter would take minimal time. He made it sound like they'd all be slackers. Chelsea preferred to think of it as a well-earned rest.

"Have you ever traveled, Chelsea?"

She blinked his face back into focus. "Sure. I've been to Mexico several times. Belize twice."

He leaned forward, eyes lit up. "With what mission?"

"Mission?" Surely she'd heard him wrong. "On vacation with my family at all-inclusive resorts."

"Oh." The fire seemed to fizzle out.

"Look, my parents tithe. My church back home supports missions." She'd been about to say the youth went on church-building trips, but he'd ask if she'd ever gone. Somehow his opinion mattered, even with the gulf wide open between them. "I don't have much personal income right now at the farm, but I tithe, too." Had she cut enough defensiveness out of her voice?

"Tithing is—" He took a deep breath. "Never mind."

"No, tell me." She might as well get both barrels now. That would help her remember why Keanan Welsh was not the right man for her. To think she'd caught herself dreaming of taking a shower surrounded by those tiles they'd bought. Yeah. So not happening. Her first instinct had been correct. This guy was not only on a different wavelength but also from a different planet.

"We are raised with so much privilege here." Keanan studied her from serious green eyes. "Even those with little have vastly more than most people in third world countries."

Hard to argue with that, so she nodded. Thank God she'd been born in Portland to Tim and Sandra Riehl. It could've been much worse.

"But we aren't given wealth to hoard it. God expects us to see the needs of others and to do what we can."

"I told you I tithe. That's not hoarding. I do my duty to others." What gave Keanan the right to make her feel guilty about her lifestyle? "I'm not in pursuit of big money, anyway. We're all about community at Green Acres. We teach stewardship and caring for God's creation. If I wanted a fat paycheck and a big house, I wouldn't have moved to Idaho. I'd have stayed in Portland."

Keanan opened his mouth and closed it again. Then he stared down at those giant hands of his for a long moment.

Should she back down? No. A relationship with a guy like him had no future. Best to know this at the outset. Let him go to Africa. Let him do his thing and be better than her. Maybe she'd even send her tithe his way and enable him to do more good deeds.

Was that what it meant in the Bible to heap coals of fire on someone's head? She couldn't remember. Probably not, but hey.

"Did you want to finish your dessert or shall we head back to Green Acres?"

Chelsea looked down. Man, she had mashed that cake into nothing. She set the fork carefully at the edge of the plate. "I'm done, thanks."

The waitress had deposited the check at the edge of the table some time ago. Keanan picked up the vinyl folder just as Chelsea reached for it. "I'll pay," she said.

"No." Keanan's eyes narrowed. "We came to buy tile for my home. I'll pick up the tab."

Right. It had never been a date. She clenched her jaw. "Fine then. Thank you." Probably hadn't sounded too gracious. She tried to inhale, but the sadness in his green eyes drowned her. What was she supposed to say? That she could be perfect just like him? She couldn't be. She was who she was, and she couldn't make herself into anyone else.

A man who truly loved her wouldn't expect her to change. Therefore, Keanan Welsh did not love her. No surprise there.

He stood and waited for her. Like a gentleman.

Chelsea grabbed her purse and slid out of the booth. "Excuse me. I need to use the ladies' room." Without meeting his gaze, she bolted.

o0o

"Great choice." Brent stacked the glass mosaics next to the six-inch tiles outside the bathroom door.

Keanan shrugged. "You can thank Chelsea." He couldn't force animation into his voice when only a heavy heart at the day's discussion lingered.

"She's got good taste."

"She does." Probably she had good taste in men, too. A man totally unlike Keanan would sweep her off her feet one day. He only hoped he wouldn't have to watch it happen.

Brent leaned against the wall. "What happened?"

"What do you mean?"

"Look, I'm not the most sensitive guy on the planet. I'm sure Allison could give you many instances where I've missed the boat."

Keanan doubted it. Brent had poured his soul into perfecting every tiny detail of the timber-framed house he'd built for Allison, not knowing at the time if he'd ever live in it with her and young Finnley.

"You left this morning with a bounce in your step and you've come back dragging. It doesn't take a genius to figure out the day didn't go as you hoped." Brent nudged the boxes with a steel-toed boot. "Other than the classy tile."

Was this when Keanan admitted he was ready to borrow Brent's truck and return the tile that had Chelsea's personality stamped all over it? How could he bear to see this piece of her every time he entered his bathroom?

He found his voice. "You're right. The day zipped downhill."

"How so?"

No mockery, no humor came through the other man's eyes or voice. Maybe Brent would be a good sounding board. "Chelsea didn't know I'm going to Africa this winter."

Brent tilted his head and his eyebrows rose.

"I thought she'd see the value of a mission trip like that." Keanan stared into Brent's eyes. "She doesn't."

"But she's a believer. She must have signed a statement of faith to join the community. I know both Allison and I did. Didn't you?"

Keanan nodded. "I did. I'm sure Chelsea did, too. But that's only the barest of foundations, as you know. She believes." He sighed. "I thought when she offered to help in the kitchen at Alpha that she was burdened for the lost. Instead, she felt pushed into it by Ed Graysen. You know how he is. He doesn't make it easy to say *no*."

Brent chuckled. "Too true."

"She told him she was an event planner and caterer, and he mentioned the church's need for a coordinator. Before she knew what'd happened, she'd agreed."

"God can work through that kind of obedience."

"I agree. But willingness is useful."

"Not sure." Brent looked thoughtful. "I seem to remember people in Bible times that God used, even against their desire."

"But it's so much better to embrace God's call! Stepping forward in faith to see what He'll do."

"Not arguing with that, man. Not at all."

Silence reigned for a few minutes while Keanan forced his emotions into line. "I'm sure she thinks I think I'm better than her. I may have said things that were inappropriate." Keanan scrubbed his hands through his hair. "Now I'm nothing but an oaf. An overgrown hippie."

Something flickered in Brent's eyes. "She said that?"

Keanan stared at the polished concrete floor. Did he have to admit it?

"Looked in the mirror lately?"

"What?" Keanan reared back, narrowing his gaze at the shorter man.

"I'm sure you don't look in one much. Haven't installed one in here yet." Brent shook his head, chuckling. "You look fine to me, but hey, I'm a guy. I understand testosterone."

"What are you talking about?"

"There's nothing wrong with long hair and wearing socks in your sandals. You know what they say. Be yourself; everyone else is already taken."

"I am not a hippie, no matter what she says." Visions of dope-smoking free-love advocates in tie-dye sprang to mind. He wasn't that kind of man. So he was big. He couldn't exactly help his size. Could he do anything about her other assumptions? It didn't matter. Not unless his opinion of her changed as well.

"My friend, may I pray with you? For you?"

Keanan looked at his friend. His brother in Christ. He bowed his head. "I'd be honored."

Chapter 12 --

She'd managed to avoid Keanan Welsh since Saturday. It had taken some doing. Skipping church, sneaking plates of leftovers, and holing herself up in the duplex to work on the big Christmas fundraiser event in Portland. Chelsea had organized it every year for the past five. She didn't need to be on location to get the basics rolling. Besides, work helped push away not only thoughts of Keanan, but reminders of how tight he was with God.

"Yes, everything is fine. I'm just busy." She'd all but lied to Sierra, Gabe, and Claire. No one else had seemed to notice or, if they had, they'd counted on her sister to talk to her. To act as a bridge.

Bridges were unacceptable. Crossing even one would topple this house of cards. Inside herself, a war waged, but she'd ignore its existence as long as she could. She didn't embrace the chasm. The battle. But how could it be solved?

Maybe it couldn't.

Chelsea slipped into the straw bale house early on Wednesday morning, carrying her keys and a note, which she set on the peninsula while she helped herself to a few assorted leftovers from the fridge and a canning jar of soup from the larder.

A quiet *snick* sounded behind her, and she whirled.

Keanan. She blinked. With a haircut?

He stood just inside the door watching her across the dining room table, across the peninsula.

Chelsea's heart clenched at the sadness on his face. She swallowed hard, her mouth suddenly dry, and placed the jar inside her basket on the island. "Keanan. What are you doing in here so early?" He had as much right to be here as she did.

"Sleep has been elusive. You?" He rounded the table and took a seat at the peninsula, his hands folded on the tile countertop, his gaze fixed on hers.

She forced a nonchalant shrug and looked away. "Ditto. I got a little hungry so came for a snack."

Keanan's large hand gestured at the basket of food she'd collected. "That looks enough for a day or two."

Busted. "So, um, you got a haircut." She peeked up from under her lashes. From a thick mass that had flowed past his shoulders to an almost preppy cut. Not a buzz, thank the Lord for small mercies. The shock was big enough as it was.

"Yes. Rosemary cut it for me."

Chelsea tucked two rolls into the basket. "She did a good job." But why?

The question must've showed on her face. "I'm not a hippie, Chelsea."

Words stalled, but her thoughts ran free, albeit in circles.

I never said you were.

A lie.

You cut your hair because of me?

Too personal.

I've missed you like crazy.

Way too personal.

Help me find a passion for Jesus like you have.

Right. Like she could ever say those words.

"What's this?" He picked up her keys from the counter in front of him. Unfolded the note.

She *had* written his name on the outside. "Oh, that." She forced a laugh. "I didn't expect to run into you. I know it's Wednesday, but I can't make Alpha tonight. Wanda has the meal covered, but you can take my car if you like." Her eyes caught on his like an industrial-strength magnet.

"I'm sorry for how I handled our conversation on Saturday."

Chelsea wasn't sure how much more nonchalance she could feign. "No problem. I always knew we were very different. That's cool. God's into variety." But, seriously... Keanan had cut his hair because of what she'd said?

"I never intended to hurt you. To cause you pain."

Her heart blipped. Did she imagine the slight inflection on the word *you*? "Keanan, don't worry about it. I'm a big girl." A big girl who wanted to grab this basket of food, bolt past him, and spend the day crying in bed with her curtains drawn. Big girl indeed.

"A woman." His green eyes were steady on hers.

She looked down, fiddled with the basket, and bit her lip. She was going to draw blood if she didn't escape soon.

"I am praying you'll find peace in your relationship with God."

That did it. "I'm fine. Really. Save your prayers for the people in your group. They're the ones who need it." She grabbed into thin air and came out with more. "Pray for Tracy. Now there's a girl for you. A woman."

Keanan shook his head slowly. "Chelsea. Don't you see? It's not Tracy I'm interested in. It's you."

Chelsea snapped her mouth shut. *Look anywhere but at him. Anywhere at all. Measure the distance to the door. To freedom.* Would he step in her way? A giant like him could block the entire gap without hardly trying.

"So much seems to be troubling you. I can't stop praying for you. The sunshine — the joy — has gone from your face. I can't deny I'm attracted to you, nor do I want to."

She would not even glance his direction.

"But while I pray God will restore our friendship, I ask even more that He'll woo you into a passionate love affair. With Him."

Chelsea's soul resonated with those words. She wanted that kind of passion, too. But it wasn't Keanan's place to assume it was missing in her life. He judged her.

Of course, she had judged him for being a hippie, which, technically, he wasn't.

"That's great, Keanan. I see why you're such a great missionary. But save it for where it's needed, okay? I'm fine. I've been a Christian since I was a kid. Never a moment of doubt."

"I'm not a great missionary."

"Oh, come on. You care about people, not only me. Just—" she fluttered her hands "—just go do your missionizing. I'll even send you my tithe, such as it is."

"Chelsea." He rounded the end of the peninsula and came closer.

Whichever side of the island he took to get to her, she'd move to the other. She could escape.

She hadn't counted on him simply reaching across the worktop and clasping both her hands in his. She stared down at his thick, tanned fingers, rough from work. The neatly trimmed nails. He wore no rings. No watch. There was no pretension in his hands, just warmth. Security. Nervousness as he gathered her hands and gripped them. His thumbs rubbed hers.

She should pull away. She should tell him once again all the reasons this was a very bad idea. He'd just recited the litany to her. Had he forgotten it already?

"Chelsea." He whispered her name like it was a precious gem. Like a caress. Like the sun peeking out between heavy clouds.

She looked up. He'd dropped both elbows to the island so his face was at her height. So close. She swallowed hard at the intensity of those endlessly deep eyes, green like a glacial lake.

He leaned a little closer and his lips swept her forehead. "My prayers are with you every moment of the day." One large hand lifted and tucked her hair behind her ear, cupping her cheek. The ghost of a smile cracked his face. "And many moments of the long night hours."

Then suddenly, he released her and turned away. Soundless for such a big man, he left the kitchen and crossed to the outside door. Seconds later the door closed behind him.

Chelsea's fingers went to her forehead where his lips had touched. Over the past weeks, he'd awakened a passion in her for a man's love. Was there any hope God would awaken a passion for Him? Maybe it was a good thing Keanan prayed. She had little faith in her own prayers.

o0o

Halfway across the yard, Keanan jerked to a stop. What had he gone to the house for? The reason had fled from his mind. He'd been hungry. That was it. Once the reclaimed countertop in his small kitchen had been installed, he'd be set to keep a bit of food over there. For now, there was still a lot of dust.

As if on cue, his stomach growled, but he couldn't return to the kitchen while Chelsea was still there. He'd already said too much. His hands tingled. Touched too much.

A door closed behind him, the click clearly audible in the still morning air. He turned.

Chelsea walked across the deck, down the few steps, and across the yard toward the duplex, carrying her basket. She caught sight of him not far beyond, and her step faltered. Then she strode the remaining distance and into her home. This time the click of

107

the closing door was considerably louder.

Keanan remembered to breathe, though his feet remained rooted. He needed a time of prayer, of basking in the presence of his Savior. Of pleading with his Lord for Chelsea's spiritual peace.

His stomach reminded him he also needed food. One day soon perhaps he'd fast and pray for her. Today, however, had too many community tasks for that kind of focus. He turned on his heel and strode back to the house.

Keanan let himself in and turned toward the kitchen. Past the peninsula, by the island, Claire stood in a fuzzy pink bathrobe, a jar of pickles and a block of cheese in front of her. From behind, Noel nuzzled against the curve of her neck, his arms wrapped around her, his hands rubbing circles on her abdomen.

Something about that scenario... Keanan narrowed his eyes. He might not be the brightest bulb in the box, but the intimate scene made him wonder.

Claire caught sight of him. Her hands stilled Noel's, and Noel glanced up as well.

"Good morning, Keanan." Noel's hands dropped as he shifted to stand beside his wife.

"Good morning." Keanan looked away.

"Hi, Keanan." Claire picked up a knife and began to slice cheese.

Did he imagine a flush on her cheeks? "I'm sorry if I'm interrupting something."

Noel winked. "No worries. Hungry?"

"I am." Keanan approached the kitchen archway. "Mind if I scramble some eggs?"

"Be my guest." Noel chuckled. "Not that you're a guest."

Claire finished preparing her plate and turned toward the hallway leading to the bedroom wing. Cheese, pickles, crackers. A cup of tea, its minty aroma lingering in the air.

Leaning against the doorway, Keanan raised his eyebrows at Noel as she disappeared.

"Uh, yeah." Noel glanced toward the sound of a closing door and scrubbed a hand through his already tousled hair. Then he offered Keanan a sheepish look.

Keanan waited.

"We hadn't meant to tell anyone yet."

Ah, his hunch had been correct. "Then don't. I don't need to be the first to know." He rounded the island toward the large refrigerator.

Noel clapped him on the shoulder. "Thanks, man. What do you want in your eggs? I can chop up some onions and peppers."

"Want to join me?" Keanan peered into the fridge and pulled out a large zucchini and a yellow pepper.

"Sounds good. I'm hungry for more than a handful of crackers and a few slices of cheese." Noel took the vegetables from Keanan, who turned back for eggs and milk.

"Not to mention the pickles."

Noel chuckled. "That was probably the giveaway."

Keanan gave his friend an answering smile. Why did the thought of a new life growing inside Claire affect him so deeply? Watching Zach and Jo with little Madelynn hadn't ever done so. Not even watching Jo's belly swell with their second child, due in just a few weeks.

Those things had happened before he'd become aware of Chelsea. With his emotions tuned toward her, thoughts of babies brought to mind images of him holding her the way Noel had held Claire. Of a quiet moment savoring their child to come.

"We've been trying for nearly a year now."

Why did couples speak of *trying* as though attempting to create a life was some sort of hardship? "Remember I don't need to know." It was true in more ways than one. He didn't need the visual aids that sprang to life in his imagination. Visuals that included Chelsea's blond curly head, her true blue eyes, her—

"Sorry, man. What are you going to do with that zucchini?"

Keanan blinked the large vegetable in his hand back into focus. "Uh, I'll take a couple of inches off and put the rest back. Chop it finely. That okay?"

"Sure." Noel's knife whacked the onion into bits.

They worked quietly for a few minutes. "Noel, how did you know Claire was the woman for you?"

His friend glanced up with a questioning look. "I knew it from the moment I first saw her. Didn't stop me from fighting it, of course."

"Why did you fight?"

"It didn't seem like we had much in common." Noel scraped the chopped onion aside with his blade and started on the pepper. "I wasn't a believer, and she was. I had the travel bug, and she couldn't be pried off this farm with a crowbar." Knives made the only sound for a moment. "There was more, but those were the main issues."

"How did you come to Christ?"

"A lot of it was Claire's deep faith. She had something I needed. But then I fought it because I knew surrendering to Jesus because of her wasn't enough. She'd see through it, or it wouldn't last."

Keanan had rarely met a man more passionate about God than Noel, at least on this continent. The man prayed for others, fervently and verbally, with the slightest provocation.

"As for the desire to travel, that's a mixed bag. I love living here. Guiding hunters and fishermen and hikers into the mountains. But I do sometimes miss scuba diving and tropical beaches." He grinned at Keanan. "I just about had Claire convinced to spend a few weeks in Hawaii this winter. Now I'm not so sure."

Why didn't it bug him to think of his friends vacationing? Why had Chelsea's admission irritated him so much? Because of the angle the conversation had come from. From the sense of entitlement he'd caught.

"I'm no expert, but it seems you have time before travel restrictions would apply to your wife. It'd likely do you both good to get away." Keanan began cracking eggs into a large bowl.

"Good thought. We should have been doing what you're doing before this. I don't know why I never thought of joining missions trips in the winter. That window of opportunity is closed now."

"Someone was required to keep the home fires burning. There weren't many of you here at first. I'm thankful to be unneeded for a few months, knowing my presence won't be missed." He added milk and seasonings to the bowl.

"You'll be missed, my friend. Trust me on that. But we'll be praying for you. You're our ambassador in the name of Jesus."

That sounded good.

"Is it my imagination, or is there someone who'll miss you more than the rest of us will?"

"It's doubtful." Keanan whisked the eggs.

"I'm no expert." Noel chuckled. "To quote you. But we're not blind or stupid, Keanan. Or deaf."

Deaf? Keanan stared at Noel.

"Didn't mean to overhear your conversation with her this mornign." Noel held up a hand. "And I only caught a bit of it before shutting the door again. Seemed like a tender moment."

If only. Keanan sighed. "It's extremely unlikely anything will come of it."

"I remember the feeling."

"No. In this case, it's true. We're miles apart."

Noel clapped him on the back. "I remember that feeling, too. We will pray." And he did, right then and there.

Chapter 13 --

A huge sheet of stainless steel with rolled edges covered the dining room table. Claire dealt out cutting boards like playing cards. Gabe sharpened several long narrow knives. Boning knives, Noel called them when showing Gabe how.

Chelsea was as ready as she was going to get for a day of cutting and grinding up raw meat. She'd tied a floral scarf around her head, taking care to tuck the loose ends in. A T-shirt meant she'd never have to worry about her sleeves getting gross. She wore T-shirts so rarely that she didn't much care what happened to this one.

Allison and Brent had prepared a large breakfast for the crew. Chelsea had nibbled some toast. Just the thought of what was to come had been enough to turn her gut sour.

Sierra sprang for the door upon Noel's shout. He entered, carrying a large slab of beef. "Here's the front shoulder. Trim it out for stewing meat or ground."

Chelsea reached for the knife in front of her. Clenched it. Thankfully Keanan worked outside, helping Zach and Noel carve the beef quarters into manageable pieces for the inside crew.

She was going to screw up one way or another. She'd either puke, cut herself, or invent a new way to embarrass herself with this experienced crew.

Portland had never looked so good.

"Here you go." Claire dropped a hunk of raw meat in front of Chelsea.

The metallic stench rose, and Chelsea's gut flipped over. "What do I do with this?" she got out through gritted teeth.

"I'll work beside you and show you." Claire poked at the meat. "See this part has a lot of lines of fat running through it?"

Chelsea nodded. Maybe if she considered this a biology lesson it would help.

"We'll turn those parts into ground beef. For now, trim off the hard layer of fat and cut the meat small enough to fit in the grinder. Like so." Claire demonstrated, tossing the fat into one bin on the table and the beef chunks into another. "Don't worry too much about the softer fat. We're not trying for particularly lean hamburger. That's so last millennium."

"Okay. What about the parts without fat?"

Claire turned the remaining piece. "This is good for stew. Trim off any gristle and cut the meat into bite-sized pieces. Those go here." She dropped a few cubes into a third bin. "When we have enough to get started, someone will start weighing and wrapping it. That won't be right away, though."

Noel came to the door with a large bowl of trimmings. Allison and Brent each lifted pieces of meat to their cutting boards. Noel leaned over to Claire and brushed a kiss against her cheek. "How are you doing, love?"

"I'm fine."

Why wouldn't she be? Of all the women here, Claire likely had chopped the most raw meat. She'd been a chef for how many years now?

Chelsea glanced at Claire as the door closed again behind Noel. Her friend did seem a little pale, her skin carrying a slight sheen. Then Claire's knife clattered to the floor, and she bolted toward the bedroom wing. Everyone froze around the table, looking at each other. Allison. Brent. Sierra. Gabe.

Sierra set her blade down. "Excuse me." She followed Claire at a more sedate pace.

"Did she say she wasn't feeling well?" asked Gabe of no one in particular.

Allison glanced toward the hallway. "She didn't mention anything to me."

Chelsea frowned. What had Noel just said? *Click.* "Is she pregnant?" She met Allison's gaze as the other woman's eyes widened slightly.

Brent chuckled. "I guess that would do it."

Gabe stared at his cutting board.

Yeah, anything to do with pregnancy or babies hit her brother-in-law hard.

Chelsea dug into her meat. Jo, finding it difficult to work around her large belly, had opted to care for Maddie and Finnley up at their log cabin today. If Claire was out of commission, too, that left a dwindling number of workers to complete the day's tasks.

She chopped the chunk into smaller bits and sorted them before reaching for another piece. A few minutes later Sierra returned just as the outside door opened with Noel and another bowl of meat.

Noel glanced around. "Where's Claire?"

Sierra, re-entering the dining room, jerked her thumb over her shoulder. He strode past, and Sierra leaned against Gabe, who slid an arm around her. "She's pregnant." She closed her eyes.

"Kind of what we figured." Allison raised her eyebrows at Chelsea.

Chelsea shrugged and turned back to trimming meat. There wasn't much she could say to Sierra and Gabe. Though only married a few months, they wanted a baby in the worst way, and it was unlikely to happen with Sierra's endometriosis. To top it off,

Gabe's first wife had been pregnant when she died in a car accident. If Chelsea could snap her fingers and make it happen for her sister, she'd do it in a heartbeat. Even if it meant she'd never have her own.

She jabbed her knife into the slab. Sure, she was only twenty-six and had plenty of time to meet the right guy before her fertility clock wound down, but she wasn't going to hold her breath.

An image of a baby with red curly hair popped into her mind. Would he have blue eyes or green?

Chelsea bit her lip and savagely chopped a chunk of meat off the piece in front of her. Those were definitely thoughts that led nowhere at all. Keanan might be powerfully attractive in ways she was unable to parse, but if he knew what was good for him, he'd get out of her head and stay there.

Whack. Too bad she couldn't tell him that.

oOo

Zach wiped a sleeve across his forehead. "Where did Noel go?"

Keanan glanced up. They worked hard enough that even the November air couldn't keep them from working up a sweat. "He delivered a bowl of meat inside a few minutes ago, but isn't back yet."

"That's not like him," Zach muttered. "Here, want to take the saws-all and cut the ribs into pieces maybe four inches long?"

Keanan eyed the electric saw. "Sure."

"Then they can go inside for wrapping, too." Zach turned the front quarter on the worktable. "Here's a good shoulder roast. I'll bone it out. The boss says we want soup bones by the mega-canner full, so when you're done with the ribs, want to start slicing through the pile? Just keep in mind the size of the soup pot."

"I can do that."

Zach glanced toward the door again, shrugged, and picked up a knife. "Good thing about soup is that we don't have to trim out the bones too thoroughly. Want some meat in there, too."

Keanan nodded and flipped the switch on. The saw easily cut through the ribs, which he then stacked into another large bowl before starting on the soup bones. He'd gotten nearly all the way through the collection Zach had created when he caught a glimpse of Noel's return from the corner of his eye.

"Everything okay?" asked Zach as Keanan shut off the saw.

Noel offered a lopsided smile. "In a manner of speaking."

Zach turned to look at the other man. "What's that supposed to mean?"

"It means Claire's pregnant and the smell of the meat got to her. She'll be okay."

"Oh, man. She barfed?"

Noel nodded.

Keanan's gut roiled. If he were ever an expectant father, he was pretty sure he'd suffer a sympathy stomach. He pushed the image of Chelsea from his mind. He didn't want to think of her in such discomfort, all his fault. Though, if it were some other man's fault, that would be even worse.

Ugh.

"Rough to see her like that?" asked Zach sympathetically.

"Yeah. We were going to wait to tell everyone, but I guess this tipped our hand. We're due in May." Noel nodded toward Keanan.

Keanan nodded back. The secret they'd shared only lasted a few days. The bond that had made him feel like he belonged.

"Well, congratulations!" Zach lifted his fist to Noel's.

Keanan raised his own to both men. Was this something like clinking wine glasses in a toast? Must be. Part of the inside circle, a place he'd rarely belonged, thanks to being raised more by Ivan than by either parent.

He didn't belong in this circle either. No wife. Definitely not about to become a father.

"Nothing like having a child," said Zach.

"We're looking forward to it," replied Noel. "Hopefully she'll feel better soon."

"Don't count on it."

The mysterious beginning of life. Did these men not feel the immensity of the moment? The very presence of God blessing their marriages? The incredible awe at creating an eternal being?

Noel picked up the bowl. "Want me to take the ribs in for wrapping?"

"Sure." Zach grabbed the saws-all and turned it onto the remaining soup bones.

Keanan shook his head slightly and turned to the task of bagging bones. There'd be time to boil them down for soup later in the fall. Today's job required they get the entire animal into meal-sized packages in the freezer.

o0o

Chelsea kept a close eye on Claire, who worked beside her.

"Don't worry about me. I'm fine. Really."

That smile looked more like a grimace, and the tone sounded none too convincing. Yeah. Chelsea would keep right on watching. Her friend wasn't going to faint away on *her* watch.

"What's for lunch?" asked Brent when they'd cleared the first quarter of the animal. "Hopefully not anything with beef in it."

"You guys are hungry?" Claire leaned on the table.

Chelsea glanced at the clock. Twelve-thirty. Now that Brent mentioned it, she was starving. "What's the plan?"

"I figured on BLT sandwiches," Claire said. "There's lots of bread, and we'll soon be out of ripe tomatoes. Might as well enjoy them."

Nightly frosts had arrived in the past couple of weeks, and they'd picked the remaining tomatoes off the vines and layered them onto shelves in the larder.

"Want me to handle it?" asked Chelsea. "I think you ought to go lie down."

Claire looked about to protest.

"I'll help Chelsea," said Sierra. "Want me to bring you a sandwich when they're ready, or would you prefer something else?"

Chelsea laid her knife on the table and headed into the kitchen. It was going to take a full minute of soapy water under the faucet to get the stench of raw beef off her hands enough to tolerate being near herself.

"A sandwich would be great. Thanks." Claire walked through to the bedroom wing.

Chelsea heard water running there as she flipped up the kitchen sink lever. A moment later her sister's hands joined hers under the tap. "You okay?" Chelsea asked in a low voice.

Sierra shrugged. "Sure. Why not?"

"Because—"

"Never mind, okay? I knew this was bound to happen sooner or later. Next it will be Allison then probably you. I'll get used to it."

The bleakness in Sierra's voice belied the words.

Chelsea leaned over and rested her head against her sister's shoulder for a brief moment. She hoped it provided solidarity and some sort of comfort. "Not likely me, thanks, anyway."

Sierra pulled away. "Want to make toast or cook bacon?"

"I'll do the toast if that's okay."

"Sure. That's why I asked." Sierra turned to the fridge and pulled out a pound of bacon.

Chelsea dried her hands, turned on the broiler, and lifted two loaves of bread to the island, where she laid slices out on oven sheets.

Her sister did something similar across the workspace with the bacon. Good thing there were two ovens. They used both regularly with this size of a crew.

From the corner of her eye, Chelsea caught a glimpse of Allison washing tomatoes. She took a deep breath. Did she need to worry about Allison, too? Or was it enough to be concerned for her sister, for Claire, and for Jo?

She shoved the thought of Keanan from her mind. There was enough to think about with her woman friends. Bemoaning the lack of a romance with a guy like Keanan would get her nowhere.

She put the first pan in the oven and glanced toward the dining room, where Brent and Gabe still whacked meat. Keanan stood in the doorway. Watching her.

Chelsea let out a shaky breath and focused on not letting the toast burn. Explaining how that happened would be tough.

Chapter 14 --

*W*elcome! Come on in." Keanan stood beside the green door to the grain bin — his own home — as his friends trooped through. Would a dozen people even fit in here?

"Thanks for inviting us all over." Allison bumped his arm. "Brent has been telling me all about the finishing touches."

"Is this your house, Uncle Keanan?"

He squatted beside young Finnley. "It is. Do you like it?"

The five-year-old nodded as he turned, taking it all in. "It's round."

Keanan ruffled Finnley's hair and stood, leaving his hand on the boy's shoulder as the last person filed in.

Chelsea.

In the background, he could hear Brent explaining how they'd cut a section from an old gymnasium floor to fit the curve needed for the kitchen counter. Everything dimmed to background noise.

"Hey." She glanced up at him then thrust a container his direction. "I brought some snacks for your party."

"Thank you, Chelsea." That she was here at all came as a relief. She hadn't set foot inside the door since she and Sierra had fitted the window coverings several weeks before.

"Look at me!" hollered Madelynn from above his head.

He looked up to see her peering through the stair railing.

"You get down, Maddie." Jo plunked her hands on her hips. The woman looked about to give birth any day now.

"It's fine by me," Keanan said quietly, setting the container down. He didn't want to undermine Jo's authority, but he'd meant for everyone to see his entire space. "You can go on up, too, if you like."

Jo nudged him. "Are you saying you don't think I can manage those stairs in my advanced state?"

He crinkled a grin down at her. "Not at all."

Zach slid his arm around Jo from the other side. "Come on up. Bet you Keanan's got his tent pitched upstairs so he'll feel at home." He winked at Keanan.

If his tent wasn't currently in Argentina, he might've done that. Little footsteps ran circles upstairs as Zach led Jo up.

"Keanan! How in the world did you get a king up here?" she called.

He went up a few steps until he could see the next level, where Maddie jumped on his mattress. "Brent and I managed it before we put the stair railings up. It wasn't easy."

"I'm sure it wasn't." Jo elbowed Zach and winked at Keanan. "And see? No tent. Our Keanan isn't a barbarian."

"Do barbarians live in tents? I thought it was caves."

"Are you going to block the access all evening?" asked Sierra. "We want to see, too."

Keanan stepped aside as Sierra and Chelsea ascended. Chelsea looked good tonight. Who was he fooling? She always did. Jeans, a flowery top that swirled at her hips and wrists. A whiff of her perfume lingered, luring him back up the steps and into his bedroom.

He and Brent had fitted a closet along the part of the curved upstairs wall directly above the outside door. Two tall, narrow windows provided a view up the mountain from the head of his bed, with two more flanking the space.

Sierra dropped onto the foot of the bed, bouncing a little. "It looks amazing up here. Bright and airy."

"I thought you were crazy." Jo motioned out the window that looked west across the valley. "But this whole place turned out really nice."

"I couldn't have accomplished this without Brent's expertise." Keanan watched Chelsea as she looked around, not meeting his gaze. "If it hadn't been for him and some of his contacts in the construction business, this would look more like a winterized camping pad."

Jo shook her head. "I was kidding, Keanan. I figured you had better taste than that."

"And Sierra picked the fabric for the window coverings. Chelsea picked out the tile in the bathroom downstairs. Really, I couldn't have done it without everyone."

Chelsea flicked a glance his direction, biting her lip.

She must be remembering that day, as he did. The day things began... and ended between them. Only not ended. Like her perfume, the essence of an almost-relationship lingered and would continue to do so.

Good thing he was leaving for Africa in just over a month. He'd see out the Alpha course, play music for Brent's wedding to Allison, and leave before Christmas. Possibly before the farm lay covered in a blanket of white snow. Perhaps when he returned in the spring, they would both have moved on from the attraction. She might have met another man.

His heart panged. *Not that. Please, Lord, not that.*

Maddie jumped off the bed and ran for the stairs. Zach surged after her, Jo in his wake. Sierra winked and followed.

Keanan's hope that Chelsea would hang around was dashed when she ran the short distance to descend ahead of her sister. He fisted his hands then relaxed them. And again. How could he do this? Having Chelsea in his home — in his very bedroom — was torture.

Why hadn't he taken her in his arms and kissed her that day a few weeks ago now? Why had he let her go when she'd stiffened and turned away? Perhaps with his lips, with his soul, he could have said what his words had bungled.

Yet they could never be one if she did not share his passion for the needy, for the lost, for the broken. For Jesus.

He'd stayed in one spot long enough for the other half of the group to ascend to view this upper floor.

Allison gripped Brent's hand, swinging it. "Wow. You guys did a great job."

"It was all Brent."

"Not so, and you know it." Brent shook his head. "You had the vision, and I had the skills to pull it together."

Keanan chuckled. "Your vision was bigger than mine. Left in my hands, this would have been a basic habitation sealed from the environment. Now it's a home."

"Fit for a magazine." Allison leaned against Brent. "But I can't say that I mind this project is done. Now you can help me make centerpieces for the reception."

Brent tugged her close and grinned at Keanan. "Sure you don't want a tiled backsplash in the kitchen, man? See what you could save me from?"

Was he serious? Keanan couldn't tell. "Thanks for sharing his time, Allison. I can't tell you enough how much I appreciate it."

oOo

Chelsea made herself small on the floor, her back to the wall near the compact wood stove that radiated heat. Probably not needed tonight with so many people packed into the space. How had Keanan made this grain bin into such a welcoming home? He and Brent had worked miracles.

She'd peeked into the bathroom when Keanan was still upstairs. The men had done an amazing job installing that tile. It looked at least as good as she'd imagined.

The wooden counters, the open shelves with a few white dishes on them, the two-burner cook top, the small fridge. Everything in proportion. Almost elegant. Even in the sitting area, a love seat shared space with a mammoth recliner. Every surface now overflowed with team members. Finnley lay on his tummy on the floor, Maddie bouncing on his back yelling, "Horsey!"

The strum of a guitar made her look up.

Keanan leaned against one of the counter stools, watching her as he tuned up.

She'd heard all about the frequent fireside sings the group had enjoyed beside Keanan's tent over the summer. They'd ended abruptly when she arrived — not because of it, surely, but because he'd been busy building. He'd played with the worship team a couple of times since. She'd been fascinated by the quick, accurate movement of his big hands. The exquisite music he'd made.

Was he playing her, too?

It seemed no one else was in the room, though the background chatter remained. Her forehead still tingled from the brush of his lips days ago. She caught herself before she touched the spot.

A smile crinkled Keanan's face as though he sensed her thoughts. He looked down at the guitar and began to pick out a song she knew from church. Noel began to sing along then a few others joined in.

Chelsea leaned back, closed her eyes, and soaked up the atmosphere. Why couldn't she feel passionate about Jesus the way Keanan did? And Noel, Allison... all the others, likely. Those three were simply the most vocal.

God? Are You there? Maybe the question was more like, was He *here.* Inside her, like she'd always been taught. The visual of Jesus standing at a door, knocking, sprang to mind. She'd invited Him in as a child. She remembered doing it. She'd never *not* believed.

Then where was the sense of purpose? The feeling of His love surrounding her and filling her?

Maybe she'd had a cup of tea and a nice chat with Him, thanked Him for coming, then shown Him the door. She'd gone on with her life, having taken care of the question of heaven and hell.

There was more. Keanan sang right now of being filled and walking in the Spirit. His voice rang with conviction, with adoration, with passion.

She peered at him without flickering more than her eyelids.

Longing spread through her, not just for the man, though that was always close to the surface. But for the sense of God that filled the room. It shuttered Keanan's eyes, caused Noel's hands to rise, and made Sierra sway and smile as she sang. Where had her sister found this deeper relationship with Jesus?

Chelsea had been missing out. Reading her Bible occasionally because that's what Christians were supposed to do. Praying a bit more often, asking God's blessing on those she loved. Going through the motions, barely remembering the passion could descend from on high like rain. Until now.

Wasn't it a gift of God, not something she could earn by striving? Where was the balance?

"Key of C," murmured Keanan, changing tempo as he nodded at Noel.

Noel responded by pulling a harmonica out of his shirt pocket and joining in. Claire shifted a little closer to Jo on the love seat, probably to give Noel elbowroom.

Jo looked a bit wan, come to think of it. One hand rested on her belly. Wait. Was that a ripple across the bump?

Chelsea opened her eyes the rest of the way as Jo shifted slightly. Uncomfortably. No one else seemed to have noticed. Maybe not even Jo.

A few songs later, Chelsea was sure.

This time, Jo's eyes widened when her belly clenched. She might have caught her breath, but Chelsea couldn't hear above the music. Jo gripped Zach's hand, and he bent toward her.

Jo's gaze caught on Chelsea's just past Zach's blond head.

Chelsea raised her eyebrows.

Her friend offered a grimace and a nod as Zach slid his arm around her and adjusted his wristwatch. Maddie now lay on her back on the floor beside Finnley. Would they send her next door to Allison's house? The plan had been to drop her off with Zach's parents, but they went to bed early.

The next time Jo's belly rolled then eased, Zach stood. "Sorry to break up the party, but we need to get going."

Maddie sat up, crossed her arms, and pouted. "I no want to go home."

"Sorry, kiddo." Zach reached for Jo with both hands, helping her upright.

Allison unfolded from her spot on the floor. "I should head out, too. It's past Finnley's bedtime."

"Come on, squirt." Brent reached for Finnley's hand.

Noel tucked the harmonica away, but Keanan kept playing, his fingers flicking over the strings as he watched the group begin to disperse.

Chelsea stood, and his attention swung to her. "Come on, Maddie. Do you want to walk home with Auntie Chelsea?"

Jo gasped.

Everyone froze except Zach, who reached for Jo's jacket. "Time to go."

"Wait, you're in labor?" Sierra rushed to Jo's side.

The cacophony erupted. Chelsea picked Maddie up off the floor and elbowed her way through the pack. "Seriously," she said to Zach. "Do you want me to put Maddie to bed and stay until you get home?"

He glanced at Jo then back at Chelsea. "Think it's that close to time?" The guy's fingers went white as Jo squeezed.

"I think we can—" Jo inhaled sharply "—put Maddie to bed first. Are you sure? I can call Rosemary."

"I don't mind. Really."

Maddie reached for Jo. "Mama!"

Chelsea tried to rebalance the squirming tot. "Mama's fine, baby girl. Where's your jacket? It's cold outside tonight."

Maddie was having none of it. As the door closed behind her parents, she kicked and yelled.

Great. Trying to help was backfiring big time. She should probably have let one of the others step in. Someone Maddie was more familiar with. But it wasn't like Chelsea was a stranger.

Someone plucked Maddie from her arms. "Here's your jacket, Madelynn." Keanan.

Maddie stopped yelling. Of course Keanan had a way with the child. Wasn't everyone putty in his hands? Even her. Chelsea shrugged into her jacket and reached for her charge.

Keanan shook his head. "Let me carry her."

Maddie burrowed into Keanan's shoulder as some of the others filed out, obviously leaving well enough alone.

"That's silly. You weren't going out anyway. I am."

His green eyes bored into hers. "She's heavy, and it's a distance to walk. I'm happy to help."

She tried to summon gratefulness when, in reality, she only felt embarrassment that she couldn't even handle a toddler.

"Besides, you'll want to stop by your place and gather a few things for overnight. Zach might not be home until tomorrow sometime."

"You're right." Of course, he was right. Couldn't he be wrong sometimes? Be anything besides a perfect gentleman?

She'd been doing her best to avoid him for the past week and more. Her lucky run had splatted against the wall.

Chapter 15 --

The little blond head leaned trustingly on Keanan's shoulder as he followed Chelsea out into the crisp November night.

"Stars?" asked Madelynn.

The black sky sparkled with tiny lights. "Yes. See them all?"

"Where moon?"

"It hasn't come up yet."

Madelynn pressed her hands against his cheeks and filled his vision. "But where moon?"

Uh. Keanan glanced at Chelsea. How did one answer a child this age?

"The moon is sleeping," Chelsea said simply.

"Where sun?"

"The sun is sleeping, too." Chelsea looked at the little girl. "Now it's time for you to sleep in your little bed."

"No want to."

Toddlers. This one had been all but dozing in front of his wood stove, even with the rousing music and singing. The air in his home had been rather close, though, with all twelve of them packed inside. Now she bounced on his arm as they approached the duplex, demanding all his attention.

He followed Chelsea inside, and Madelynn squirmed to be released. "Hold still, little one," he murmured.

"I'll just be a minute." Chelsea flicked him a questioning glance then disappeared into her bedroom.

Keanan hadn't been in this half of the building since the day Allison and Finnley had moved from here to the timber frame house Brent had built for them. Although the furniture had not been changed, the kitchenette and sitting area looked different somehow, the differences between the two women visible.

The walls remained Allison's choice of gray, but bright, slightly abstract floral prints hung in a tidy row above the sofa. Punches of color were everywhere. A stack of magazines — he'd forgotten those existed anymore — lay beside a closed laptop on her table.

"Maddie get down?"

With a start, Keanan realized he was still holding the child. "No, little one. We're waiting for Auntie Chelsea, and then we'll go to your house."

Her lower lip dropped into a pout.

In the distance, a closet door opened and closed, then a creaky drawer. A moment later, Chelsea came toward him in an oversized sweatshirt and stretchy pants, her hair tied back, as usual. She slipped her laptop into a purse the size of an airline carryon then shrugged her jacket back on.

"Ready," she said, without looking at him.

"Go Maddie house?"

"Yes, little one." Keanan held the door for Chelsea then followed her back into the night. "I like the personal touches you've made in there."

"Thank you." Chelsea's face lay in shadow. "Your place looks good, too."

He couldn't help but tease her. "For a grain bin?"

"Yeah. Listen, Keanan—"

Not far away, Zach's pickup rumbled.

"Yes?"

"Never mind."

What had she thought to say to him? Well, there was no reason for him to leave the log cabin again immediately after delivering Madelynn. Perhaps Chelsea would even welcome his presence and help with the toddler. Then he could ask her again.

They rounded the final turn in the driveway to see Zach toss an overnight bag into the truck's backseat. The headlights pierced the distance to the porch light.

"That's okay, Mom. Chelsea's got it." Zach must be wearing his Bluetooth headset. "Yes, I'll make sure she has your number. Do you have hers? ... Thanks, Mom. I'll let you know ... Love you, too."

"Daddy! Where Mama?" Madelynn kicked to get down, but Keanan held tight.

"Hey, kiddo." Zach reached for the toddler and gave her a little whisker rub. "You be a good girl for Chelsea and Keanan, okay?" He turned to Chelsea, an apologetic look on his face. "Jo wanted to tuck Maddie in herself before we left, but, honestly, I don't think she's able. We need to get going. Maddie's pajamas are in the top drawer. Just brush her teeth and read her a story, if you don't mind. I hope she'll settle down quickly for you."

"It's fine, Zach." Chelsea rested her hand on Zach's arm, the rings on her fingers glinting in the red glow of the taillights. "I've taken Babysitting 101. Don't worry about a thing."

"Zach?" Jo called.

He glanced at the truck. "Gotta go." He passed Madelynn back into Keanan's arms and raced around to the driver's side.

"Want Daddy!" Madelynn hollered, pounding small fists against his chest. "Want Mama!"

oOo

It took longer than Chelsea would have dreamed to get Maddie settled. The little girl had fought her every inch of the way, demanding her parents. It had been impossible to pry her mouth open for the toothbrush. Whatever. One night wasn't going to corrode the kid's teeth to nothing.

Finally Maddie curled up in her toddler bed with her stuffed moose clenched tightly in one arm, a quilt lovingly sewn by Zach's mother tucked up to her chin.

Chelsea might not have needed to stay in Maddie's room until the child was asleep, but she wasn't sure. The longer she stayed, the more likely that Keanan would have left already. No, he wouldn't leave without talking to her. Therein lay the problem.

The little eyes drifted shut.

She couldn't put this off much longer. *Lord, what do I say to him? The attraction is powerful, but it just doesn't make sense.*

A soft sigh came from Maddie.

Chelsea tiptoed to the door, opened it, and glanced back. The tot didn't stir. This was so strange, tucking a little one into bed while a man waited in the other room. Couples — families — did this sort of thing all the time. She and Keanan weren't a couple. When she was thinking clearly, she knew it wasn't meant to be.

The big question was, was she thinking clearly tonight?

She took a deep breath. She'd better be.

oOo

Keanan turned at the muffled whisper of Chelsea's slippers on the short hallway's wooden floor. "I made you some tea."

She eyed him pensively. "Thank you."

"It's mint. I put in a bit of honey and cream." He'd seen her doctor a teacup often enough. He poked his chin toward the sitting area. "Have a seat? I'll bring it to you."

Chelsea chose a deep armchair and curled up in it, feet tucked beneath her. Domino, Zach's Border collie, padded over and sprawled beside her.

Keanan reached across the dog to set the cup and saucer on the end table beside her then settled across with his own tea.

A grin twitched at her cheeks when her eyes landed on the huge mug he'd chosen for himself.

"I don't want to break one of those fragile little things." Was that a metaphor for his relationship with Chelsea? Might be.

"Then why did you bring mine in china?"

He met her gaze. "I know you like pretty things." Yeah, so why was he even pretending? There was nothing *pretty* about him, even in a manly sort of way. He'd looked in the mirror. Sure, shorter hair changed his look some, but he wasn't exactly handsome. Or cute, or whatever a woman wanted to look at.

She lifted the teacup and had a sip. "Thanks for noticing."

He'd observed all that and more, but perhaps it wasn't the best time for the litany. Just like she shouldn't be attracted to him, the reasons he shouldn't be attracted to her were many. Pink nail polish. Four rings glimmered on her fingers. Glittery eyeglasses. Flowers as far as the eye could see, most days.

Not tonight. Neither the stretchy black pants nor the yellow Ducks sweatshirt made her any less feminine. He couldn't take his eyes off her.

"Chels—" he began, just as she said his name. They stared at each other.

"Go ahead," he said.

She bit her lip and stared into her tea.

Was this when she would tell him to leave the log cabin, leave the farm, leave her life? *Please, God, no.* But it was too much to hope she'd provide him any welcome. She'd made it clear enough, but somehow he couldn't help torturing himself with her nearness.

"That song you played tonight. About the God-song inside a person."

Keanan blinked. So not what he'd expected. "You mean *Hallelujah! Your Love is Amazing.*" He hummed a few bars.

She nodded, not meeting his eyes. "That sounds like the one."

He crossed the room and pulled out Zach's guitar case then lifted the instrument out. Sitting back down, he tuned it slightly and began to pick out the chorus.

"I didn't know Zach had a guitar."

Keanan glanced up, his fingers continuing to flick out the melody. "It's his dad's. Steve used to play a bit, years ago. I've been teaching Zach a few chords and such."

"Oh." Chelsea's face disappeared behind her teacup until only her glasses showed.

He focused on the guitar and began to sing, closing his eyes and feeling the worship well up inside him. When the final strum died away, he rested his hand across the strings, glancing over at Chelsea.

She dabbed a tissue behind her glasses then drew both knees up, burying her face behind them.

Oh man. Now what was he supposed to do? Something told him it wasn't his comfort she sought. That the problem — for once — wasn't with him.

His fingers began another song, and it took a few seconds for his mind to clue in where they were going. Ah, yes. Good choice. *Come and Fill Me Up.* A prayerful request to the Holy Spirit to fill a thirsty soul. A song of desire for a closer relationship with God. He sang through the whole song three times then drifted into *Holy is the Lord* by Chris Tomlin.

Keanan had never played for an audience of one. Sure, he often lost himself in praise when he was alone, and leading a group in worship was a sensation he never tired of. But to sing in front of one person, someone he was coming to cherish, someone with tears streaming down her face... that was a new one.

He was on the fifth song when Chelsea took off her glasses and scrubbed at her eyes with the tissue. He let the song drift away then silenced the strings, staring down at the curving wood on the instrument.

"I don't know how to do this." The words erupted as she uncoiled from the seat and strode down the hall.

Water splashed in the bathroom. Silence.

Lord, what do I do now?

We're not waging war against enemies of flesh and blood alone. The words he'd read in Ephesians 6 this morning came to mind. Keanan rested his forehead on the guitar and prayed the protection of spiritual armor over Chelsea. Yes, she knew Jesus, but somewhere in her everyday life, the lifeline had been squeezed until little of God's power trickled through. *God, help her.*

It wasn't his battle. It was hers. All he could do was pray.

o0o

Chelsea sat on the bathroom floor, arms wrapped around her knees as she leaned on the log wall. Slowly the words of Keanan's songs dispersed, and she took a shuddering breath. Longing for that kind of relationship with God didn't do any good. Hadn't she asked God so many times to make Himself real to her? Dozens of times. Hundreds of times. And what had she gotten for her efforts? Pretty much nothing.

Okay, she believed in God. She believed Jesus was one with God and that He'd died to redeem her. She'd accepted the gift of salvation as a child. She'd even felt close to Him as a young teen. Then she'd gotten busy. Still plugged in. She'd gone to a private Christian school with chapel every morning. Her dad led a family devotional time every evening. Her friends were all in the same boat. They went through the motions, but the fervency had dissipated.

Chelsea hadn't realized it was gone. Not until she met Keanan. Sure, she'd seen it in others from time to time, but not like him. Keanan breathed his beliefs.

She heard her cell ring in the distance. It was in her bag in the living room. Maybe Keanan had the same ring tone on his. If so, the sound would get cut off.

It rang seven times then stopped. A moment later it started again. Who on earth would be calling past midnight?

Zach, that's who.

She jumped to her feet and sprinted for her phone, ignoring Keanan. "Hello?"

"Chelsea? How's Maddie? Did she go to sleep for you okay?"

What on earth? "She's fine." Chelsea gripped the phone. "How about you guys? How's Jo?"

"Okay." He sounded tired. "She keeps asking about Maddie, so I told her I'd call you and make sure."

"She settled down in under twenty minutes. She's been asleep for—" Chelsea checked her watch "—two hours or more now."

"Okay." He let out a long breath. "I'll tell Jo. Maybe now she can focus on pushing the baby out."

"Is she making good progress?"

Zach laughed, and she could picture him running his hand through his hair. "It's going to be a while yet. Could be a long night. You sure you're okay there?"

Did she come across that inept? "Everything's under control, Zach. Forget about us here and concentrate on Jo and the baby. I'll catch some sleep on the sofa. If you're not home when Maddie wakes up in the morning, I'll take her down to the house. We'll be fine."

"If you're sure." He paused. "Sorry. It's just that we've never left her with anyone but my parents overnight. And Dad's really not been feeling well lately, and with it being so late..."

"I understand. Get back to Jo, will you?"

"Thanks, Chelsea. We owe you one." He ended the call.

She turned a cheery face toward Keanan. "You might as well head back to your place. Zach says it looks like it could take all night."

He searched her eyes.

If he wanted to talk to her about those worship songs, she wasn't ready. Chelsea yawned, covering her mouth, and unfolded the bright quilt from the back of the sofa. "I'll just sleep right here. Thanks for helping out with Maddie."

Keanan rose and tucked the guitar back in its case before coming so close to her she could feel his body heat. He tucked his finger under her chin, pushing her to look up at him. Surely he was smart enough not to kiss her. She raised her eyebrows and looked up at him, head tilted to the side.

"Goodnight, sweet Chelsea. My prayers remain with you."

Chapter 16 --

*F*innley Mama? Where Mama? Daddy!"

Chelsea groaned and started to roll over before remembering that would likely land her on the floor of the Nemeseks' log cabin. Wow, her neck hurt and so did her back. She pushed her hair back from her face — where had her scarf gone, anyway? — and swung her legs over the edge of the sofa.

"Maddie?"

"Where Mama?" The little girl stood beside the sofa glaring at Chelsea, her chin quivering.

If Zach had returned while she slept, he'd have heard his daughter, wouldn't he? In the first place, Chelsea would have heard him return. So, he wasn't back yet.

"Your mommy and daddy are at the hospital getting your baby brother or sister." Chelsea shoved her glasses on and fumbled for her phone. Had Zach left a message? Didn't look like it. "Need to go potty, Maddie?"

"No! Want Mama."

Chelsea forced out a smile. Hopefully it wouldn't scare the tyke. She was never at her best first thing in the morning. What time was it? A hint of daylight lightened the darkness beyond the windows. That made it too early to be awake, no matter what time it actually was. She squinted at the clock. Six forty-five? Ouch.

"Want a snuggle?"

The toddler set her little jaw and crossed her arms.

Chelsea needed a cup of Earl Grey and a shower before she'd be able to cope. Guess that wasn't going to happen. What was Maddie's morning routine? It was too early to take her down to the house. She'd wake up Claire and Noel, and for what? Because Chelsea couldn't cope? Yeah, she'd muddle through. One way or the other.

"Well, Auntie Chelsea needs to go potty." Chelsea came back out a minute later, having also splashed water on her face and run a pick through her hair. Spying her scarf, she tied her hair back.

"Okay, let's see what's for breakfast." Jo didn't always bring Maddie down, so it stood to reason there'd be food somewhere. She opened the small fridge. "Want an egg?"

"And bacon."

Whew. If the little one was going to cooperate, life would be much easier. "Scrambled?" She lifted Maddie to the counter and turned on the kettle before getting the ingredients out. That somehow reminded her of Keanan making tea for her last night. Everything flooded back. She shoved the memories into the dark recesses of her mind. No time for that now.

Her phone beeped with an incoming text, and she surged for it. Zach?

No, Allison. *Saw yr light on. Baby?*

Haven't heard. Maddie woke me up.

Keep in touch. :)

Will do.

"Who talking to?" Maddie peered at the phone.

"Auntie Allison."

"Play Finnley?"

"Maybe after breakfast." Chelsea turned on the element farthest from Maddie and laid two pieces of bacon in a skillet. She wasn't particularly hungry herself this early, but who knew how the morning would go? *Lord, watch over Jo and Zach.*

As if in answer, her phone beeped again. She glanced over to see a message from Zach.

It's a boy! Is Maddie up?

Congrats!!! We're up! Phone?

Soon.

Chelsea whisked a couple of eggs with a slosh of milk and a dash of salt and pepper then poured the mixture across the skillet from the bacon. A couple of minutes later she settled Maddie at the table with her plate and a glass of milk.

Why didn't Zach call? Probably too busy phoning the world. Was she supposed to tell Maddie? No. Better if her daddy did.

She texted Allison. *Boy. No details.*

Yay!

Chelsea picked at her egg while Maddie all but inhaled hers. The phone rang. "Hello?"

"Hey, Chelsea. Can you put us on speaker? Is this an okay time?"

"It's great. Just a sec." She pressed the button and laid the cell on the table. "Look, Maddie, your daddy is calling."

"Daddy?"

"Hi, kiddo. Are you being a good girl for Auntie Chelsea?"

Maddie nodded. "Where Mama?"

"Right here, baby."

"Maddie want Mama." Her lip protruded.

Zach spoke again. "Maddie, Daddy will come get you in a little while, and you can meet your baby brother, okay?"

Chelsea couldn't wait any longer. "What's his name?"

"John Steven."

The Steven was likely for Zach's dad. But John?

"John was both our grandfathers' name, Jo's and mine. We thought it was fitting."

"Well, congratulations! When was he born? Did everything go all right? How much did he weigh?"

Jo laughed. "He was born just after four o'clock. Seven pounds two ounces. Remember he's a couple of weeks early. And yeah, we're all good."

Chelsea had rarely heard Jo's voice so emotional. So... soft.

"That's great. Do you want me to bring Maddie there, Zach? She's eating breakfast now."

Actually, Maddie had cleaned off her plate during the call. She might miss her mama, but food came first. Good to know.

"No, it's okay. I'll have a quick shower while I'm there and then bring her back here with me."

"When are you coming home, Jo? When do the rest of us get to meet John?" Johnny sounded more like a baby's name. They'd trimmed Madelynn to Maddie. Surely they'd call the baby Johnny.

"We'll be home in a few hours, I think," said Zach. "We'll stop by my parents' place on our way by. Then we can have a meet-and-greet at Green Acres, but I count on you to help me keep it short, Chelsea. We didn't get any sleep last night."

"If you let me know when you're coming, stop by the big house and we can have a little welcome home party there. I'll get everyone together." Her mind already churned planning the details. "Then it will be easier for you guys to break away and come up to your place when you're ready. Easier than kicking everyone out of the cabin, I mean."

"Good idea." Jo sounded like she was fading. "We'll give you a heads-up. Maddie, are you being a good girl for Auntie Chelsea?"

"Maddie good girl."

"Okay, kiddo. Daddy will see you soon." Jo made a kissy noise.

Maddie puckered her lips.

"Bye for now." Zach disconnected the call.

Chelsea ate the last few bites of her breakfast. "Come on, Maddie. Let's go see Auntie Allison."

oOo

"Congratulations!" Keanan opened the truck door for Jo. He'd been on his way to the big house when they drove in.

Jo smiled up at him, pale but relaxed. "Thanks."

Zach opened the back door, released Maddie from her car seat, and came around the vehicle.

Keanan thumped him on the back. "Happy for you both."

"Uncle Keanan!"

Madelynn attacked his leg, and he swung her up. "Madelynn! Are you a big sister now?"

She nodded, pointing at the truck. "John brother."

Zach chuckled as he pulled the baby's car seat out of the back then held out his hand to Jo. "Ready, love?" He glanced at Keanan. "The troops are assembled?"

"I assume so. I was only just arriving, myself." He shut the truck doors and glanced at the seat swinging from Zach's hand. A fluffy blanket covered the baby's head. All in good time. He'd catch a glimpse in a minute, probably after the women had passed the little guy around. He swung Madelynn in circles as he followed them into the house.

Chelsea only had eyes for the baby as Allison unbuckled the harness and lifted out the newborn. Claire reached over and touched his tiny cheek.

"That Maddie brother," Madelynn informed Keanan, one little hand pressed to each of his cheeks as she got in front of his eyes. "Brother little."

"Yes, he is very little. But he will grow."

Finnley crowded close to Allison, and she lowered the baby for him to see. Madelynn squirmed out of Keanan's arms and ran to join them. "That brother," she told Finnley.

Jo lowered herself to an armchair gingerly, wincing as she settled. She caught Keanan watching and shook her head with a little grin. "Might be a few days before I can sit like a normal person."

"Then lie down." He pointed at the love seat. "No one will argue with your right to take up more space than usual."

"If I lie down, I'll fall asleep. I'll be okay for a bit here."

"Can I get you a coffee? Tea?"

"You're so thoughtful, Keanan. If there's apple juice in the fridge, I'd really like some."

"You, Zach?"

His friend scrubbed his hand through his hair. "Coffee. Black."

Keanan nodded and strode toward the kitchen, passing the women and baby. His step faltered. Chelsea cradled the little one, her curly head bent low. Keanan's heart squeezed and his mind took a leap into the future. Would she ever hold his child? *Their* child?

Right. His mission. He poured juice over a few ice cubes in a tall glass then turned to the coffee urn and poured two cups. Something smelled good in here. Beef soup simmered on the stovetop, but a sweet aroma surfaced.

He turned as Chelsea opened one of the oven doors. Keanan let his gaze linger. "Can I help?"

"No, I've got it." She lifted out a pan and set it on the island.

"What did you make?" He'd noticed she was often in on the kitchen action. More than Allison or Jo, for sure.

"Plum upside-down cake." She didn't look at him. "It's one of Jo's favorites. We'll serve it after lunch."

"It's one of my favorites, too."

She glanced at him, her expression unreadable. "Good to know."

"Can I help you serve lunch?"

"Looks like you're busy. Besides, Claire said she would." She looked across the peninsula.

Noel cradled the baby in one arm while the other tucked Claire close. The three heads were mere inches apart.

Keanan had never expected to feel this left out. He glanced at Chelsea, who bit her lip, watching them, too. "I'll help you," he said softly. "Be right back." He gathered the juice and a coffee and carried them out to Jo and Zach then returned.

Chelsea sliced a long loaf of French bread, glancing up when he lifted a stack of bowls from the shelf above the peninsula.

Everything was such a jumble. What could he say to her after last night? So many subjects seemed taboo. Even talking about that baby could quickly lead to an impenetrable wall. "Did Madelynn sleep well?" Hopefully that was safe enough.

"She slept through until six forty-five."

"And you?"

She grinned, a bit lopsided. "So did I."

"The sofa was comfortable?"

"Not particularly."

They'd exhausted the only topic he'd come up with. Now what? Keanan ladled soup into bowls and set them on the peninsula. Wait a minute. He looked more carefully around the great room. "Are Gabe and Sierra coming for lunch?"

"I-I'm not sure."

Keanan swung to meet Chelsea's gaze.

"Sierra's finding this all difficult. It's not just that Jo and Zach are on their second, but finding out Claire's expecting hit her really hard. She wants a baby so badly."

"But keeping apart from the group won't make it easier."

"I know that. You know that." Chelsea hesitated. "I think

Sierra knows, too. But it's still hard."

He nodded slowly. Such varied emotions in their group to the birth of one small child. Allison probably looked forward to having a child of her own. Her marriage to Brent was mere weeks away. Watching them interact with Finnley proved the good parents they would be.

"I'd like to have children one day." How had those words come from his mouth? But he couldn't take them back.

Chelsea's eyes flared behind her glasses before she looked down at the bread. "Me, too."

The words were so quiet, he wasn't sure he'd heard them or dreamed them. *Lord, please work a miracle.*

"Keanan?"

He turned to Noel's voice, but his gaze fixed on the babe in his friend's outstretched hands.

"Here. Your turn to hold the little guy. I'll finish with lunch."

His throat closed. "Me?"

"Sure, why not? They tell me he's not fragile." Noel grinned and laid the bundle in Keanan's hands. "Hey, man. Looks good on you."

Keanan drew the baby closer to his chest. Brown fuzz crowned the little head. A teensy yawn split his face, and a tiny fist waved. Keanan couldn't take his gaze off the miracle in his hands as a sensation of fierce longing swept through him.

He'd never thought to fall in love. Marry. Have a family. But meeting Chelsea had tipped his world upside down. The ordinary things of life — the things most people took for granted — shone with a new light, beckoning him in.

He looked up and met Chelsea's eyes. For the first time in days — weeks, perhaps — she didn't turn away immediately.

Keanan couldn't hold back the emotion that surfaced from touching this baby. He blinked back moisture in his eyes, and sucked in his lips.

Chelsea's gaze dropped to his mouth for an instant then back up. Something passed between them. What, exactly, Keanan couldn't say.

"Soup's on!" called Noel.

The baby startled and gave a thin wail.

The moment was broken, but something new had happened.

Chapter 17 --

*C*helsea checked over the numbers from the caterer then approved the file before forwarding it to Greta, her liaison at the church in Portland. It would be good to be home for a few weeks.

She rotated her shoulders. Hadn't she come to think of Idaho as home even after ten weeks? Apparently she still had one foot in Oregon. The duplex felt like a rental, not like her own nest. Not that different from living in her parents' basement suite, especially with Sierra and Gabe in the other half.

They'd dropped by the house the other day just as Jo and Zach prepared to leave for the cabin. Whispered congratulations and a pat on the baby's head were as far as Sierra seemed able to get. She'd even turned down a piece of plum upside-down cake.

Upside down. Just like life. Had Chelsea made a mistake coming to Green Acres? She'd jumped from one safe place to another. It might've been better to get an apartment in Portland.

Keanan would say she should stop playing safe and go to Africa but, even now, her insides cringed at the thought. Not everyone was adventurous like he was. Many countries weren't safe for a woman traveling alone.

That word again. But wouldn't she be safe at his side? He was

147

so big. Surely not many bad guys would mess with him.

The real question was, was God safe? A line from *The Lion, the Witch, and the Wardrobe* came to mind from when the beaver spoke of Aslan. *Safe? Who said anything about safe? 'Course he isn't safe. But he's good. He's the king.*

The phone rang, and she picked it up.

"Chelsea, I'm sorry but I won't be able to work the kitchen tonight at Alpha," said Rosemary. "Steve is really not feeling well today, and I hate to leave him."

Chelsea gripped the phone. "That's okay. I can do it." She'd bailed for two weeks, trying to avoid Keanan. He'd even ridden in with Rosemary once, but she could be a big girl and do the duty she'd agreed on. "I'm sorry about Steve, though. Tell him he's in my prayers." Fat lot of good that did, but hey. It was the right thing to say. *Lord, please heal Steve.* See? She hadn't lied.

"Thank you, Chelsea. That's so sweet of you. You are in our prayers, too."

Uh oh. What did it seem she needed prayer for? "Thank you."

"I will have a pot of chili ready to send in with you, if you want to stop by for it."

Back on solid ground. "That's perfect. Jean said she'd bring one as well. And Barb Smith. Three should be enough."

"Okay, well, I'll let you get back to it."

Get back to it. She glanced at the clock. That probably meant heading over to the commercial kitchen and putting on a triple batch of cornbread for the Alpha supper. She hadn't found a volunteer for that part and, really, once she was in the mode, it wasn't any harder to make three pans than one.

She clicked out of her email program and closed the laptop. If she were going to pray about anything, it should be about how to handle this annoying awareness of Keanan Welsh. Seeing his humungous hands holding that baby the other day, seeing that goofy grin on his face as little John squirmed, seeing the intensity in his eyes when he caught her watching... talk about overload. Way too much.

So many things lately — no, she wasn't going there. She grabbed a jacket, slid into a pair of shoes, and headed across the yard. This first week of November was bringing in an icy wind. Winter on the way. Portland was sounding better and better.

oOo

"It's good to have you back." Keanan glanced across at Chelsea in the driver's seat of her car.

"Rosemary says Steve isn't feeling well."

Keanan released a long breath. "I know. It's hard to see him in so much pain. It's like all his nerve endings are on overload."

She flicked him a look. "You still go over there a lot?"

"At least twice a week." How was Steve going to manage when Keanan left for Africa in little over a month? Rosemary couldn't do all the things Keanan had been doing. She simply wasn't strong enough. Zach was busy with a veterinary practice and a young family, and his parents didn't want to bother him. Keanan figured Zach ought to know, but it wasn't any of his business to do the telling. Not yet, anyway. That might soon change.

"They'll miss you when you're gone."

He angled his whole body toward her, hard to do in the confines of the small car. "Will you?"

The question hung in the air, nearly visible, for a long moment.

"I'm going back to Portland."

The words hit him like a sucker punch. "You don't need to. I'll stay away if I make you that uncomfortable." Could he give up everything?

"I didn't mean permanently."

He dared to breathe.

She glanced his way, shaking her head. "This is confidential, by the way, but I'm still getting requests to coordinate events in the city, and it seems there's not much I can do here, after all. Getting people to volunteer a few meals for Alpha doesn't count."

"Why doesn't it count?"

She shrugged. "Anyone could do that. It's a pity assignment."

Keanan swallowed the growl that wanted out. "Do you have any idea what we really do at Alpha?"

Her eyebrows angled up as she looked at him.

She couldn't still be on that Tracy thing after all this. "Do you know that Wesley is *this* close to making a decision for Jesus?" He pressed his thumb and forefinger together. "Maybe tonight will be the night. Do you know that Tracy's two friends are asking deep questions about faith? That they're grappling with Scripture and who God is and why Jesus died? Do you know that in the Graysens' group, two people have committed their lives to Jesus in the past week? Coordinating meals for Alpha is not a pity job, Chelsea. A lot of important bonding takes place over food. You're helping to make a real difference in people's eternal destinies."

Something swept across her face. "Really?" All the longing he'd seen when he played worship songs for her last week spilled out in that one word.

"Really. There are front lines all over the world, and this is the front line right now in Galena Landing."

"I had no idea."

He barely heard those words, they were so quiet.

A few minutes later they pulled into the church parking lot. As usual, they were among the first to arrive so Chelsea could set up the meal. Keanan didn't mind the extra half hour. He'd take some time to study and pray. Pray for Wesley. For Diana and Rylee. For Chelsea.

"Lord, I've fallen in love with her," he murmured into the

quiet fireside room. "I don't know whether it's Your plan or not. I know she believes, but something is holding her back. I pray Your Holy Spirit will descend on her and fill her with Your presence. Your love. Your peace."

Her attitude was not something he could change. Nor could he modify her history or personality.

Keanan dropped his head into his hands. "Jesus, heal her. Lift her up." He had no idea what to say. Was this where Jesus, at the right hand of God, could intercede for him? "She's Yours, God. You know what I want, but underneath I want what You want. Grant me patience and peace."

A door opened, and he heard Pastor Ron's voice. "Keanan? Sorry if I'm interrupting."

"No, please. Do come in." There was nothing left to say to God, anyway. Either He'd answer the prayer, or He wouldn't. More to the point, Keanan would either like the answer or prefer a different one.

Pastor Ron lowered himself into a chair across from Keanan. "Is there anything you want to talk about?" His deep brown eyes radiated understanding.

How could the pastor know? He couldn't. "Sometimes it is difficult to know how to pray," Keanan said at last, shaking his head. "Sometimes having faith is more painful than not having it."

"You are referring to Miss Riehl?"

Maybe Ron did know. Keanan sighed and nodded.

"Are you speaking of matters of the heart, or matters of faith?"

Good question. But having admitted this much, there was no point in pretending otherwise. He met Ron's gaze. "Both?"

"Are the matters one and the same?"

Keanan pondered. "Not exactly. But they are certainly related."

"Would you care to explain? Forgive me if I shouldn't ask."

"No imposition, but I'm not sure I can clarify. I don't understand fully myself."

Ron leaned back in the chair and crossed his feet. "Try me."

"She believes. I don't doubt that for a moment. She was raised in a Christian home and environment. She's trusted Jesus for her salvation."

The pastor nodded, his gaze not leaving Keanan's face.

"But it seems perhaps... superficial. It has molded who she is in much the same way living in Portland has. Or being of European ancestry. But I'm not certain what effect it has on her day-to-day living."

"I see."

"I'm sorry, Pastor Ron. I feel I'm passing judgment, and that's not my place as a fellow-believer." Keanan stared at his hands as he clenched one over the other. "Only God knows her heart."

"But then there's the romantic interest."

Keanan sighed. "Yes, there is that."

"So the question of her faith comes into this aspect as well."

"Exactly. For a romantic interest to grow—" Keanan felt the flush creep up his neck "—we need to share a deep spiritual bond. Right now, that bond isn't present." How had he allowed this to happen? He hadn't been seeking romance. His first instinct had been correct, but in between he'd fallen in love. There. He'd admitted it to himself. How could he go back to the way it had been before?

"I don't know the young lady well." Pastor Ron watched Keanan. "How deep is her interest in you?"

"It definitely goes both ways. But she might be more reluctant than I am to see where this might lead us."

Ron's head tipped to the side as his eyebrows pulled together. "Not what I expected to hear."

"I'm only a man, pastor, and she's a beautiful and charming woman."

The ghost of a smile creased the other man's face. "I can't deny that. But I was more thinking of the fact that she's the reluctant one. Why do you suppose that is?"

Besides the fact that Keanan was an oversized oaf with no redeeming qualities? "Maybe... maybe I've created something in my mind that doesn't exist. I'm too big. Not handsome. I don't express myself well to her but find myself tongue-tied. I don't do grand things for her to prove my feelings. Perhaps she's immune to me, and I read her wrong." He caught the bemused expression on the other man's face. "What's so funny?"

"Keanan, your humility is as inspiring as it is misplaced."

"I don't understand."

The pastor chuckled. "I hardly know where to start."

Keanan crossed his arms and raised his eyebrows.

"Okay. You are tall, but since when was that a flaw? It's how God made you. You aren't handsome? You don't hear the women whisper around you, I suppose, but I've heard a comment or two around the church. Although I understand the word *handsome* is outdated. *Cute* and *hot* are the words I hear."

Hot? Only if his cheeks were any indication.

"As for speech—" Ron shook his head "—I've rarely met a preacher with a more eloquent tongue. I have seen you carry supplies for Chelsea, open doors for her, and assist her with her coat."

"But I'd do that for any woman," Keanan protested.

"With that same look on your face? I don't think so. Tracy Grindle told me she'd been rather interested in you and worried when I paired you together to lead a group, but her concern had been unfounded."

How was he to follow that? Keanan shook his head. "I don't get it."

"She saw how you watched Chelsea, and she set aside her own preliminary interest. You know she has been seeing Tyrell

Burke for the past few weeks?"

"No, really?"

The pastor grinned. "No reason for you to care, right?"

"I suppose. Though I'm happy for her and wish them all the best. Isn't Brent building a timber frame house for him?"

"Yes, one and the same." Ron leaned forward, elbows on his knees. "But back to Chelsea. I think we've established there is a mutual physical attraction."

That Chelsea found him in any way appealing was still difficult to believe. Pastor Ron didn't know the half of it.

Keanan nodded. "And yet she avoids me. I don't know what to think."

Ron steepled his hands. "Your best guess?"

He had no reply.

"Let me offer a thought. I might be wrong, as I do not know your hearts nor your history together. But I wonder if she sees in you such a passion for Jesus that she is jealous." Ron held up a hand. "Not jealous in that she thinks you'd love her less because you love the Lord more, but in that she sees her own lack of relationship with Him in comparison."

Keanan stared at Ron as gears clicked in his mind. Could he be right? "But anyone can ask Him."

"It's not always that simple. Yes, confession and request are all that is needed. I'm not arguing with your theology. But I can tell you many people do not *feel* forgiven. Do not *feel* close to God. Feelings don't alter reality, but they are very real even so." Ron rose to his feet. "I heard the outside door. Our Alpha guests have started to arrive for dinner."

"Thank you, pastor."

Ron's hand rested on Keanan's shoulder. "My prayers will be with you."

Chapter 18 --

I guess you're wondering why we've called you all together like this." Steve Nemesek looked around the great room of the straw bale house.

Chelsea would hazard a guess Keanan knew, but she wasn't looking at him. He sat in an armchair not far from Steve. Chelsea dropped onto a dining chair she'd dragged into the space.

Zach rested his elbows on his knees and looked at his father. Jo perched on the sofa arm beside him with baby John asleep in a wrap against her chest. "Go for it, Dad. What's up?"

"Well, it's been nearly five years since I contracted Guillain-Barré Syndrome. Most people who get it recover fully." He glanced at Rosemary, who sat next to him. "I guess I'm special."

Rosemary squeezed his hand.

Yeah, he was. Chelsea didn't know him all that well, but she'd heard about how much pain he was in and knew he rarely complained. He was what, not quite sixty? And hadn't been able to hold down his job since it hit. It couldn't have been the way he planned to retire.

Zach's jaw worked as he watched his father.

"Anyway, your mother and I have been talking and praying, and we've come to the decision that it's time to sell the farm. I know you kids have worked the land for five years now, and I hope you're interested in buying it."

It was like Steve and Zach were the only two people in the room. Had Zach seen this coming? Why wasn't this talk between the two of them in private?

"I'd always hoped to pass the farm on to you, son. Even when I wasn't sure you wanted it. But I never expected the toll GBS would wreak on us." Steve clenched Rosemary's hand. "I expected to stay healthy well into retirement."

Rosemary took over. "What Dad is trying to say is that we need to move into town. The old house wasn't built for someone who struggles with stairs. It's in decent shape but will need a new roof in the next year or two. The veranda needs some repairs, too. And I suppose you could say the whole place needs some TLC."

Zach surged to his feet. "Why didn't you tell me it was coming to this?"

Chelsea's gaze caught on Keanan's across the room as Zach paced. Keanan had known.

"You're so busy, son." Steve's voice held no reproach. "You have a thriving veterinary practice and a beautiful family. You oversee the entire operation here."

She wouldn't go so far as to say the *entire* operation, but Chelsea knew he was the only one in their whole crew who'd grown up on the farm. He'd been the one to teach others how to manage the equipment, how to fix the fences, and how to butcher meat for the freezers. Meanwhile, he spent less time at Green Acres than any of the rest of them. Yeah, she could see Steve's point.

Zach stopped in front of his father. "But I never meant to be too busy for you."

Rosemary reached for Zach's hand. "You've always been right there when we needed you. This isn't intended to be a guilt trip in any way. Instead of pushing us aside, you've built a log house right next door. You've allowed us to be a regular part of Maddie's life, and now little John's. Your father and I have always felt that we gained more sons and daughters through your friends." She looked around the gathering, her gaze lingering on Chelsea. "You all have made our lives so full of blessing."

"Then why?"

"Because it's time," Rosemary said simply.

"We've found a little house in Galena Landing," Steve said. "It's fairly new and well-maintained, all on one level." He grinned at Rosemary. "Even has a little yard your mother can dig up to plant tomatoes if she wants."

She leaned against him. "Or I'll just keep coming out to Green Acres and garden with the kids."

Jo shifted from the sofa arm to her feet. "We'd like that." The baby whimpered and wiggled in the wrap, and Jo's hand rubbed circles on his back as she swayed from side to side.

"So this is a done deal?" Zach demanded. "You've already bought a house?"

Chelsea's heart went out to him. It was probably rough accepting his dad's medical situation had worsened. Plus, the whole doing-this-in-public thing. Only — she glanced around at the gathered team, pointedly not looking at Keanan — this wasn't public. This was the group Zach had promised to make decisions with. So it kind of made sense.

"The way I see it, there are a few ways we can do this." Rosemary looked around at the group. "We'd like to offer you the farm at the same cost as the house we want to buy. The farm is valued considerably higher, but we don't need more. If you, as a team, decide not to purchase the farm, we'd like to put it on the market early this coming year. Gary Waterman has always been interested in this part of the valley, and he'd make a good neighbor for you if that's how it went."

Zach's mouth opened and closed. "Any other options?"

Rosemary nodded. "We've talked to a real estate agent about zoning, and we can subdivide the property. We can sell the farmland to you and the front five acres, including the house, to someone else."

"I see. Do you have numbers in mind for any or all of those options?"

Rosemary handed a manila envelope to Zach as she rose. "Everything should be in there." She reached for Steve's hands and helped him stand. "We need to get home, and you kids have plenty to discuss. If you've got any questions, you know where to find us."

Steve straightened slowly. "Nothing needs to be done in haste. The house we've chosen isn't going anywhere right away. It's been on the market a while, and the owners have delisted it for the winter. Tammy, the real estate agent, knows them and has spoken of our interest. So there's time to figure it out."

Chelsea considered the farmhouse next door. Was that the kind of place she'd like to live in? It had a certain amount of charm, but she couldn't see it. Way too big for a woman alone. It must have been a great place for Rosemary and Steve to raise four kids, though.

"How about my sisters?" Zach shook his head. "Not that I imagine any of them wanting to buy a farm. But maybe the house and yard?"

"I don't think so," Rosemary said slowly. "Cindy and Tom are established in Denver, of course. Heather and Andrew in Seattle. They all seem settled."

Steve slid his arm around his wife's waist. "And who knows about Liz? She's been in Thailand a long time now. I don't think it's her permanent plan, but it's hard to know when she's in touch so rarely."

Chelsea knew that had been a sore spot for Zach and Jo. Liz hadn't come to their wedding and only sent a gift — a pair of carved elephants — a year later. She'd barely acknowledged the birth of her niece and, to Chelsea's knowledge, hadn't yet sent congratulations for little John.

"We'll email Liz once you kids have had a chance to talk," said Rosemary. "You certainly have first dibs if you want them. Of course, we'll let Cindy and Heather know, too. But don't let thoughts of your sisters interfere with your decision."

Steve swayed, and Rosemary's arm around him tightened.

So in tune were they with each other. Chelsea could only hope she'd find their kind of love one day. She peered at Keanan from behind lowered lashes. His gaze was fixed on her. Oh, man. Was this the beginning of a relationship like Zach's parents had? Had they fumbled around in the beginning, not sure if they had enough in common to build a marriage? A family?

What was she going to do about Keanan?

oOo

"I can't believe I didn't see this coming." Zach came back from walking his parents out to their car and scrubbed his hands through his hair before fixing a sharp gaze on Keanan.

Keanan raised his shoulders slightly and let them drop. He could see it both ways. He nearly always could. Whether that was a blessing or a curse, he'd never been certain.

Zach opened the brown envelope and drew out several sets of papers stapled together. He glanced through them and shook his head. "A copy for everyone." He dealt out papers around the room.

Silence for a moment while the team members absorbed the material. Keanan had seen it all yesterday. He'd printed out the copies. He watched as Zach pulled Jo and the baby close and they scanned their papers.

Keanan shifted restlessly. He definitely couldn't fault Zach. How long had it been since he'd been in touch with his own father? Or his mother? He needed to start rebuilding those relationships before leaving for Africa.

His gaze found the top of Chelsea's curly head. She adjusted her glasses as she read. Longing surged through him, a no longer unfamiliar emotion.

Chelsea looked up and met his gaze. A pink flush crept up her cheeks and she turned back to the papers, creasing the corners.

"Well, what does everyone think?" Zach asked at last.

Claire glanced around. "For starters, can we afford to buy the farm?"

Allison's hand swept down and away. "Easily. With or without the house."

"We'd be hard put to feed this gang if we lost that land." Noel's fingers twined around Claire's.

"I hate to see it going out of the family." Jo rubbed the baby's back then grinned. "I consider all of us family in that regard."

Zach nodded. "My first instinct is to say yes to the farmland, but I don't want to move out of the log cabin we've built and into my parents' house, no matter how full of childhood memories it might be."

"It's a decent place as far as older farmhouses go, I'm sure." Allison shrugged before giving Brent a sweet smile. "But we, too, have a home."

Zach glanced at Keanan. "So do you."

Keanan nodded. The less he said, the better.

"Claire? Noel?"

The couple glanced at each other. "Our place is here in headquarters," said Claire. "Unless someone thinks we'd be better off elsewhere."

"No, not at all. We value having you guys in residence. Unless you think the baby will change things?"

Noel laughed, his face glowing. "The baby will change everything... and nothing. We're good with continuing our current roles." He tangled his fingers with Claire's. "We'll need some pinch-hitting from time to time, of course."

"Done," said Jo.

Keanan choked back a chuckle. Jo understood better than any of them, but had the least time to take on new roles. Although she did watch Finnley quite a lot, saying he kept Madelynn company and out of trouble. So, anything was possible.

Zach turned to his childhood friend. "Gabe? Sierra?"

They glanced at each other and Sierra looked down. "We need to talk about it, I guess," said Gabe. "The duplex has never been considered a permanent situation for us, but I hadn't thought of taking on your parents' home. You all might be surprised to know I don't consider myself much of a handyman."

Keanan grinned and held up both hands. "I suppose it goes without saying that I have all the home I need in the grain bin."

"That's great for now, man." Noel leaned forward to see him better. "But one day you'll have a wife and family."

In Keanan's periphery, Chelsea folded her papers twice more. He held Noel's gaze steady. "If that happens, the best answer for me is an additional pair of grain bins with a passageway joining them. I'm no more up for renovating than Gabe is. Ask Brent if I'm even capable of it."

Everyone chuckled. He'd learned a lot working with Brent, but nothing had been structural save installing the second floor.

A sudden thought struck him. What if Chelsea fancied a fixer-upper? Could he do that for her? Give up his cozy home and learn to replace shingles and repair verandas? His heart expanded just a little. For her, he could, but he couldn't imagine her asking it of him. Could barely imagine her accepting him at all, regardless of the smoldering looks that passed between them on a regular basis.

"Chelsea?" asked Zach.

Her curly head tilted up sharply, and her mouth opened as she stared at Zach. Clearly she had not expected to be asked.

"I, uh. No. I can't take on a house. I wouldn't know the first thing to do with it."

Zach flipped to the third page of the report and tapped on a spot Keanan knew held the estimated value of the house and required repairs. "We can probably afford to hire Brent and his crew to fix the house up, if that makes a difference to you. Or to anyone here."

Chelsea shook her head so quickly her curls flared out around her head. "No, thanks. It might be a great opportunity for someone else, but not for me."

"It might be a year or so before I can clear my schedule to do a full renovation," said Brent. "But it's a definite possibility if that's what the team wants."

Gabe cleared his throat. "I think we need to take a week or so to pray through this and make sure we're making the right decision. We can buy the whole property and rent out the house, too. Maybe new team members will come and it will be perfect for them. Or maybe someone's situation will change."

Noel nodded. "I agree that this isn't the type of decision we should make in haste. Let's commit to asking God's direction." He launched into a verbal prayer.

Several of the team members spoke out in prayer before Zach closed.

When Keanan opened his eyes, his heart hitched. Chelsea met his gaze from across the room, more openly than she'd ever done. It looked like an invitation to him. He wanted to cross the space, take her in his arms, and ask her what she was thinking. What her deepest desires were. If he could kiss her.

Whoa. None of those things were happening here tonight. Especially not with the whole team present.

Chapter 19 ---

Chelsea helped Rosemary set up a fourth folding table in what had once been Zach's bedroom. Tables lined the perimeter of the small room with one in the middle.

"There," the older woman said with satisfaction. "Now I can sort everything out to which child it pertains."

"Everyone's coming for Thanksgiving?" That didn't give Rosemary and her much time to sort a lifetime of memories.

"Everyone but Liz." Rosemary's eyes clouded. "I haven't had an email from her in several weeks. I know the Internet is spottier in Thailand than here, but..."

Chelsea gave the older woman a squeeze. How could the unknown Liz not realize what a treasure she had in her parents? If Chelsea didn't have a great family of her own, she'd adopt this one in a heartbeat. As it was, her parents and younger brother were making the trek to Idaho for the holiday, too. She hadn't seen them since her move in early September, but they texted, Skyped, or emailed often.

"Anyway. Thanks for giving me a hand today." Rosemary looked around the sparse room. "Zachary and Jo have taken the last of his things over to the log cabin. That gives us at least part of a table to set items any of the kids might want." She sighed. "We will be carrying a lot of boxes up these stairs and back down again, but there just isn't room to leave everything set up on the main floor. Not with all the supplies Steve needs."

"It's fine. We can do this."

"Keanan said he'd be over later to carry the heavy ones. That boy is a gem."

Chelsea's heart caught. "Right. Where do you want me to start?"

"Cindy and Heather's room is next door. Pictures off the walls, things out of the drawers, boxes off the shelves in the closets." Rosemary bit her lip. "This is going to be difficult."

"I'm sure." Chelsea eyed the older woman uncertainly. She could hardly stand the thought of her own parents downsizing, but it was inevitable sooner or later. Wasn't it? After all, both she and Sierra had left home, and Jacob had all but moved out.

She went into the next room and lifted pictures off the walls. Bits of wallpaper came off when she removed posters held on with yellowed tape. A bulletin board still covered in teenage photos came next. She carried everything to Rosemary.

"If the girls wanted these, wouldn't they have taken them already?" Rosemary let out a long breath. "The posters can go in the recycling box, I guess."

Chelsea spent two hours carrying assorted items from various rooms for Rosemary's judgment. The older girls' room had been stripped of everything but the double bed and an empty dresser. Floral wallpaper had faded around the brighter spots where things had hung on the walls.

Liz's room, smaller than Chelsea's walk-in closet in Portland, held more mementoes. Chelsea watched Rosemary blink back tears as she arranged the items on Liz's table.

"Tell me about Liz." Maybe talking would be like therapy.

"How old are you, dear?"

"Twenty-six."

Rosemary nodded. "She's a little older than you, then. The

baby of our family, three years younger than Zachary. Cindy and Heather were practically twins, just sixteen months apart, and had no room for a little sister in their busy lives. They were six and seven when she was born."

The Nemesek family was a lot like Chelsea's would have been if her parents had another girl after Jacob. She'd never thought of Zach and her brother having so much in common with two older sisters, though she and Sierra were a bit farther apart in age.

"Liz always struggled to fit. I'm not sure what Steve and I could have done differently. We certainly loved her as much as the others. Heather accused us of loving Liz more, actually. Our baby..."

"It must have been hard."

Rosemary's unfocused gaze stared out the window as though the four children played outside on the farm. "Oh, we had many happy times, too. Even Liz." Rosemary looked at Chelsea. "I pray for her daily — constantly — that God will soften her heart and bring her home. I don't mean that selfishly. If He wants her to serve in Thailand, I'm good with that, but right now she's not listening. She's cut herself off from everyone. I just want to see her again. My baby girl."

Chelsea blinked back a tear of her own for this young woman she didn't even know. Liz had been braver than Chelsea. Instead of putting on a front and doing what was expected, she'd tossed everything and gone her own way. A tiny bit of Chelsea envied that.

"As parents, we do our best to raise our children." Rosemary fingered the edges of a crocheted afghan on Liz's table. "Sometimes we're too tired to fight for what's right. Life comes at us from all sides. It's been very difficult to accept that I can't change Liz's choices. She's a grown woman who was raised to know the Lord. What she does with that is her choice."

"I can't imagine."

Rosemary dabbed her eyes. "I asked you one time if you brought everything to God in prayer — little things and big things. This is where I've learned to depend on Him moment by moment through every day and night. I guess it hasn't been a complete waste."

Chelsea reached for Rosemary and enveloped her in a hug. She'd have to remember to do the same for her own mom next week when they came for Thanksgiving. Unlike Liz, Chelsea didn't want to cut her family ties. If anything, maybe she was a bit too dependent on them, even now.

Rosemary hugged her back. "Thank you, dear. Now, where were we? Is there anything left in Liz's closet?"

"A few things. Let me get the rest." Chelsea whirled out of the room.

"Anyone up here?"

Keanan's voice. She'd been half waiting for it all morning.

"Come on up!" called Rosemary.

His measured tread came nearer. Chelsea fought the impulse to run, not that there was anywhere to go. Maybe it was guy trouble that had sent Liz packing for the Far East.

oOo

"I brought the boxes you wanted," Keanan said as he entered the room at the head of the stairs. Then he blinked. Chelsea? What was she doing here?

"Thank you." Rosemary moved things on one of the tables. "I have tape here somewhere... Aha!" She brandished the dispenser. "Shall we go down to the kitchen and start on the china cabinet?"

Chelsea eyed him. He smiled at her. She looked away.

Baby steps.

"Certainly."

Rosemary brushed past him and started down the stairs.

"Seriously?" Chelsea's eyes were wide. "She's getting rid of her china? Or just packing it for the move?"

"The house in town is quite small. She feels this is the best time to downsize their belongings."

"But one of her daughters will probably want it, right?"

Keanan scratched his head. "They are only things, Chelsea. Dishes to eat from. Pretty bowls, too, I suppose."

"I wouldn't expect *you* to understand." Chelsea hurried past him and jogged down the stairs.

No, he didn't. Keanan sighed and followed the women.

"This box would be a good size," Rosemary said as he entered the kitchen. She hefted the tape dispenser.

"Allow me." Keanan assembled the box. "Which would you like me to lift down first?"

She turned to the cabinet. "We'll set it all out on the table. Maybe the dinner plates first. Chelsea, dear, would you mind shredding paper from that box? Old paperwork from decades ago. It will make good packing material."

"Okay." Chelsea looked from one to the other then started the shredder.

"How's Steve today?" asked Keanan as he lifted down stacks of dinnerware.

Rosemary grimaced. "Tired. Even though he can't do much to help other than sorting papers, he's as exhausted at the end of the day as I am. Now that we've embarked on this move, I can't wait to see it through. Once we're settled again, he'll do much better."

Chelsea turned off the shredder. "Where did you get this lovely china?"

Rosemary stroked the floral pattern at the edge of a plate. "Much of it was a wedding gift from my aunts. In those days every bride needed china and crystal, no matter how big or fancy her house was."

"It must hold many special memories."

Keanan bit his tongue.

"It does. I hope one of the girls will want to take it home. If not, I've heard of people selling things like this on eBay. Maybe I'll give that a try."

"You're getting rid of it?" Chelsea's voice held a tremor. Keanan couldn't be quite certain, but he didn't think it was faked.

"It's time, I think." Rosemary aligned the top plates. "We rarely have dinner parties here anymore. Everything has moved next door to Green Acres." She smiled at Chelsea. "I don't mind. The straw bale house has so much more room. We'll be, what, twenty-five people next week for Thanksgiving? Even in our best days, we couldn't hold that many here. Besides, it's good for Steve that we can come home when it becomes overwhelming. We don't have to wait for everyone to leave."

"I get that, but surely these dishes still hold sentimental value."

No wonder Chelsea had looked down on his grain bin home. There certainly wasn't room in his space for non-utilitarian items. Things that had more than one function were even more valuable. She'd never be able to adjust to his lifestyle.

Could he adjust to hers?

She pursed her lips as she stacked plates inside a box, smoothing a handful of shredded paper between each.

No, he couldn't. Not really. God had challenged him to hold earthly goods loosely. Looked like Chelsea wasn't interested in that lesson.

"Chelsea, dear, it's not that we couldn't wedge the china cabinet into the new place, but I want to free myself from things I don't need. From clutter. It seems better to sort through things now rather than make the kids deal with it all after we die."

"But you're not that old!"

"Age has little to do with it. I thought Steve's number was up four and a half years ago. God spared him, and I'm so thankful.

But none of us knows when we will die."

Chelsea moved on to the next box.

Keanan taped the first shut then grabbed a felt pen and labeled it.

"Under the table on the left side of the room upstairs, please," said Rosemary.

He nodded and carried it up. Remnants of the family's history lay spread across the tables. Maybe he should cut Chelsea some slack if she'd had to deal with all this.

She'd lived a life of privilege. He'd wager her parents' home was at least the size of his father's house in Beverly Hills. Mom'd had no trouble walking away from it all when she'd had enough of Dad, and she'd never regretted it.

Keanan had left for different reasons, of course. But he had just as few regrets.

He should invite Mom for Thanksgiving. He couldn't very well head to Oregon right now with all the Alpha meetings and the other loose ends he needed to tie up before Africa. She probably already had plans — it was only two weeks away — but what did it hurt to ask?

Without giving it any more thought, he pulled his phone from his pocket and tapped her icon.

"Keanan! It's good to hear from you. All is well, I hope?"

"Hi, Mother. I'm doing well. And you?"

"Fine here. Not as busy as some years in November, but I have enough Christmas orders to keep me occupied."

Was that a good sign... or not? He took a deep breath. "I was wondering if you'd like to come to Idaho for Thanksgiving. You could fly into Spokane if you wanted. I'd be happy to pick you up." Uh, that would require borrowing a vehicle, but it shouldn't be too hard.

"Really? I'd love to see where you're living now before you head off on another adventure."

"So you'll come?"

"Let me look into flights, and I'll let you know."

He crossed the room to look out of the window at the late fall day. "That sounds wonderful. I can't wait to introduce you to everyone here."

"Oh?" There was a lilt to her voice. "Anyone special?"

"No." Oh, who was he kidding? "Maybe." Even though it didn't seem there was any way he and Chelsea could find a level playing field.

"In that case, I'll make every effort."

"Don't start ringing wedding bells yet, Mother. I really don't know if things will work out but, yes, there's someone special."

She laughed, a sound that warmed his heart. "Should I start designing an engagement ring?"

"It might be too early for that." If only. If ever.

"I'll talk to you as soon as I can figure out how to get there. I love you, Son."

"I love you, Mother." He pressed to end the call then pivoted to return downstairs.

Chelsea, eyes wide, stood in the doorway clutching a box. Her face flushed as their gazes locked.

Keanan's mind scrambled. What had she overheard? Had he said too much, or had his mother done all the jumping to conclusions on the other end?

Wedding bells. He closed his eyes for a second. Those had been his words. He'd admitted there was someone special. He took the box from Chelsea and set it with the other before looking at her again.

"My mother might come for Thanksgiving."

Her jaw clenched. "So I heard."

"Chelsea..."

She flicked a glance at his eyes then turned away.

"Chelsea," he repeated, and she stopped with her back to him.

Why did words fail him now? He'd told her weeks ago he found her special. Nothing new had happened. But now he'd said it out loud to his mother. And Chelsea had heard him.

"What?"

He touched her arm, and she shifted slightly away. Would gathering her in his arms and kissing her break through her reserve, or would she slap him hard and never speak to him again?

He wasn't willing to take the chance. He swallowed hard. "Nothing. Let's go help Rosemary."

Chapter 20 --

*C*laire pointed her pen toward the bedroom wing. "We can put Cindy and Tom and their kids in the guest rooms down the hall. Rosemary has space for Heather's family, and Sierra wants your parents to stay with her and Gabe."

Chelsea nodded. "That leaves Jacob with me. I haven't had a good visit with my baby brother in months."

"Well, that's the trouble." Claire glanced up. "Keanan's mom is coming, too."

"And that's a problem how?" She'd kept the emotion out of her voice. Pretty sure.

"Well, you've got an actual guest room, and Keanan doesn't. Your brother would probably be fine with a foamie on the floor at Keanan's, but I'm sure his mother would like more privacy and a decent bed."

"No." Chelsea surged to her feet. "You can't do this to me."

"Do what?" Claire leaned back in her chair, the pen still tapping on the table. "What do you mean?"

Was she faking that innocent look? Chelsea couldn't tell.

"I don't want Keanan's mother staying with me. That's just too... weird."

"Oh? How's that? I thought you said there was nothing

between you. It shouldn't be any weirder to you than having Noel's mother."

"If she's coming, I'll take her. In a heartbeat."

Claire shook her head. Was that a grin poking at the corners of her mouth? "Noel and I are leaving for his mom's in Missoula tomorrow. His sister and brother-in-law are flying in from Flagstaff."

Chelsea slumped back into the chair. "Hope you have a great time."

"We will, I'm sure. Are you really saying you'd prefer a middle-aged woman to sleep on the floor with no privacy?"

"I'm saying Keanan should have thought about having company before building something that small."

"Seriously."

Chelsea was going to give in. She knew it. Claire knew it. But, man, did she have to do it graciously? How could they force her into this situation? Probably laughing all the way. She peeked at Claire. Not laughing. Just waiting.

"Did Keanan ask? Because he should have talked to me first. Himself." Maybe he'd tried. She'd spent the past week avoiding him since helping Rosemary. She'd been getting pretty good at avoiding him, actually. Practice made perfect. Who knew.

"No, he didn't say anything about that. He mentioned she was coming and I asked if I should find a place for her. He seemed grateful."

I bet. Chelsea bit off the words before they came out.

"If you don't care about him, why does it bother you if his mother sleeps in your guest room? I'm sure she'll spend most of her time at Keanan's or over here. It's not like you need to entertain her every minute."

Chelsea felt herself sliding a little closer to the edge of the precipice. "Good point."

"So it's okay then?"

"Not precisely." Chelsea pinched the bridge of her nose. "But whatever. I'll take one for the team."

A smirk played with the edges of Claire's mouth. "The team thanks you." She made a note and laid down the pen before folding her arms and looking at Chelsea. "Want to talk about it?"

"Not really."

"Sounds serious."

Chelsea took off her glasses and cleaned them on her hem. What could she say that wouldn't incriminate her one way or the other?

"I've noticed Keanan watching you."

That was the best her friend could do? "That's interesting."

Claire chuckled. "Sounds like you've noticed it, too. Have you two talked about the reasons for this phenomenon?"

There must be something she could do right now. Make lunch, maybe. Or whatever meal was next.

"Chelsea."

Chelsea stared at her friend's hand on her arm. Trimmed, unpainted nails. She should offer a manicure.

"There's nothing wrong with falling in love, you know. I did it myself. Yes, reluctantly at first. I'll admit it. But God knew what He was doing in my life. In Noel's."

"Who said anything about falling in love?"

"It's not like it's something new at Green Acres. I've watched Jo and Sierra and Allison. Even watched myself. And now you."

"Oh, no, you don't. It's not that easy. You can't drop me in a mold with everyone else. You all are married. Except Allison, but that's in less than a month."

"Are you honestly denying any sort of attraction to Keanan Welsh?"

Chelsea opened her mouth and closed it again. Lying was a sin, and telling the truth wasn't really an option.

"I hope you'll be glad to know Noel and I have been praying for you two."

Nice. Now they were a topic. A prayer request.

"Do you want to know what I think the problem is?"

Not really, but Chelsea kept her mouth zipped.

"I'll tell you." Claire leaned closer. "I think you're fighting it on a spiritual level. I think you find his deep faith unsettling."

"I'm not sure I like what you're insinuating."

"It's not my intention to hurt you. Please believe me."

Intention or not, the words stung.

"You're bottling something up, holding pain close to your chest. I don't know what it is, Chelsea, but if it's affecting your ability to love, it's affecting everything in your life. I'd be honored if you chose to confide in me, but you might feel more comfortable with your sister."

Chelsea shook her head. How had Claire guessed what even Sierra hadn't mentioned?

Claire put her hand on Chelsea's. "Father God, I bring my sister Chelsea into Your presence. You know what is holding her back. You know what she needs from You. I pray that by the power of the Holy Spirit, You will touch her life and restore to her the joy of Your salvation. In Jesus' name, amen."

Chelsea blinked back tears. "Where do you get that kind of faith?" Oh no. She'd said it out loud. Whispered, but loud enough for Claire to pick it up.

"I ask Him for it, and He supplies," Claire said quietly.

"I've asked. Maybe it takes faith to get faith."

"Have you asked Jesus to forgive your sins? Have you asked Him to be in control of your life?"

She should be offended at the questions, but it would take too much effort. Besides, it seemed a relief to come clean. "Yes, I have. But it still doesn't feel real."

"Did it ever?"

Chelsea nodded. "When I was a kid. A teen. Digging into the Bible was a joy and a challenge."

"What happened to change that?"

"I wish I knew." She wiped a tear from behind her glasses and glanced at Claire. Had she expected to see judgment? Triumph? In her friend's eyes was only a sober sincerity.

"I don't know the answers." Claire squeezed her hand. "But I know who does. I'll pray for you."

o0o

"So this is where you're living now." Keanan's mom peered out the window of the borrowed car. Allison's. He hadn't dared ask Chelsea, even though Claire told him Chelsea would be happy to have his mom stay with her for the weekend.

Somehow he doubted that was completely true. In return, he'd get Chelsea and Sierra's younger brother at his place. An ironic twist of fate, for sure.

"Keanan?"

"I'm sorry, Mother. Did you say something?" He stopped the car in the parking area by the farm school. The half-dozen students had left last week at the close of the fall term.

"I'm thankful you've finally found a place to call home."

If only Chelsea... no, he wasn't going there. Not right now. "I am, too. I can't wait for you to meet everyone. It may be somewhat overwhelming, though, as there are other families visiting from out of town."

"I'm sure I'll manage just fine." She waited for him to round the car and open her door before stepping out. She hugged her light jacket tighter. "Quite a wind you have here."

"It is November," he reminded her. "Sometimes there's snow by Thanksgiving."

Mother shivered. "I can think of plenty of reasons to live in Salem. Winter is a good one."

"I hope we get snow before I leave for Africa. I haven't experienced much of it in my life, other than a few ski trips."

"So where is your house? You said it was round..." She turned slowly, taking in the various buildings.

He pointed at the farm school. "Just behind here. But maybe we should get you settled first? Chelsea Riehl lives in the right-hand duplex there." He swung his hand. "And she's got a spare room you're welcome to stay in."

"Sounds very nice, son."

Keanan popped the trunk and picked up his mother's luggage. He hadn't been inside that duplex since the night before the baby had been born.

His hands felt clammy and his heart beat faster as he escorted his mom across the yard. Was Chelsea even home? If she wasn't, could he walk right in? No. He couldn't do that. He set the luggage on the stoop and knocked.

"Coming!" Chelsea called.

Keanan's heart hiccupped at the sound of her voice.

The door swung open and there she stood, lovelier than ever in a multi-toned pink top that matched her glasses. Her curly hair framed her perfect face. Skinny jeans ended in high heels.

He blinked. Heels? Only Chelsea.

"Hi! You must be Keanan's mom. I'm Chelsea. It's so good to meet you. I hope you'll treat my home like your own." She extended her hand to Mother's without sparing a glance in Keanan's direction.

"Why, it's lovely to meet you, too. My name is Fernanda, but please call me Fern."

"Come on in, Fern. Your room is the one to the right of the hallway. Feel free to come and go as you wish while you're here."

"Thank you. You're so sweet."

Chelsea's face flushed as she bit her lip. "No problem. It's the least I can do as we all have quite a bit of company for Thanksgiving. It only makes sense to divvy everyone up according to the best use of space."

Keanan stepped forward. "I really appreciate it, Chelsea."

Her eyes did not meet his. "If you'd like to take your mom's things through to her room that would be great."

He pulled in a deep breath and managed to exhale soundlessly before nodding and doing as he was told. The green and gray room looked a lot different without the bright mural Brent had once created for Finnley on one wall. Chelsea had painted over it without him. Surprise.

He set the suitcase on the folding stand. Chelsea and his mother talked in the other room. He closed his eyes. Oh, God, what was he going to do? If Chelsea were immune to him, she'd think nothing of looking at him and talking to him. As it was, she barely acknowledged his presence and then only when he forced her to. But how could he break through the wall she'd built? He needed to talk to her — *really* talk to her — before he left for Africa. He couldn't bear to be halfway across the world with all these questions unanswered.

"Ready to go, Mother? I'd like to take you over to the main house and introduce you to whoever's in at the moment, and then we can go back to my place. I can't wait to show it to you."

"That sounds lovely." Mother squeezed both of Chelsea's hands, smiling at her. "I'll be back later. Again, thank you so much."

Chelsea stepped back with a little smile of her own. "No problem."

Back outside, Mother tucked her hand behind his arm. "Now do tell me, son. Is that the lovely woman who's won your heart?"

Keanan's feet stopped working, and he nearly tripped on his face. "Whatever gives you that idea?"

She chuckled merrily. "If your words don't tell me, that response certainly does. She seems very sweet."

"I'm not sure what clues you think you saw."

Mother squeezed his arm as they started to walk again. "You couldn't take your eyes off of her, and the reverse was also true."

Chelsea was watching him? When? She'd had little opportunity when his own gaze had been averted.

"Besides, she loves jewelry. That girl will be a pleasure to design pieces for. I can already see a an engagement ring with an entire set to match."

"Mother."

"Yes, Keanan?" She looked up at him, batting her eyelashes.

"Don't overstep. The situation is... difficult."

"I will be careful, my son. But I may not be able to resist giving a helping hand." She looked over the big house as they mounted the steps to the deck. "You said this building is made of straw bales? How quaint."

Chapter 21 ---

*T*he Green Acres kitchen bustled with preparations for a bountiful feast. Chelsea peeled potatoes at the sink, trying to stay out of the way while Rosemary directed her daughters in creating the various side dishes she'd planned. It seemed very strange not to have Claire and Noel in charge. Guess they needed a break same as anyone else.

"May I be of some help?"

Chelsea looked into Fern's eyes. Great. Last evening she'd avoided a heart-to-heart with Keanan's mother by feigning tiredness after Alpha. She managed a smile. "Sure. There's another peeler in the drawer to your right. It takes a lot of potatoes to feed this large a crew."

The fatigue last night hadn't been completely fake. Everyone at Alpha had been on such a high after a weekend retreat a few days before that it had reminded her yet again of the relationship she did not have with the Lord.

Fern reached into the sink. "My goodness, these are huge. I can't think when I've seen potatoes this size."

"Idaho is known for its potatoes. We had a bumper crop in the garden this year." Strange. She really felt a part of it after all the digging and sorting she'd done beside the other team members.

"I think it's delightful that you grow your own food here, but I'm sure there are still plenty of things you need to buy at the Super One."

"You'd be surprised how little." At least, Chelsea had been amazed. Part of that was Jo's militancy. She urged everyone to find local substitutes or do without. Somehow coffee and chocolate — organic and fair trade — still found their way into the house to Jo's tight-lipped annoyance.

"This meal," Fern said. "Everything is from the farm?" Her voice reflected curiosity.

"Pretty much. Let's see. We raised the turkeys. They're more difficult to raise than chickens, but it takes several chickens to feed our core group at one meal, where one turkey will do it and offer leftovers." Of course, two of the largest ones were roasting at the moment, one of them up the hill at Allison's to leave space in the second oven here.

Fern held up another potato. "And these."

"Yes. The stuffing ingredients are homegrown, other than the salt. Bread, celery, onions, sage—"

"The bread?" Fern looked astonished.

"Several of us alternate baking batches of six loaves at a time. Usually every second day."

"I had no idea."

"Keanan makes excellent bread." It pained her to admit it.

The peeler dropped from Fern's hands and clattered into the stainless steel sink. "Really."

"Yes, he does." But it wouldn't do to dwell on him with his mother so interested. "We also grew the green beans and mushrooms for the casserole. The beets. We're able to get salad greens from the greenhouse most of the year." Or so they said. She hadn't experienced a full Green Acres year yet.

"Now you have me intrigued. What about dessert?" Fern leaned closer. "I saw a row of pumpkin pies on the shelf when

Keanan showed me the larder."

"Most of the ingredients for that are from our farm, too." Our farm. The words sounded good. Maybe visiting Portland would be enough after all. Maybe Keanan would meet some woman in Africa and not bother coming back. Then her life would be sweet right here.

"Pumpkin pie has always a favorite of Keanan's."

Chelsea chopped a potato into smaller pieces than was likely required. "Interesting." Hers, too, but this wasn't the moment to mention it.

"I'm so glad he's found a place to call home. He seems very happy."

Surely no reply was needed.

"He hinted on the phone that there was someone special here. Yet, strangely, he hasn't introduced me to anyone like that. Do you know if it's someone from the church instead of the farm? He really didn't say much."

Chelsea's knife slipped and a drop of blood welled from her finger. "Excuse me." She squeezed her finger and edged past everyone on her way to the washroom for an adhesive bandage.

Drat that woman.

Chelsea stared at herself in the mirror. Did Fern know she was the one Keanan had referred to? Was the woman hinting, guessing, or merely oblivious? Good grief. If Chelsea hadn't given it away by any other means, slicing a deep gash in her finger would be a massive tip-off.

Lord? This would be a really good time to answer some of my prayers. Take Your pick which one. Make me stop caring about Keanan. Make him stop caring about me. Or there's always the big one: teach me how to feel my faith.

That last prayer might nullify the other two. Maybe... maybe she didn't want the spark between her and Keanan extinguished. Maybe she wanted it to grow into something real. Something big.

But that seemed as impossible as breaking down the invisible barrier between her and God.

It was all or nothing.

God, are You listening?

The only reply was a knock on the washroom door. "Anyone in there?"

That figured.

oOo

Keanan leaned against the pole shed in the still night air. Above lay a canopy of dark velvet studded with tiny but brilliant diamonds. Enough light came from the nearly full moon that he could see his breath billowing in the freezing air.

Stupendous. Magnificent. God-affirming. "The heavens proclaim the glory of God. The skies display his craftsmanship. Day after day they continue to speak; night after night they make him known."

A soft voice murmured, "I wish that were true."

Keanan jolted so hard he bashed his head on the overhang. Now there were stars of a different sort.

"Sorry." Definitely Chelsea.

He rubbed his head and looked down at her. She stood nearby — not quite close enough to reach out and touch — huddled in her down parka, its fur-rimmed hood pulled up over her curls and casting her face into shadow.

"Chelsea?" Not because he didn't recognize her voice, but because she so rarely sought him out or even acknowledged his existence.

"Yeah. It's me."

Questions tumbled through his mind. So many things he wanted to ask her, just so he could hear her voice. About her family, her brother — who seemed like a nice enough young man

— about how it was going with his mother, about what she was thankful for. He latched onto her words. "If what were true?"

She slid her hands into the opposite sleeves' cuffs. "That the skies make God known."

Keanan lifted his hand toward the sparkling sky. "How can this all be an accident of nature? Randomness? It speaks of a creator."

Did he imagine the soft sigh? Then he'd missed the point of her question.

She tipped her head back. If only he could see the stars reflected in her eyes, but he didn't dare take a step closer. She was like a fawn in the forest. What had lured her near he had no idea, but any quick movement and she'd bolt.

"I believe in God. The Creator. But how can a person really know Him? Not from studying the moon and stars is my guess."

Words, please, Lord. "Acknowledging His existence is a good first step, and we do learn something of His nature from seeing the works of His hands." She didn't move, so he plunged on. "The first chapter of Romans tells us that creation itself makes His undying power and divine identity clear."

"That's not the same thing as knowing Him."

"No, you're right. It points us to His existence and power. To His love."

She turned his direction, but he still couldn't see her face.

"But to really know Him requires a relationship. Spending time together. Conversing with Him."

"Conversing." Her hood moved from side to side. "It's so one-sided. I talk to Him, but I don't hear Him answer. He's a million miles away. Like the moon or stars."

Keanan bit his tongue before providing more accurate distances. Her point held, and this wasn't the time. "Sometimes we have to simply trust Him. Read His word, pray, ask Him to reveal Himself."

"And when the Bible seems like a dry ancient book?"

"You carry on, believing your faith is relevant and that God will speak through it to you."

"Fake it 'til you make it."

He barely heard those quiet words. "It's more like stepping out in faith than faking it. Remember trust doesn't have to be large to be real. Jesus talked about faith the size of a mustard seed."

"I don't know what faith is, Keanan. Oh, I get the definition, the theory. But Christian faith just seems like the comfy thing to accept, you know? It's what I was raised with. And yeah, I believe it. It makes more sense to me than anything else does. But deep inside? Not so sure."

Comfy? If only she could see the terrors many Christians around the world lived in. Being a believer was only comfortable for a tiny percentage of the world's population.

And yet, she was speaking to him. Opening her heart in a way that must be distinctly *un*comfortable. Searching. Reaching out.

"Chelsea?"

She turned toward him fully.

He took a step closer and tipped the hood away from her curls. Her glasses and her eyes behind them came into sight. If only he could remove her spiritual hood as easily. "Chelsea, I'm praying for you every day. Many times a day."

"Why?"

Keanan's hands cradled her face. "Because I care about you."

"At the risk of sounding like a toddler, but why?"

He grinned at the allusion to Madelynn's incessant questions. "Why do I care about you?"

Chelsea nodded. Her silky curls brushed his fingers, tantalizing him.

"I'm not sure. At the beginning, I didn't want to care. I focused on outward things that annoyed me. You always being

185

dressed up like a city girl for farm chores."

"That's because I was a city girl. You annoyed me, too."

"Because I was a hippie?"

She reached up and touched his hair. "Is that why you cut it?"

Keanan tried not to lean into her fingers as he nodded. "Brent asked if I'd looked in a mirror lately."

"You talked to Brent about me?" She dropped her hand, and his head felt chilled.

His breath caught. "A little." He ran his thumbs across her cheeks. "It just kind of came out. I'm sorry." Or at least he would be if she minded. If it made a difference to her.

"Seems weird."

"Does it?" He tucked a thumb under her chin and tipped her face up. "I want to tell everyone what I think of you."

Chelsea's eyes caught on his. "What's that?"

"I think you're very special. I see you pitching in with whatever is needed, whether you've ever done it before or not. Whether it's messy or not. You watch people and see what they need, then you help them if you can."

Her shoulders lifted and dropped as she broke eye contact. "Anyone would—"

"No, Chelsea. Not everyone would. You saw that Jo needed help the other evening and stepped up. No one else had noticed."

"They would have."

"You're also..." Dare he say the words? "You're also very pretty. I can't take my eyes off you when you're nearby. I can't stop thinking about you when you're not." His fingers tangled in her soft curls. They felt just the way he'd imagined.

Chelsea looked down where her boot scuffed the frozen ground.

His hands felt a tremor cascade down her body. He cupped her shoulders with his hands and tugged her closer. For an instant she resisted then she leaned against him, one cheek resting against his chest. Surely she could feel his erratic heartbeat even through his winter coat.

Dear Lord, thank You for this woman.

Slowly, gently, he slid his arms around her. If she pushed against him, he'd release her, but there was no push. After a few seconds he rested his cheek on the top of her head then closed his eyes to savor the moment. He'd dreamed of this. Could spend all night standing right here cradling her in his arms, even with the wind chill factor plummeting the temperature.

"How can I have faith like yours, Keanan? Why does God feel so far away?" Her voice was muffled against his coat.

Forgive me, Lord. All I want to do is kiss her, but this moment is here to draw her closer to You, not to me.

"Read the word. Memorize it. Meditate on it. Ask Him to reveal Himself to you through it."

She shuddered. "It sounds so easy."

"It's not easy. It's simple, but not easy."

"I don't get it."

He rubbed his hands up and down her back. "Do you... do you want to get together and spend time with God?" *Too forward, Welsh. Way too forward.* But she'd be the judge of that. He held his breath.

Chelsea pulled back enough to look at him. "Really? You'd do that for me?"

As though it might be an imposition. He massaged her shoulders. "It would be an honor. We have a few weeks before..." Oh, man. He didn't want to think about leaving. Not now. But changing his plans wasn't an option. Too many were depending on him. He'd given his word.

"If you think it might help..." Her words trailed away.

"I'd be honored."

Chapter 22 --

*C*helsea slipped in her front door. With any luck, Keanan's mother would have retreated to her room already. But no.

"There you are." Fern looked up from her tablet and raised her glasses to rest on her hair. "If I'd have known there was still so much cleanup to do, I'd have stayed longer."

Chelsea pushed out a smile. "No worries. We finished it up a bit ago." If Fern hadn't looked out the window and seen her and Keanan standing under the full moon, Chelsea certainly wasn't going to mention it. Why couldn't she savor the moment in private? Yet this was the woman who'd given birth to Keanan and raised him, at least in his pre-teen years.

"Would you like a cup of tea?" Chelsea crossed to the kitchenette.

"That would be lovely. Something herbal if you have it."

Chelsea opened the cupboard and peered in. "Chamomile? Mint?"

"Let me guess. Both were grown here at Green Acres."

"Yes, they were. I particularly like the chamomile with a dab of our honey."

"That sounds wonderful."

Chelsea felt the older woman's gaze on her as she heated water and got down two teacups.

"So what's your position here at the farm? I haven't figured out yet what everyone does."

"We all do whatever is needed, I guess." She glanced over at Keanan's mother. "I spent five years building an event coordination business in Portland. I thought I'd be able to use those skills here, but instead I've pitted a lot of plums, canned a lot of tomatoes, and trimmed out a lot of beef for grinding."

"Ah, Portland. I live not far out of the city myself. I'm a jewelry designer." She held up her hands, where half a dozen rings gleamed from various fingers.

Chelsea crossed the space for a closer look. Fern's work was exquisite. Bold. "These are gorgeous."

Fern reached for Chelsea's hands and held them, examining her rings. Did Keanan's mother notice that none of hers lived on the third finger of her left hand?

The kettle whistled, breaking the intense concentration. Chelsea whirled and finished making the tea. After passing a cup to Fern, she settled into the other easy chair.

"An event organizer. That's not unlike an artist," Fern mused.

Chelsea raised her eyebrows over her teacup.

"You have an eye for beauty. For design. For how things fit together."

Well, since she put it that way. "True. I've done a large fundraiser for my home church for several years. I've been doing the organizing from here this year, but I'll be going home to finish pulling it together right after Allison and Brent's wedding next weekend."

"What church is that, and what kind of a fundraiser?"

Chelsea named the congregation. "People buy tickets to attend. So there's a program, a dinner, a silent auction — a variety of ways to raise the money. It's been quite successful."

"So is this for a charity?"

"Yes. I'm not sure what the committee has chosen this year. There have been a variety of projects they've underwritten."

Fern leaned forward. "I love being part of endeavors like that. Depending on the recipient, of course. Let me know. I might be able to offer a set of jewelry for the auction."

"Really? That would be spectacular. I'm sure your work would bring in good bids." She'd probably bid herself if it didn't go too high. A new enthusiasm for the fundraiser simmered in her.

"I'll leave you my card, and you can let me know what's decided. When and where and any details I should know."

"I'll do that." Chelsea took a sip of tea. "I've recommended to the committee they support Keanan's trip. Send solar cookers to Africa for the mission to distribute."

Fern grinned. "Now that's a cause I can get behind." She eyed Chelsea speculatively.

Uh oh. "They make the final decision on that."

"Of course. My son tells me you picked out the tile for his bathroom."

Chelsea tried for a bright tone. "Do you like it? I think it turned out rather nice. He and Brent did a great job on the installation."

"It surprised me. The rows of glass mosaic reminded me of jewelry setting off what would have been a simple but classic outfit. They add just the right amount of bling. I was quite certain Keanan hadn't come up with that by himself."

"You're right." What a sweet way to describe the mosaics. "He went straight for the first tiles we saw in Wynnton and figured they'd be good enough."

Fern's eyebrows rose over her teacup. "Oh, you went shopping with him?"

How not to admit too much. Chelsea feigned nonchalance.

"Yes. He asked for input. Turns out that was a good idea on his part."

"Well." Fern tucked her feet under her on the cozy chair. "I must admit to some surprise. It's not like him to care how things look, and it's really not like him to ask a woman for an opinion."

Alarm bells rang in Chelsea's mind. Dangerous territory. "I guess anyone can change." Only she knew *why* Keanan had changed. Did his mother get it? How well did she know her son?

"I pay attention to details that others might overlook."

Oh, no.

"Is your finger better where you cut it earlier?"

"Um, yes. It will heal just fine. The adhesive came unglued in the dishwater. I left it off since the bleeding had stopped." Chelsea chuckled. Even to her it sounded brittle. "Can't believe I cut myself chopping potatoes. That was sure clumsy of me."

"I wondered why, too. Did I startle you with my question about Keanan?"

Silence hung in the air for a long moment, Chelsea's gaze riveted to Fern's.

"I've been praying for my son for many years. That he would find the woman God has chosen for him. That this woman would know she was cherished by God as well as by Keanan. My son lives an abundant life. He has a lot to share."

Chelsea drank more of her tea. What could she say to this woman?

"I see I've made you uncomfortable, Chelsea. That was not my intent. I wonder if you might be that woman. If you or my son realizes it."

A few hours ago it would have been much easier to laugh and deny it. Now, after their talk outside and the way he had held her in his arms? The way she'd allowed it and even leaned against him? She wasn't so sure.

Chelsea stood. "I guess there's a lot to wonder about." She walked to the kitchenette with measured steps and set the teacup in the sink. "If there isn't anything more you need this evening, I'm off to bed. It's been a long day." The yawn behind her hand may have started as a pretense but quickly turned real.

Fern nodded. The older woman's eyes held something that was not quite a twinkle and yet wasn't amusement, either.

Chelsea wasn't about to analyze it too deeply. Her sleepless hours were more likely to be filled reliving the moments in Keanan's arms.

oOo

Keanan pressed his forehead against the warm flank of the Guernsey cow as he squeezed her milk into the stainless steel bucket. Strange how he was going to miss this early morning ritual when he went to Africa. Not that he did it every day, but swapped out with Gabe and Noel. Even Sierra and Claire stepped in at times.

Not Chelsea though. Not yet. Maybe he could teach her, his arms around her and his hands guiding hers. He took a deep breath, remembering last night.

Down the way, the barn doors creaked open. Keanan shifted enough to see Gabe and his father-in-law entering. Chelsea's dad. He'd made sure to meet the man and chat a little then make good his escape. It hadn't been that difficult to melt into the large group gathered for Thanksgiving dinner.

"Morning, Keanan," Gabe said.

"Good morning, Gabe. Tim."

The cow fidgeted, and he crooned to her as he kept his hands moving, listening to the milk shooting rhythmically into the bucket.

"I haven't seen a cow hand-milked since I was a boy." Tim stepped a bit closer but kept a respectful distance. "My grandparents had a farm out in Waco County."

"I'd never milked before moving to Green Acres," Keanan responded. "But it's a vital part in keeping our food sources close to home."

Gabe chuckled. "Your daughter has become quite an avid cheese-maker, Tim. She's got a few small wheels of cheddar aging which we haven't had a chance to try yet."

The *zing zing* of milk hitting the bucket lightened as Keanan squeezed the last few ounces of milk from the teats. After a final massage, he moved the bucket and three-legged stool off to one side before releasing the cow from her confinement. He patted her flank as she ambled past him.

"Need a hand with the chickens?" he asked Gabe.

"No, I think Tim and I can manage."

"Every time Sandra and I visit the farm we see a whole new aspect of what you kids are doing here." Tim grinned. "I use the word kids lightly, you understand."

"Zach's parents are looking to sell the home place." Keanan eyed the older man. "Maybe you folks should think of buying them out. Moving up here." Oh, man, what was he saying? All he needed was another pair of interested eyes watching his fragile relationship with Chelsea.

Tim shook his head. "Sandra has a thriving optometric practice, and it's where my job is, too. I don't think we're leaving Portland until we retire, and that's a few years off yet. Maybe not even then."

Gabe turned to his father-in-law. "So long as you remember you're always welcome to visit as often as you like."

"I appreciate that, son." Tim clapped his hand on Gabe's shoulder.

When was the last time Keanan's own father had treated him that well? He hadn't thought about marriage — well, at all, really — but especially not as the possibility of gaining a set of parents who could speak truth and love into his life.

The urge to escape the barn nearly overwhelmed him. Keanan lifted the milk bucket.

"I haven't had a lot of chance to speak with Chelsea one-on-one since we got here," Tim went on, and Keanan froze in place. "Seems she's been a bit pre-occupied, but we're headed out for a family day together in a few hours."

Keanan dared a glance at the man. Behind him, Gabe smirked. Not that there was anything funny. "I hope you have an excellent day together. I'll be spending it with my mother. I don't see her as often as I'd like, either." Why had he added that? Likely so Tim wouldn't get any ideas to invite him along, yet there was no reason to suspect he might have done so.

Tim nodded. "Sandra is quite interested in talking with your mother about her designs. I'm sure there will be plenty of time yet this weekend for everyone to get to know each other."

"Uh, yes." Keanan didn't dare glance at Gabe. "That would be great. My mother is quite outgoing. She'd be happy to visit."

He should never have allowed Claire's innocent-sounding idea of having Mother stay with Chelsea and Jacob with him. Not that Chelsea's brother had been a problem. Far from it. But having Mother's watchful eye on Chelsea was something else entirely. And yet, Claire had been right. His mother shouldn't have to sleep on a mat on the floor with no privacy. The question remained, was she allowing Chelsea solitude or was she inspecting her with a magnifying glass?

Keanan eyed Tim again. The father of the woman he loved. Yet it was too early to admit such a thing openly. Definitely not with Gabe present.

Chapter 23 --

Chelsea slid into a vinyl booth at The Sizzling Skillet between her brother and her mother. She shivered against the November chill that had pelted her on their walk along Galena Lake. No doubt she'd be shedding her jacket soon thanks to their seats near the kitchen.

Her dad leaned onto the table and looked past Sierra at Gabe. "I must say this Thanksgiving has been much different than last year."

Sierra's elbow caught Dad's ribs. "Don't even start."

Gabe slid his arm across the padded back of the bench, his eyes twinkling with his grin. "It was a difficult time in our relationship." His hand cupped Sierra's shoulder. "But we got past it."

Chelsea remembered all too well how pig-headed her sister had been. She'd invited her other boyfriend to dinner at the farm, fully knowing she was going to break up with him. And not knowing Noel and Claire had invited Gabe.

The waitress dropped off menus and asked for their drink orders.

"I hear Tyrell Burke is dating Tracy Grindle from church," Chelsea said.

Sierra rolled her eyes. "That's nice for him. I wish them the best of luck."

Gabe chuckled. "Brent says he's matured a lot." He leaned forward to meet Dad's gaze. "Brent is building a house for Tyrell this winter. Now that he's out of my personal life, I do hope and pray he finds peace and joy."

"A lot can change in a year." Sierra eyed Chelsea across the table. "A year ago you were making a ton of trips out to see me. Now you live here, and I hardly ever see you."

Chelsea poked her chin toward Gabe. "You're too busy with *him*."

"It's not just that. Sometimes I think you're avoiding me."

And she had to bring this up with the whole family present — why? "I'm not avoiding you." She fixed a narrowed gaze on Sierra. "We just have different tasks. The farm keeps all of us so busy."

"Huh. And here I thought it might be because of Ke—"

"Mom, did you want to talk about the church fundraiser? I'll be driving home after the wedding. Probably Monday so I can help with the cleanup. That still leaves ten days to finalize everything before the event."

The waitress slid water glasses and teacups down the table and took their orders.

"I'm kind of curious what Sierra was going to say," commented Jacob from beside Chelsea.

Chelsea kept her gaze fixed on her mother. *Please, Mom. Help a girl out here.*

"Fernanda said she might have some pieces to donate for the silent auction." Mom stared back, not giving an inch. "That woman seems to have a rare gift."

A rare gift for meddling, much like Sierra. "Yes, she's quite talented."

"I've noticed the arts run in some families." Sierra leaned forward on her elbows. "She makes such fabulous jewelry, and her son is a terrific musician. Isn't he, Chelsea?"

What was this, gang-up-on-Chelsea day? It wasn't like she could pretend Fern had any other son. "Yes, he is quite musical."

"We had many great evenings around the campfire with him and his guitar over the summer," Gabe agreed. "Keanan has done a lot to deepen the spiritual focus of our team."

"And now he's going on a missions trip." Sierra picked up the baton. "Where is he going again, Chelsea?"

"South Africa, I believe."

"He's taking solar cookers and teaching people how to use them." Gabe took a sip of his water. "Firewood is quite scarce in many parts of Africa."

"Solar cookers." Jacob sounded thoughtful. "We discussed those in one of my environmental engineering classes. I heard of a mission that provides solar panels for villages. Hooks them up to wells as well as providing power for schools. I wonder if it's the same mission?"

"I don't know. Maybe you should go to Africa, too." Chelsea couldn't quite keep the bite out of her voice.

"Maybe I should. One more semester to go before I leave Portland State. I might take a year overseas to get a better idea of possibilities. Of where God could use my skills."

Since when was her baby brother a grownup?

"Good idea." Gabe still rubbed Sierra's shoulder. "I spent three years in Romania. It's amazing to see how little some people have and yet they can be so happy in the Lord. I can't tell you how much I wish adoption from Romania were possible. The kids in that orphanage still haunt my dreams."

Chelsea's status as spoiled American rich girl was likely confirmed when Sierra nodded at her husband with tenderness in her eyes. Was it so wrong to want to stay in her own country and continue to enjoy the rewards her parents and grandparents had worked for? So confusing.

Keanan sure didn't look at it that way, but he was a guy. Used to roughing it. How long had he slept in a tent and not even cared? See, she wasn't like that. She valued her creature comforts.

But Keanan's deep green eyes, full of compassion, wouldn't leave her alone. If she moved forward with him, he'd keep challenging her comfort zone. Why couldn't she pick someone more like Gabe? Yeah, he'd gone overseas and worked in an orphanage, but he'd gotten it out of his system and now he was home, content with Sierra and Green Acres Farm.

"He seems like such a nice young man." Mom's voice drifted into Chelsea's reverie.

Oh no. Were they back to Keanan?

"He is." Sierra winked at Chelsea.

"A bit unconventional, perhaps," Mom went on, "but that's not necessarily a bad thing. I appreciate when someone thinks for himself and then acts upon what he believes is right."

Ouch, Mom.

"He's not exactly a saint," Chelsea blurted.

Sierra leaned on the table across from her. "Oh? Tell me his faults."

"Sierra Ann!" said Mom. "We don't gossip."

"No, really." Sierra grinned straight at Chelsea. "I'd love to know what my sister has to say about that."

Chelsea pinned Sierra with her gaze. "You heard Mom. No gossip."

Sierra tipped her head back and laughed. "Nice try. I'm willing to make a bet that the only faults he has involve how uncomfortable he makes you feel."

"That doesn't even dignify a reply."

Dad's eyes crinkled in amusement. Gabe's fingers tightened on Sierra's shoulder.

Good luck keeping your wife in line, buster.

"You could sure do worse than him, sis." Jacob nudged her with his elbow. "That's quite the place he built on a really low budget. He thinks outside the box."

Sierra tittered. "Outside the box. Good one, Jakey, for a round house."

Juvenile.

"Is there something we should know, Chelsea?" asked Dad.

All five pairs of eyes honed in on her. Why couldn't she simply slide under the table? "N-not really." Oh man. Sounding more definite would have helped.

Sierra smirked.

"Your mother and I are very happy that God brought Gabe into your sister's life." Dad glanced down at Gabe and nodded. "We've been praying for both you girls since you were young that He would send the right men at the right time."

Jacob fidgeted, bumping Chelsea.

"And a bride for you." Dad grinned at Jake. "In no hurry for that one, though. All in God's time." His gaze switched back to Chelsea. "We've only heard good things about Keanan. If he's the man we've been praying for, we'll be very happy. But that's between you and him and the Lord."

Chelsea stared at the water glass in front of her with blurring eyes and bit at her lip.

"Now, who ordered the chicken quesadilla?" The waitress stood at the end of the table, loaded with plates.

"Me," said Sierra.

Chelsea peeked at her dad through lowered lashes. He was watching her with a concerned expression. *Thanks*, she mouthed. And meant it.

oOo

"Isn't he the sweetest little thing!"

Mother made smoochy faces at the baby in her arms as they sat around the straw bale house great room. "There, I think he smiled at me."

Holding a baby looked good on her. Keanan kind of liked holding the little fellow himself. Had he ever been so tiny? So dependent on his parents? Must've been.

"He's only seventeen days old." Jo sounded tired. "It's most likely gas. He has a lot of that."

His mother glanced at Keanan. "Surely you could be doing something about getting me grandchildren of my own."

Jo laughed then hid her mouth behind her hand.

He gulped. "Surely you could be more tactful."

Mother scrunched her face at the baby as she jiggled him. "Mothers don't need to be tactful. I think you should marry that nice girl and get to work making babies." She dropped a kiss on John's forehead. "Wouldn't you like a playmate, little man?"

"Claire and Noel are providing a buddy. No pressure from here, Keanan." Jo's eyes danced.

"I don't know them," his mother said. "And I'm pretty sure their child won't be my grandbaby. Don't let Keanan off so easily, Josephine. Do you know he was thirty years old last June? Plenty old enough to settle down, I think."

He could only hope his children would look more like Chelsea than him. Curly hair, pert nose, sparkling blue eyes...

"Uncle Keanan!" Madelynn leaped into his lap.

He tossed her in the air, and she squealed. The baby startled, but Mother cradled him close and soothed him as though she'd had far more practice than only one child of her own.

"Play with me?"

Keanan sat cross-legged on the floor and accepted the doll Madelynn thrust into his arms. She looked over at his mother then arranged his hands and the doll the way Mother held John.

"Shh," she stage-whispered. "Baby sleeping."

"Okay," he whispered back.

"He really is very good with the children," he heard Jo say.

"I see that." Mother sounded bemused.

"Finnley adores him as well. I'm not sure how many hours Finnley sat on one of the horses while Keanan worked the fields over the summer."

"You do the farm work with horses? Son, there's so much you haven't told me about this place."

He twisted to see her better. "Some of it. There's a tractor, too."

Madelynn planted herself between them then grabbed the doll from his hands. "Put baby clothes on."

Oh man. This was the hardest part of the game. Doll clothes were so tiny and his fingers so thick. He glanced over at John, who yawned, his face all scrunched and red. A real baby wasn't much bigger than this doll. Dressing a doll was good practice.

His big fingers struggled to get the doll inside the clothes. Finally, he succeeded and handed the doll back to Madelynn.

She cradled the toy. "Thank you, Uncle Keanan."

"Excuse me a moment. I need to use the washroom." Mother stood and leaned over Keanan, handing him the baby.

He froze as the infant settled into his hands and he met his mother's twinkling gaze.

"Baby John," Madelynn informed him as she perched on his left knee.

Keanan shifted the baby into a more comfortable position on the crook of his arm and Madelynn sagged against his chest, touching the baby's hand. "He soft. Be gentle."

Mother's heels clicked away.

From behind him, Jo chuckled. "Your mom is right. Holding a baby looks good on you."

Wherever he went, it was always the children that drew him. The little ones growing up without enough food, without clean water, without a safe place to sleep. The two in his arms were loved and cared for. Yes, he wanted his own — what man didn't?

"I'll go put on another pot of tea while you've got him, Keanan. Want a cup?"

"Sounds good."

Her footsteps padded away. Madelynn bounced off his leg and ran after her mother, begging for a cookie.

It was just him and the baby, who weighed almost nothing, his warmth and frailty hitting Keanan solidly in the gut. "Hey there, little fellow." He stroked the dark wispy hair with one finger, nearly as thick as the child's forearm.

John opened his dark eyes and stared into Keanan's. He waved a tiny fist. When Keanan tucked his finger against the babe's, the fingers clenched around his.

Please, Father, do You have a gift like this for me? Maybe one with curls and stamped with Chelsea's features?

He became aware of vehicle engines turning off, of doors slamming, of voices and laughter coming nearer. Of footsteps on the wooden deck and the door opening with a whoosh of November air.

"Auntie Chelsea!" yelled Madelynn.

John startled, his little face puckering for a good cry. Keanan jiggled the baby as he glanced up to see the entire Riehl family troop in the door, shedding jackets and boots.

Chelsea froze with her coat half off when she caught sight of him. Her eyes widened as she noticed the infant in his arms.

Sierra slipped an arm around Chelsea's waist and smirked at Keanan. "Look who's natural with a baby. Looks good on you." She pulled Chelsea's coat the rest of the way off and hung it before giving her a nudge.

The room narrowed to just him and Chelsea as she walked toward him. John squirmed, reminding him of the babe's presence.

Chelsea sank onto the ottoman a few feet away, watching the child. Was the rosy hue of her cheeks from the cold outside or from proximity to him?

"Do you want to hold him?" he asked quietly.

She shook her head slowly, her gaze fixing on his. The raw emotion on her face hit him below the belt.

He wasn't the only one with these strong swirling sensations.

Madelynn launched at Chelsea, breaking the intensity of the moment. The other people in the room crept back into his awareness. His mother, leaning against the doorway with a bemused expression. Tim and Sandra looking as dazed as she was. Jo with a tea tray. Sierra and Gabe grinning at each other. Jacob at the back, eyebrows raised.

He looked back at Chelsea as she tickled the toddler. Let them all think what they wanted. They weren't far wrong.

Chapter 24 --

*C*helsea twirled a curl around her finger. She sat with Keanan at the little table in her duplex, their Bibles open in front of them. Deep inside, she knew this was the last big hurdle. Well, maybe the second to last one. If she could just reach into that love relationship with God Keanan spoke of, she'd be free to love the man, too. The whole matter of him gallivanting off to the far parts of the world was another issue entirely, the elephant in the room that loomed larger with each passing day.

First things first.

Keanan covered her hand with his large one and began to pray. "Father God, please reveal Yourself to Chelsea in a new way. I thank You, Jesus, for Your love and Your gift of salvation for her. I ask You, Holy Spirit, to commune with Chelsea's spirit and brand her with Your love and Your peace." He hesitated a moment. "Thank You. In the name of Jesus, thank You."

This felt so strange. Before he'd come over, before Fern had excused herself for the big house, she'd been torn between the thrill of spending time with the man and the anticipation of what they were about to do together. Pray. Talk about the scriptures.

A dispassionate part of her reminded her not many women would think of this as a hot date. And yet her spirit craved to be loved by God as much as to be loved by Keanan.

She glanced up to find his gentle green eyes watching her.

"I want to talk to you about love." The crinkle lines around his eyes appeared as his lips curved into a grin. His fingers tangled with hers on the table. "God's love. The most important love of all."

"I know."

"When did you become a believer?"

"I was just a child. Maybe four or five. I learned about Jesus dying for me in Sunday school and asked my dad about it afterward. He prayed with me."

"How did it make you feel?"

Chelsea thought back. "I don't remember. It was such a natural thing to do. So expected." Was that all this was today? Trying to take an expected step? No. Deep in her soul, she needed this.

"What happened then?"

"We had family devotions at bedtime every night where Dad would read a Bible story and pray with us. When I learned to read, I was expected to do a devotion on my own in the morning. Mom kept us supplied with little books for our age." She tried to remember what the readings had been like and failed. "We had chapel every day at school. And Bible class." She twisted her mouth and looked at him. "Lack of biblical knowledge has never been my problem."

Keanan tilted his head to one side. "Have you been baptized?"

She nodded. "The summer I was thirteen. Sierra wanted to, and I thought, yeah, me, too. It wasn't so much copycatting as that I hadn't really thought about it before. When it came to my attention that it was something a believer should do, I followed through."

"An act of obedience, then."

Chelsea narrowed her eyes. "Yes. Is that so wrong?"

He held up both hands, and hers chilled where his touch had

been. "That is not what I said or even meant. I'm seeking perspective."

"Sorry." She folded her hands in her lap. Perspective on what, then? Why else would a person get dunked in a barely-heated tank? It certainly wasn't for the fun of standing in front of the church with no makeup, dripping wet.

He was quiet. Probably praying.

How could she think this was going to work? He had an actual relationship with God, and it mattered to him. She'd lost her way. She'd tipped her hand so he knew her faith was a barren wasteland. *Fake it 'til you make it* was no longer an option.

Lord, where's the sweet water in this desert? The oasis where Keanan gathers strength and refreshment? Please, Lord. I want to want more of You. I want to love You like he does.

It wasn't the first time she'd prayed similar words. It wasn't the first time she sat there, waiting, and felt nothing stir. If God were really all-powerful, couldn't He give her at least a whisper inside her to show the way? Maybe He didn't love her as much as He loved others. She was still His child, just a second-rate one. Maybe it was okay to sit on the sidelines. Not everyone could crowd onto God's lap and be His favorite, after all.

Her heart clenched. It was *not* okay. Not when she caught a glimpse of how much adoration Keanan felt for his Savior.

"Does God love you, Chelsea?" His words were so quiet she barely heard them over the voices in her head.

She knew the right answer. "Yes. He loves everyone. That's why Jesus died for us." At least she had salvation.

Keanan nodded slowly, his green eyes holding hers. "But you. Personally. Individually."

"In theory." She shrank back. He knew too much.

"In reality?"

Her hands, twisting in her lap, required her attention. "Not so much."

"Accepting that love, embracing it, is an act of faith that will set you free."

Chelsea's chin shot up. "And where does one find faith? Can you conjure it out of thin air? You think I haven't tried?"

"If I took you mountain climbing, would you wear a blindfold?"

"Not a chance."

"Not even if I promised you'd be fine? There'd be no way you could fall, because I would catch you. Every. Single. Time."

She shook her head.

"What if I were God?"

"You're not."

Keanan nodded. "You're right. There is a chance something might go wrong, and I couldn't save you from pain. But God can keep that promise. For sure. No ifs, ands, or buts. Do you believe that He is able?"

Chelsea took a deep breath. "Yes."

"Then step out on the ledge."

"What ledge? Stop talking in riddles, Keanan. You aren't making any sense."

"If you say you believe—"

She leaned forward, mouth open in protest.

"Just hear me out. If you say you believe but don't live like it, then you are implying that God isn't trustworthy. That He's lying."

Chelsea surged to her feet. "You're saying I'm not even a Christian?"

"No. Not at all. I'm saying that the evil one wants you to believe you are not worth anything to Jesus, but it's not true. You are wearing the shackles when they cannot hold you. Faith is an action, Chelsea. It's not enough to say, *I believe*. It is up to you to learn the facts that God has put in His word."

He tapped his open Bible, drawing her gaze toward the book.

"Then, when the doubts come, you can point to the words that counter the doubts. You can announce and claim God's promise. Repeat as necessary, asking God's help. He will do it, Chelsea. Jesus said, *ask and it will be given to you. Seek, and you will find.* It's a promise He can keep."

She crossed her arms and leaned against the counter. "That sounds like *fake it 'til you make it* to me."

Keanan shook his head. "It's not. The difference is that you're not pretending everything is fine. You are claiming God's promises, taking a step of faith that He will hold up His end. And He always does."

He shifted his Bible over, revealing a few index cards. He slid them to the place she'd been sitting, the little chain holding them together whispering across the tabletop.

"What's that?" Yes, she could take the few steps closer and see for herself, but did she want to?

"Promises, Chelsea. Promises He's made to you. Promises you can read and claim every single day. As many times a day as you need to."

She eyed the cards. "Like what?"

"Like this one from Psalm 103. Measure how high heaven is above the earth. God's wide, loving, kind heart is greater for those who revere Him."

Chelsea bit her lip. "What else?"

Keanan turned a few cards over. "This is from Romans 8. No matter what comes, we will always taste victory through Him who loved us. For I have every confidence that nothing — not death, life, heavenly messengers, dark spirits, the present, the future, spiritual powers, height, depth, nor any created thing — can come between us and the love of God revealed in the Anointed, Jesus our Lord."

"What version are you reading from? That doesn't sound like anything I've heard before."

"It's from The Voice." He held her gaze. "There are several others that put God's words into today's terms, that can cut through some of the archaic language we've heard forever. Sometimes new wording can bump our brains into seeing things a new way."

Hadn't Claire said the same thing? Was a renewed relationship with God as simple as reading an up-to-date translation? Going over the verses Keanan had copied out for her and claiming them as God's promises to her?

His bold, even scrawl across the white note cards caught at her breath. He'd done this for her. Because he cared more about her spiritual life than about them as a couple. She couldn't be offended by that. She wouldn't want to hold him back from being the man God wanted him to be. But maybe — just maybe — there was hope for her yet. She couldn't focus on the possibility of a relationship with him as a reward. This craving for a deeper life — didn't the Bible call it an abundant life? — had been present before Keanan had strolled into her life. Before she'd come to Green Acres.

She took the few steps to the table and sank back into her chair before touching the stack of cards. She flipped through them, unable to make out the words through tears that blurred her vision. "Thanks." The word came out in a croak.

Keanan's hands covered hers overtop of the promises he'd copied for her. "Chelsea, I want to pray over you from Ephesians 3. May I do that?"

She choked out the word, "Sure."

His thumbs caressed her palms. "This is only a very slight paraphrase of verses sixteen through nineteen from The Voice. You'll see when you read the verses again later, okay?"

She nodded, still staring down.

"Father, out of Your honorable and glorious riches, strengthen Chelsea. Fill her soul with the power of Your Spirit so that through faith the Anointed One will reside in her heart. May love be the rich soil where her life takes root. May it be the bedrock where her life is founded so that together with all of Your people she will have the power to understand that the love of the Anointed is infinitely long, wide, high, and deep, surpassing everything anyone previously experienced. God, may Your fullness flood Chelsea's entire being. Amen."

That was in the Bible? Really? Oh, not with her name exactly, but Keanan was right. The words spoke deeply into her soul. *Please, God, may Your fullness flood my entire being.*

She swiped at tears dribbling down her cheeks from behind her glasses. Was this the start? Could she really feel God's love and presence in a tangible way? Keanan said he did. Claire. Sierra. Surely it was open to her, too. Why wouldn't it be?

Keanan pressed a cloth handkerchief into her hands, and she dabbed at her face. He'd seen her with blotchy makeup before. If it hadn't scared him off before, it wouldn't likely today.

She managed to get out one word. "Thanks."

"Chelsea, I'm going now."

"No!" She clutched at his hand. "Please stay."

"This is between you and God, sweetheart. I promise I'll be praying for you."

"Oh. Kay."

"Text me later?" His thumb caught a tear on her cheek and wiped it away. A moment later the door quietly clicked shut behind him.

Chelsea took a deep breath and focused on the open Bible and note cards on her table. She riffled through the stack. References from Isaiah, from Psalms, from John, from Zephaniah caught her eye. She pulled the Bible, open to Ephesians, closer. She'd start with rereading that prayer.

Chapter 25 ---

*K*eanan picked up his guitar. Fingers caught the strings, creating melodies without conscious thought. He might be sitting in his own little house, but his heart, his thoughts, his prayers surrounded Chelsea at her kitchen table.

He worked his way through favorite worship songs by Chris Tomlin. Matt Redman. Phil Wickham. Others. Doerksen's song *Hallelujah! Your Love is Amazing* was one that had gotten to Chelsea a few weeks ago. He could only pray that the God-song would rise up in her, too. That God's love would make her sing.

As he played and rested in the words, he prayed for Chelsea.

She'd reached out to him, of all people. This was both exhilarating and terrifying. Hosting Alpha for so many weeks, watching Wesley, Diana, and others slowly grasp a new life in Jesus had been one of the most amazing experiences of his life. Right up there with some of the mission trips he'd been on and the teaching moments those had brought him.

But... Chelsea.

So much was at stake. He had to give that to God, too. He couldn't beg God on her behalf for his own sake, for the hope of their potential future together. Thankfully Chelsea wasn't playing that card. She knew this moment in her life was about far more than him.

It didn't stop his thoughts from sidling to that future. He'd been rehearsing the songs he'd play and sing for Brent and Allison's wedding next weekend, all the while dreaming of singing them into Chelsea's upturned face, her love for him shining from her sparkling blue eyes.

He'd seen glimpses of that love as a tiny seed. Would it gain ground, grow, blossom?

Keanan stopped the strings' vibration with one hand across the sound hole and touched his forehead to the curved wood. *Lord, help her feel Your love! Then show us the way forward. If there is one.*

He didn't want to go to Africa with this unresolved between them. He was flying in just over a week, and it was too late to back out.

A light tap sounded on his door, and he surged to his feet. Chelsea?

The door opened and his mother's head poked around. "Keanan? Oh, good, you're home. I hoped to catch you here."

"Come on in." He leaned the guitar on its stand.

"Oh, please. If you were playing, continue. I've missed listening to you."

He'd been playing for Chelsea. For a quiet time with Jesus. "Maybe later. May I fix you a coffee? Tea, perhaps?"

"Whichever you prefer." She followed him across the space and climbed onto a stool at the island. "I can hardly believe how beautiful your home is. When you told me you were fixing up a grain bin, I didn't imagine this."

He turned the kettle on and chuckled. "Chelsea didn't either." He bit his tongue, but his mother didn't need more of an opening than that.

"Funny you should mention her. I stopped by her place on my way here, but the door was locked. I'm surprised she felt it necessary, whether she was in or out, especially as her car was parked out front."

Keanan eyed his mother. "Chelsea had some things to pray through this afternoon. She probably didn't want to be disturbed." Had she turned the lock to keep *him* out? No, he wasn't letting his thoughts go there. Nor did he wish to elaborate to his mother. That wasn't fair to Chelsea.

Mother nodded slowly, her gaze fixed on his. "I understand. She is the girl you spoke of on the phone a few weeks ago, isn't she?"

There was no reason to deny it. "Yes."

"She seems a lovely girl."

He nodded.

"I've offered to donate some items to her Christmas fundraiser in Portland, so I'll be connecting with her again in a couple of weeks."

"I'm glad to hear that." He poured boiling water over the coffee grounds in his French press. There was silence for a few minutes while the brew steeped. He pushed down the plunger, poured coffee into two mugs, and set one in front of each of them.

She cradled it between her hands and looked up at him. "I don't want to pressure you to talk about her, but I'm willing to listen if you want to."

"There isn't much to say at the moment. We have acknowledged a mutual attraction, but she has things to work through, and I'm leaving soon. God alone knows how this will end. If we are destined to be together." *Or not.* But he couldn't say those words out loud. "My one request is prayer for her. For me."

"I can do that." She sipped the coffee. "So tell me more about your life here. I didn't believe you would ever stay in one spot until you texted pictures of this place looking like a real home."

"Can you call it staying in one spot if I'm still planning trips?"

She chuckled. "Perhaps. What does Chelsea think of that?"

"Let's just say that it's part of the bigger issue."

Mother nodded. "I see."

Most likely she did not. "But yes, I've found a home base here. Good friends who value God's creation. Honest work growing and preparing food. A local church where I can serve in various ways."

"Alpha?"

"That and music." Keanan glanced over at the guitar. "I also teach Sunday school from time to time. But, yes, Alpha has been the big one recently."

She reached across the island and laid her bejeweled hand over his. "Have I told you lately how proud I am of the man you've become? I'm sorry your father and I ripped your world apart when you were a child. I feared we'd done permanent damage to you."

He'd felt the same at the time. Broken. Torn.

"But God has answered my prayers for you." She smiled. "At least since I came to know Him and began to pray at all. He is so good."

"Yes, He is. Thank you for sharing your faith with me. For modeling it in my life." Like he was trying to do for Chelsea, maybe.

Mother sipped her coffee. "I asked Sandra Riehl when they were driving through Spokane to see if they could drop me off at the airport. To save you a trip, you understand."

He tilted his head at her.

"She offered me a ride the whole way, and I was able to get a credit on my airfare."

"I have to say that the thought of you with Chelsea's parents for the better part of a day is slightly terrifying."

She smirked. "I'm not sure what you have to be afraid of. They're a lovely family. We're leaving early tomorrow morning."

"I'm glad you could come to Idaho on such short notice."

"Me, too. Thank you for inviting me back into your life. You'll find that I'm quite hard to get rid of, now that I know where you live."

"As it should be."

oOo

The doorknob rattled a second time. "Chelsea?"

Mom's voice. They were leaving in the morning. She really couldn't hold to the private time she'd indulged in since Keanan left. She glanced at the clock. It had been two hours? No wonder people were looking for her.

"Coming." She crossed the space and unlocked the door to see her mother's worried frown.

"Chelsea? What's wrong? You've been crying."

It turned her face blotchy. Always had. "I'm okay. Really." She stepped aside as Mom came in then closed out the November wind.

"Tell me, sweetheart."

The same word Keanan had used. Chelsea ran her fingers through her curls. She must look a sight.

"Did that man break your heart?"

Chelsea stared at her mother. "What?"

"Keanan Welsh."

"Break my h—? No." Not yet, anyway. Maybe it would be the other way around. At least they'd finally acknowledged their hearts were both engaged, though.

"Then what happened?"

Chelsea rubbed her temples. "It's just... Mom, how do you know God loves you?"

Her mother dropped into a chair beside the table. "This is not the question I was expecting to hear."

"I'm sure. But humor me, please."

"Okay." Mom watched her pensively. "For starters, the Bible says He does."

Chelsea nodded. Waited for more.

"He demonstrated that love by dying on the cross."

"He loves everyone. He died for everyone."

"Isn't that what we're talking about?" Mom's brow furrowed.

"Not exactly. How do you know God loves *you*?"

Mom's gaze landed on the table. Keanan's Bible lay open. Note cards with his handwriting littered the surface. A heap of used tissues crowded around the box they'd come from.

"I see..." she said slowly. "Do you doubt Grandma Riehl's love for you?"

That was easy. "Never."

"But your grandmother has fourteen grandchildren. Are you sure she loves *you*, or just everyone as a group?"

"I see what you're getting at, Mom, but it doesn't hold up. Fourteen is a far cry from the billions of people alive today, let alone throughout history."

"Grandma loves you with ferocity. She watched you kids for years while I worked at the clinic. After school as you got older."

"I know."

"She knew what made each of you kids tick. You and your cousins. She knew you were the quiet one. She didn't forget about you because you weren't pushing into the front like your sister."

It was true. Grandma always had a special smile for her, no matter what. She'd been gone for five years now, and Chelsea still thought about her nearly every day.

"So how did you feel about her?"

"Huh?" Not a question Chelsea expected. "I loved her."

"But why did you love her?"

"What do you mean? She was my grandmother."

"She wasn't perfect, you know. She had a hard time at first, accepting a career woman as a wife for her son. She was sometimes critical. I know she brought you to tears a time or two as well. But you still loved her, as did I."

"I'm not sure where you're going with this."

Mom pushed the note cards into a pile and straightened their edges. "It's possible she could have broken your trust at some point. She was human, after all. But she didn't. She loved you, and you loved her back. It wasn't about your grades at school, or whether she baked chocolate chip cookies that day or not. You loved each other because you had a relationship."

Hmm.

"God is your abba, Chelsea. He's like your daddy, only better because He's perfect. Jesus asked if a father would give a serpent to a child when he asked for bread. Of course not. No daddy would. The relationship between a parent and a child precludes that type of response."

Would God mock her, knowing her heart yet abusing her? Allison's father had, but Chelsea's never could've. And God was so much bigger. Better.

"God doesn't keep track of our wrongs, sweetheart. He forgives us when we ask Him, based on our bond. It's not by whim or by performance, but because Jesus died to provide that relationship. His love is based on our identity as His children."

The assurance was there, so close she could almost touch it. Almost, but not quite. "But it's still a group thing. Isn't it?"

Mom's blue eyes gazed into her own. They'd never had a talk like this, mother to daughter. One on one.

"It is, and it isn't." Mom rearranged the cards and bit her lip as she seemed to search for words. She glanced down, and a smile curved her lips. "Take this, for example." She held up the top card. "The Eternal your God is standing right here among you, and He is the champion who will rescue you. He will joyfully celebrate over you; He will rest in His love for you; He will joyfully sing because of you like a new husband."

217

"Zephaniah 3:17." Chelsea had read that one a dozen times today, trying to absorb it and grasp it.

"I haven't seen it in this version before. It's hard to view those words as polygamous."

Chelsea frowned. "What?"

"The visuals are very personal. A new husband only has one wife. Only one treasured person to celebrate and sing about."

Was Chelsea making this harder than it needed to be? How could she take a step of faith, not a step of fake? "Thank you," she said simply. "I think that helps."

Mom grasped her hand. "And thank you for letting me in. Not only into your home, but into your doubts. Your fears. I've been too busy and just assumed you'd found your way. I know you accepted Christ as a child and followed Him into baptism. I've heard you sing and pray and help in the church, and I can hardly believe I missed something this big in your life. Can you forgive me?"

"Of course I can. It was my choice to keep this to myself." A bad choice, it turned out, but hers all the same.

Mom wiped away a tear of her own. "Do you still love me?"

"Now that's a crazy question! Of course I do." Chelsea nudged the tissue box closer. "Oh, wait. I see what you're getting at."

Hmm. The point was taken.

Chapter 26 --

*K*eanan wrapped his gloved fingers around Chelsea's mitten-clad hand as they strolled down Thompson Road. The weak winter sun failed to provide much warmth, but at least the wind wasn't howling at the moment. He glanced down at the top of her stocking cap grazing his shoulder and nudged her slightly.

Her head tipped back and her blue eyes looked up into his through her pink-rimmed glasses.

Keanan caught his breath as she squeezed his hand. He'd never dreamed he'd fall in love, yet here he was. Here *she* was, curly hair, pert upturned nose, and pink lips curved upward in response to him. Those lips.

His gut tightened as he loosened his grip on her hand to wrap his arm around her, tugging her close to his side. *Keep walking, Welsh. No turning. No holding. Definitely no kissing.*

Her arm slid around his waist. He could feel her warmth even through his winter coat. Or else he might have an excellent imagination. Oh, he had that, all right. Kissing wasn't all his thoughts were capable of.

He was leaving for South Africa in just a few days. He'd be gone nearly three months, long enough to miss the worst of an Idaho winter. Long enough to clarify his thoughts about Chelsea and for her to grow in love for the Lord. Long enough to see if what they had was real.

If only he weren't going. If only the mission board had someone else to send instead, but they were counting on him. He was the one who'd been trained to demonstrate the cookers. He was the one prepared to share God's good news. He was the one.

Keanan had made a commitment. He had his tickets. He was going.

His grip tightened around Chelsea's slim waist. Her head bumped his shoulder as she looked up at him again. He turned and gathered her in both his arms, resting his forehead against hers. Her floral fragrance filled his senses as time stood still.

"Chelsea." His voice choked on her name.

She sucked in her lower lip slightly as her blue eyes looked into his.

"I'm going to miss you so much. I'll be counting the days until I'm home again." Yes, Green Acres Farm was home. The grain bin was home. Chelsea's arms... yes, they were home, too.

"I wish you didn't have to go."

"I know. But I do. I've made a promise." He poured everything he could through his eyes. "I keep my commitments, Chelsea. I am a man of my word. A man of honor." When he committed himself to her — when, not if — he'd pour his whole being into keeping that commitment.

"I guess that's a good quality." A touch of sadness tinged her voice.

"You know it is." Keanan wiggled a hand out of its glove and tucked his fingers under her chin, tilting her face to his. His fingers caressed her chilled jaw line.

She leaned into his touch, her eyes drifting shut.

If her glasses weren't in the way, he'd kiss those eyelids. But there was nothing between him and her lips. They were mere inches away. He'd barely have to bend.

His fingers tangled in the soft curls that brushed her slender throat. He managed to stifle the groan the tantalizing touch triggered. Better get those fingers away from her face. "Chelsea."

Keanan tucked both hands tightly around this beautiful woman, who melted against him. He rested his cheek against the top of her head, but the knitted cap was in his way.

Barriers. He needed those. But nothing was stopping him from holding her, pouring his love for her through their contact. Inhaling her fragrance. Soaking up the memory of this moment to hold him through the months ahead.

oOo

Why did he have to leave her, now when they were finally working through the things that had kept them apart?

Chelsea nestled against his chest, feeling safer in his arms than she'd ever felt in her life. She belonged here. No doubt about it.

The winter ahead looked bleak. Cold. Forlorn. He wouldn't even be here over Christmas. How could she handle watching all the couples open gifts to one another, kissing and glowing in the candlelight while carols played softly on the sound system? Aromas of peppermint and gingerbread would fill the air. Snowflakes would drift past the expansive windows of the straw bale house's great room, partially hidden by a fourteen-foot fir or pine with twinkling lights.

The perfect Norman Rockwell Christmas, dashed to smithereens because Keanan insisted on going to Africa. She wouldn't open a tiny velvet box from him and find a glittering diamond ring. He wouldn't drop to one knee and ask her to marry him like Gabe had done to Sierra last year at Christmas.

She couldn't do this. But did she need to? The church event was just a few days before Christmas. Mom and Dad would welcome her staying a bit longer.

Maybe she'd stay in Portland until Keanan returned.

He might come back having fallen in love with someone else. Or he might not come back at all.

Her heart twisted.

Maybe she'd stay in Portland forever. Now that she'd reconnected with God's love, maybe Keanan had fulfilled his role in her life. Maybe that was the only kind of love he had to offer.

But if that were true, why was he holding her so tightly, his face burrowed against her neck at an angle that must give his a crick? On the flip side, if it *were* true, why didn't he kiss her?

If she were braver, she'd turn her head and make the first move. But if she did, and he pulled away, her heart would be broken. Wasn't it better to remain in this tight embrace? Let the early December wind blast against her legs and back. Where she touched Keanan, she was warm. Safe. Better to be safe than sorry.

The man was an enigma. Surely she meant more to him than a soul to save. Someone to point to the love of Jesus. He wouldn't hold Tracy this way, or Diana from Alpha.

But the truth was, he had cared enough to share with her the personal love of God. If for no other reason than that, he would always have a special spot in her heart. If it had to be enough, it would be.

Wouldn't it?

Somehow Chelsea managed to loosen her grip around Keanan's midsection. She set her hands on his hips and pulled slightly away.

He released her the same amount and looked into her eyes.

What were those green eyes saying? If he kissed her, she'd know. If he told her, she'd know. Otherwise, it was only a guess.

She offered a wavering smile and inched backward just a little more, capturing his hands — one gloved, one not — with hers. "If we're going for a walk, we'd better get going before we freeze to death."

Something in Keanan's gaze shifted slightly, though his smile remained in place. He pulled her to walking, holding her hand.

"I need to say thanks, Keanan."

He bumped her shoulder with his arm. "For what?"

"For being so patient with me. For caring enough to point me to Jesus' love." She wasn't quite there yet, but she was closer. Definitely closer.

His fingers clenched around hers. "My pleasure. He is so good."

"Yes." Even though that wasn't the only love Chelsea wanted to talk about. But he had to lead the way. She wasn't going to make a fool of herself. Not again.

"We can continue to share scripture daily via email, and speak of what God is teaching each of us."

She bit her lip. "We can do that." It wouldn't seem as personal as a text, but he wouldn't have access to that medium everywhere. And it certainly wouldn't be as personal as sitting at her table with their Bibles open in front of them as they'd done several times this week. Or as personal as closing her eyes and listening to him play his guitar. She'd joined him in worship as he sang.

How could she let him go so far away? But there wasn't a choice. He had plane tickets. A giant crate of solar cookers awaited him in not one, not two, but three separate countries. He had a mission to complete that would take him halfway around the world. And he wasn't exactly asking permission.

She was going to create an event for wealthy people in tuxedos and ball gowns. She was going to spend Christmas in the lap of luxury.

Keanan's voice broke into her thoughts as he told her what he'd read this morning in the book of Ephesians. How old truths had come home to him in a new way.

The guy ought to be a preacher, not a farmer. Sure, something new flickered in her own life but, in comparison, his passion for

Jesus raged like a forest fire.

"I wish you didn't have to go." Oh, no. Had that come out of her mouth again?

"I have an idea."

She angled a glance up at him. "Oh?"

Keanan turned on the road and placed his hands on both her shoulders. "Come with me."

Chelsea took a step backward. The icy wind cut through her. "What do you mean?"

"Come to South Africa. I bet we could still get plane tickets for you. I can pay for them if you can't."

"But—"

"The flight goes from Spokane to Seattle then Dubai before landing in Johannesburg. I'd love to show South Africa to you. And Mozambique. You'll see what life is like there. Why it calls me so much."

She swallowed hard. "But I don't..." *I don't want to go.* Dare she simply say it?

Keanan's face fell.

Had he heard the true reluctance in her voice? How could she say no without it being a rejection of him? Because it wasn't. Not really. She wanted to be with him, but here. At Green Acres Farm. Or in Portland. But not on a distant continent.

"I should have remembered you don't have a passport." His gaze searched hers and his hands dropped to his sides. "I'm sorry. It just seemed like a terrific idea in the moment."

Chelsea had a passport. How did Keanan think she'd flown to Belize and Mexico? Didn't mean she wanted to pull it out for an impromptu trip. Even with the lure of spending the winter months with Keanan. She'd only see how much more spiritual he still was than she was. Maybe being there would help her catch more of it. But it seemed easier to be on the outside from a distance than close-up.

Besides, trips like this took months of planning, not five days. She had plans. Maybe not big plans, other than the event in Portland, but plans nonetheless.

"I'm sorry," she whispered.

"No, it's okay. I didn't think about the details. The passport. I just caught a vision of a way to stay together. I spoke out of turn."

Guilt grabbed at her heart. She should explain. Tell him she didn't want to go, that she didn't do spontaneous. She didn't do Africa. But then what would he think of her? She couldn't risk his disappointment. Better he think she would come if she could. Besides, he'd be so busy there, with no time for her in his preset schedule.

No. She'd keep her mouth shut and stay home. Safe. She pulled together a smile. "Too bad it could never work out. I'll miss you like crazy."

"And we'll email often?" Keanan's voice came as close to begging as she'd ever heard.

She reached up, running her fingertips lightly across the hint of stubble on his face. A touch of red to match his hair, now outgrowing the short crop he'd had cut a few weeks back, just because she'd called him a hippie. Soft auburn waves covered the tops of his ears and curled up at his collar.

Barely daring to breathe, she wrapped a curl around her finger. Hey, he'd started it. She'd felt his hands in her hair. It wasn't fair he knew what hers felt like, and she hadn't touched his.

Keanan's gaze locked on hers as he sidled a little closer. His hands held hers against his face. "Chelsea. Heart of my heart."

Whoa. That made hers pound a bit faster. Was he really going to say the magic words? Here and now, on a frozen Idaho road?

She couldn't pull her gaze from his. Not that she wanted to. She bit her lip, trying to think how to respond to his words. What was appropriate? "Keanan..."

He reached for her, cupping her face in his hands, leaning closer. "May I?"

Chelsea couldn't think what he was asking permission for. She couldn't think at all. But he couldn't be asking anything inappropriate, and she was pretty sure this question had nothing to do with Africa. She nodded slightly.

Keanan's lips skimmed hers, softer, gentler than anything she could have imagined. No taking. No demanding. Just a sweet brush that awakened something inside her.

She'd been kissed before. She'd once thought Robert might be the one. There wasn't any question here. Keanan *was* the one. Her fingers still deep in his hair, she tugged his face back into range and kissed him back. He needed to know how she felt, and words were too hard.

His lips responded, caressing hers with greater urgency as his fingers tightened around her face.

She melted into him, glad his hands held her up, while she eagerly tasted more. Keanan Welsh. Who would ever have guessed he had this in him?

Chapter 27 --

Keanan fingered his guitar as he stood at the side of Galena Gospel Church's stage along with a few members of his worship band. He was going to miss this group. His gaze traveled over the people gathered in the pews, more dressed up than the average churchgoers.

The group gathered for Brent and Allison's wedding consisted mostly of locals with a good representation of Brent's Irish and Korean families blended in.

Tracy gave him a little wave from the back of the sanctuary, her other hand tucked in the crook of Tyrell Burke's arm.

Keanan nodded back, his hands too busy to wave. Now that was an interesting couple. If he were a betting man, he'd bet on a summer wedding there, once the house Brent was building Tyrell was completed.

Summer wedding.

He watched the drapery at the interior window not far from where Tracy and Tyrell chatted with Ed Graysen. Zach, acting as usher, offered his arm to Tracy, and Tyrell trailed behind them to seats halfway to the front. It would have been too much to ask Gabe to usher them, the way Tyrell had once treated Sierra.

Gabe and Sierra's had been a summer wedding out at the farm. Keanan had played for it, too. That had been the first time he'd seen Chelsea, a vision in pink froth as she came down the aisle toward him. It would happen again today. Any minute, but maybe not in pink. The bride wasn't into pink.

After that soul-rocking kiss on Thursday afternoon, he'd dared to dream she might float down the aisle toward him a third time. Next time she'd be in white and he'd be in a tux, or whatever she wanted him to wear. There'd be no hiding behind his guitar. He'd be the guy coming in through the side door the way Pastor Ron, Brent, young Finnley, and Noel did right now.

He nearly missed the cue to change music for the processional. The door at the back opened. He caught his breath and his fingers froze on the strings.

Chelsea stood at the back of the church in a silky-looking black dress that hugged her curves, a multi-colored bouquet in her hands. The swooping hem of her dress exposed daringly high black heels. Her curls lay mounded on top of her head with tendrils trailing down her exposed neck. She took a step down the aisle then another, her blue eyes, so clearly visible behind her pink frames, fixed on him.

She looked sensational.

Somehow Keanan's fingers remembered the music they were supposed to be playing. He felt the strings and heard the chords as from another dimension.

Chelsea. She took his breath away with every step toward him.

At the front of the church, she turned toward center. Away from him. A cloud came across the sun. Beyond her, Noel caught his eye with a grin.

Keanan blinked and time resumed. If Noel had noticed his reaction, others might have. But a quick glance at the gathering showed everyone rising and turning to the back once again.

Allison stood alone, radiant in white, carrying a bouquet even larger than Chelsea's. She began her walk down the long aisle.

Keanan snuck a glance at Brent, where young Finnley pulled at his father's hand to no avail. Had Keanan's face expressed as much for Chelsea as Brent's did for Allison? For everyone's sake, he hoped not.

The love Brent had for his bride glowed.

One day Keanan would stand at the front of this church — or maybe the pole barn out at the farm — and watch Chelsea float toward him. Not as accessories to their friends' wedding, but for their own.

Where would he take Chelsea? Where would they go to learn to know each other with nothing between them?

Maybe it was just as well she didn't have a passport and couldn't come to Africa with him on Monday. How would he ever focus on his work with her nearby yet unattainable? As it was, he'd be counting the days until his return. He'd ask Mother to create the most spectacular engagement ring on the planet. Something worthy of Chelsea's beauty. Something that showed how precious she was to him. When he returned, he'd offer it to her on bended knee, swearing to protect her forever like a knight his princess. And then a celebration of vows like this one.

Keanan brought the wedding party back into focus. His view was mostly of Chelsea's back. The black neckline scooped, exposing her sweet neck and the strand of pearls that surrounded it.

He was vaguely aware of Pastor Ron's words on the beauty and sanctity of marriage. Could Brent and Allison focus on the words if even he couldn't? Keanan tried again. God knew he hoped to need this wisdom himself in the next few months, but it was like Chelsea's shapely form blocked the words, little more than a distant buzz, from getting to his ears.

Pastor Ron glanced his way, and Keanan froze for a second before remembering he was to sing a special number here. Another instant of panic ensued before he glanced at his stand and saw the title and tabs. He nodded to the musicians beside him as he mentally counted out the beats until the music began.

The Wedding Song by Peter, Paul, and Mary had been around for decades. He'd known it all his life, but never had the words meant more to him than now as he sang for Brent and Allison. Oh, who was he kidding? He was singing to Chelsea.

She angled toward him, the flowers in her hands trembling. She filled his vision, leaving little room for him to see the wedding party beyond her. He didn't want to see them, anyway. He poured out his heart to her with the words of the song. *There is love.*

A few minutes later Brent and Allison said their vows and exchanged the rings that young Finnley offered them. Finally Pastor Ron said the magic words Keanan knew he'd be longing to hear when it was his turn. "You may kiss your bride."

As Brent gathered Allison in his arms, Keanan could only see Chelsea's face from the few times they'd kissed. At this moment, Brent placed his seal on the woman he loved, publicly claiming her as his own. The time would come when he'd do that with Chelsea. He knew it. Felt it deep in his being.

oOo

The wedding and reception had been long and distracting. Chelsea only had one more day with Keanan before he left. She didn't want to spend hours upon hours smiling and nodding at Ed Graysen and his wife and hearing, once again, how grateful they were that she'd stepped up to coordinate meals for the fall's Alpha program. With Keanan leaving, she couldn't think of doing it again.

Chelsea could hardly think of anything. She loved the man, beyond a doubt. She could put those three months to good use digging into God's love. With any luck, she'd have it all figured out — if that were even possible without his daily guidance — by the time he got back.

. If he returned at all. Wasn't the mission field overrun with single women missionaries? One of them would surely see the gold he was, snap him up, and he'd stay there. Or he'd see some sort of need elsewhere and hurry off to help. A good guy, Keanan. A rare and precious gem. But not the kind of man she'd always dreamed of marrying.

Robert had been that kind of man except he didn't make her heart do somersaults. How important were those, anyway?

Yeah, she knew. She could never settle for like and mutual respect, now that she'd experienced Keanan's toe-tingling kisses, all the more precious for waiting so long for them. But could she trust him so far away?

She blinked.

He stood in front of her, warmth emanating from his gorgeous green eyes. "Ready to head back to the farm?"

Chelsea glanced around. Everything seemed under control. Allison and Brent had whisked away to the airport already, leaving Finnley with Claire and Noel. Cleanup was underway. As maid-of-honor, she wasn't expected to help with that. She took in a long breath and let it out. "Yes. I'd love to."

"Let me get your coat."

She slipped off her heels and jammed them into the top of her large handbag before reaching for her winter boots. No snow yet, but it was imminent. Maybe even tonight.

A moment later Keanan returned and held the coat while she slipped her arms down the sleeves. He arranged the collar around her neck with a gentle touch before reaching around her and clasping both her hands in his from behind.

Safe. She leaned back against his chest with a sigh. When he was near, like this, she could believe anything was possible. But three months apart? What would that do to them?

Chelsea straightened, pulling away from him, and his hands immediately dropped. He could read her better than she could herself sometimes. That was a little scary.

She smiled up at him and dug her car keys out. "Want to drive?"

"Sure." Their eyes caught for a long moment then he touched his hand to her back, nudging her toward the door.

"See you at home!" hollered Sierra as she carried a stack of plates past them.

Chelsea waved and allowed Keanan to steer her out into the icy night air, the small of her back tingling with his touch even through her heavy coat.

He tucked her into the passenger seat, rounded the car, and slid in beside her. "I should have come out a few minutes ago and warmed the vehicle. I'm sorry it's so cold for you."

"It's okay. We'll be back at the farm in five minutes. I won't freeze to death in that short a time."

A moment later they were on the road. He glanced over at her. "You are so beautiful in that dress."

Who needed heat coming from the car vents with praise like that? "Thank you. They say every woman needs a little black dress. Now I have one."

"I wouldn't have thought black would do so much for you. You're made for vibrant color."

Heat rose in her cheeks. What could a woman say to such blatant flattery? Besides the most polite. "Thanks."

"I mean it, Chelsea." Keanan reached across the console and laid his large gloved hand over both of hers. His voice lowered. "You are so beautiful."

She couldn't keep thanking him, so she stared down at his hand in her lap until he removed it to navigate a tight corner. She felt chilled where his touch left. Just like her spirit already chilled knowing he was leaving soon.

Keanan parked in front of the duplex and came around to get her car door.

Never mind her melancholy thoughts. She'd try to enjoy the remaining time with him, hoping it would be enough to tide them both over until spring. "Want to come in for a few minutes? I'll put on a pot of tea."

He took her hand. "I'd love to."

She changed into jeans and a long-sleeved sweater and re-entered the main room of the duplex to see Keanan in the kitchen turning on the kettle. He'd shrugged out of his suit jacket and removed his tie. Now he glanced over at her in the doorway and his slow smile lit his face. "Feel better?"

"Much. Thanks for starting the tea. You didn't have to."

He lifted a shoulder in a slight shrug. "And why not?"

Was it too much to dream of a future in which they puttered around the little kitchen together? Her generic kitchen morphed into the one in the grain bin in her mind's eye. His had way more style than hers.

Chelsea entered the kitchen and opened the cupboard where she kept tins of tea. "What would you like?"

He moved in behind her, wrapping both arms around her. "Whatever you want." He nuzzled into her neck.

Her emotions skittered. She shouldn't have invited him in. No, he'd never take advantage of the situation, but... temptation. Chelsea twisted in his arms until she faced him then cradled his precious face between her hands. "Oh, Keanan."

He dipped his head and kissed her, gently at first, then more insistently.

She was starving for this man. Chelsea tangled her fingers in his unruly hair and held his head close to hers while she responded to his lips with her own.

The kettle whistled and they pulled apart, gazes locking. The green of Keanan's eyes deepened as he reached over and snapped the element off before slipping her glasses off and setting them on the counter behind her. "Chelsea." He bent again and swept his lips across her mouth, her cheeks, her throat. Her eyelids.

How could she stay upright? If it weren't for the countertop against her hips and Keanan's strong hands holding her up, she'd dissolve into a puddle of goo on the floor.

At last Keanan's forehead rested against hers, his aftershave and minty breath continuing to tease her senses.

She clutched his neck with both hands. "Keanan, don't leave me. Please don't leave me."

His voice caught. "Africa?"

Chelsea nodded. She hadn't meant right now. Tonight. Well, maybe she had, a little, but surely some sense of propriety would have intervened.

"I have to go, sweetheart." He brushed his cheek across hers. "But I'll come back before spring."

"That's so long." Tears welled.

He kissed them away. "I know. It will seem like eternity."

"Don't go." She captured his lips with hers, pouring all her emotion into the kiss. "They don't need you as much as I do." Had she really whispered those words?

"They need me in a different way." His hands tightened around her. Was that even possible? "Not like this." He kissed her, deeply, slowly, possessively.

The tears wouldn't stop now they'd started. It must be the emotion of Allison and Brent's wedding mixed with the adoration on Keanan's face as she'd walked down the aisle at the church. The thoughts of losing him now, when she'd only just found him, tore her to pieces.

"Sweetheart, don't cry. We'll email often. We can Skype. We won't lose each other." He hesitated. "When I return, we can make plans for our future together."

Did he mean what she thought he meant? She buried her face

against his chest, feeling the dampness spread on his white shirt.

He rested his cheek against the top of her curls.

The tears came faster now. Huge hiccupping sobs couldn't be far behind. She'd look a mess, all red-faced and blotchy. Why didn't he just leave her to her misery, if he was so bent on going? Why the gentle words, the caressing touch?

Chelsea pushed him away and lunged for the box of tissues on her kitchen table. Empty. Hadn't she bought another one? Where was it? Her mind was befuddled from Keanan's presence and so much emotion. Clogged with more tears than those already gushing forth.

Her bag. She had a travel-size pack of tissues in there. The irony of travel-size. She grabbed at her purse but, without her glasses, couldn't see clearly. Or maybe it was the tears. Either way, groping didn't seem to reveal the package she knew was inside.

She dumped the contents out on the table. The tissues lay under her wallet in the jumble of makeup, receipts, keys, electronic devices, and more. She slit the plastic with a fingernail, tugged out a tissue, and turned aside to blow her nose.

"What is this, Chelsea?" Keanan's voice had lost the warmth of only seconds before.

Chapter 28 ---

Chelsea turned, squinting at him. Where were her glasses, anyway?

Keanan stood beside the table, holding up a small black square with gold embossing.

Chelsea stared at him, her mouth hanging open.

"Why did you lie about having a passport?"

Her mind scrambled to catch up. "I — uh..." She pushed past him into the kitchen and shoved her glasses onto her face with shaking hands. Turning to face him was a mistake. Being able to see him clearly was a bigger mistake.

Keanan stood rigid by the table, still holding her papers. His jaw clenched. His lips a thin line. He met her gaze with glacial green eyes. "Well?"

"I-I didn't lie." Her chin rose. "You didn't ask."

"We talked about passports."

"*You* talked about them. You assumed I didn't have one, even though I said I'd been to Mexico and Belize. You didn't ask."

"You knew what I meant and didn't correct me." Keanan slapped the booklet against the table with a resounding smack. "What else is a lie that I thought was true?"

Chelsea took a step closer, drawn toward him like a magnet,

but both his hands came up to ward her off.

"Those questions about God's love? Just to gain my sympathy? My-my love?"

"What? No!" A great sob surged up her throat. "Never. It was all real. Everything."

"Except for the passport? Why didn't you just say so, Chelsea?"

"I didn't want to go to Africa. I still don't. We've made a home here." She choked on the words. "Or at least I have. I don't know what you want."

"My only desire is to do what God wants of me."

There was no turning off the tears now. They flowed like twin rivers down her face, dripping from her chin, more than a tissue could hope to stem. She swiped her face with her sleeve.

"I thought you'd come to seek God's will, too." His voice quieter, more resigned.

"Of course, I do. But that's here." She drew in a deep, gulping breath. "You told me yourself God led you to Green Acres."

"And you think God's plans for us are that simple? A one-time map with no complexity to it?" He narrowed his eyes. "You're a planner. All you have to do is decide where the event will be held, and that's all there is to it?"

"N-no."

"We can't put God in a box, Chelsea. We can't say He'll only tell us one thing is His will for us. Why can't I make my home here and still go to Africa? How are those counter-inclusive?"

She bit her lip. Keanan made altogether too much sense. "Maybe God doesn't want me to go to Africa." She could only hope she'd been right in that at least.

Keanan angled his head to one side, his eyebrows rising. "Did you ask Him?"

Chelsea let out a long, shuddering breath. "No. But why would He?"

"I don't presume to know. Maybe He just wants you to be willing, but you're not. You're still stuck in Chelsea Land, where if it's good for you, it's good for the universe. And to think—" He shook his head and reached for his jacket.

"Don't go..." The words whispered out of her without conscious thought.

He zipped up his jacket. "I'm really sorry it ended this way. When I think how close I came to asking you..." He turned for the door.

Her heart squeezed painfully. "To ask what, Keanan?"

Keanan paused, staring at his hand on the knob. "I thought we'd built a relationship on trust. On mutual love and respect. I never dreamed this would happen."

"All because I didn't tell you I had a passport?" She walked toward him, half expecting him to run, or at least wince, but he stayed rigid. "You're giving up on us because of that one little thing?"

He glanced at her then away, eyes dark. Shining. *Tears there, too, big guy?*

Chelsea rested her fingers on his arm. "I'm sorry I didn't tell you."

"What are you truly sorry about?" He stared down at her hand.

"Because—" What kind of ridiculous question was that? "I didn't realize it would be such a big deal to you."

"Chelsea. At this moment I'm not sure if I love *you* or the person I thought you were. Please forgive me. It's not my intention to hurt you. I need to go home and think and pray. Maybe I, too, have been guilty of assuming God would fall in line with my hopes and plans. My dreams."

"D-dreams?"

Keanan's eyes were so dark no hint of green remained visible. "Today all I could think of was you in a white dress, not a black one. Coming toward me down the aisle of the church as you did today, only I was not the musician but the man standing beside Pastor Ron awaiting his bride."

"Th-that's what I was thinking about, too." She slid her hand down his arm and caught at his fingers. Had she ruined everything, or could he see her remorse? "I'm sorry. Really, I am."

Keanan shifted out of reach. "Goodnight, Chelsea. Let's both ask God for healing. For restoration. It's up to Him now."

A shock of freezing air swirled around her. The door closed behind him. She hugged herself as she stared at the unyielding wooden rectangle. As she listened to his footsteps crunch away. As his aftershave dissipated.

She reached behind her, grabbed the passport off the table, and flung it across the room then collapsed on the floor while deep sobs wracked her body. Oh, dear God. Look what her selfishness and lack of faith had cost her. Was there any hope?

oOo

Keanan strode down Thompson Road. His grain bin home repelled him with its memories of Chelsea. He needed air, the colder and brisker the better. He needed to burn off some of this anxiety.

To think he'd nearly proposed tonight, even though his greater wisdom and rational thought had decided to wait until he returned in spring. That curve-hugging black dress had nearly done him in, filling him with dreams and desires.

He growled into the wind.

It's just a passport, whispered part of his mind.

She lied about it.

Not directly. You didn't ask.

I shouldn't have had to. She knew.

And you never in your life knowingly gave a false impression to someone?

That doesn't excuse her.

Did you? Or did you not?

Yes. Yes, I've been guilty. But this is different.

How so? Why is it okay if you did it, and wrong when she did?

I asked God's forgiveness. I repented.

How do you know she hasn't? That she won't?

Maybe being alone out here with his thoughts wasn't that great an idea either. Which way was the right way? Both sets of arguments were valid. But what was *God's* way? Which voice spoke for Him?

The voice of forgiveness. The voice of grace.

Okay. Keanan could forgive Chelsea. He could. But did that automatically restore their relationship to its previous bearing?

It did with Jesus. His forgiveness wiped the slate clean. Forgiven. Forgotten.

He wasn't God. His memory-wiper didn't work so well. How could an all-knowing God forget, anyway? That made no sense.

Headlights rounded the corner down past Elmer's farm. Snow angled across their glow. The same snow that drifted against his face.

Keanan trudged off the middle of the road and planted one foot in the frozen grass at gravel's edge. Why was he wearing a black parka anyway? Black pants? He was all but invisible to the driver as the vehicle careened toward him.

The car — Gabe's — passed then squealed to a stop and backed up to come abreast of him. The passenger window slid down and Sierra looked out, her eyes wide. "Keanan? What are you doing out here?"

Chelsea's sister. The second last person he wanted to see. "Just going for a walk."

"Uh oh."

He scowled at Sierra, certain the darkness hid his face. "Don't worry about me." He took a step away and his shoe slipped. He grabbed at the car to stay upright. His chore boots would've been a better choice for this icy road than dress shoes.

The far door opened and shut, and Gabe loomed beside him. "Drive on home, honey. I'll walk with Keanan."

Keanan gritted his teeth. "No need."

Sierra pushed the car door open, nearly sending him sliding again. "Okay." She cast a worried glance at him then shuffled around the car, got in, and drove off.

Gabe started walking toward Galena Landing. When Keanan didn't follow, he turned back. "Thought you wanted to walk."

The fight in him had fled. Keanan shoved his hands in his pockets. "Why are women so confusing?"

Gabe laughed. "The first man to figure that out will make a fortune." He beckoned. "Come on, Welsh. I'm freezing. Least we can do is keep moving while we try to unravel the mysteries of the universe."

"I'm ready to go back to the farm."

"You sure? I'm willing to listen." Gabe fell into step beside him. "I'll make a guess this is about my sister-in-law."

Was a reply truly required? He wouldn't fool anyone, either way. He let out a long breath, nodding.

"You two left the church a while ago looking pretty cozy. What happened?" Gabe held up both hands. "Only if you want to get it off your chest. No pressure."

Somehow, saying *she let me believe she didn't have a passport* wasn't as simple an answer as he'd like to give. "On a scale of one to ten, where would you place the importance of total honesty in your relationship with Sierra?"

Gabe shot him a glance. "You've heard our story, haven't you?"

Keanan wracked his brain. "Not really. Parts of it, maybe."

"Let's just say honesty — openness — is a ten now, but it was hard-earned. On both our parts."

They walked in silence a few minutes, the lights from the farmhouse nearing.

"Honesty is a matter of trust," Gabe mused. "Until you know beyond a shadow of a doubt that your heart is safe in the other person's hands, it's easy to hold back. Sometimes it's easy to hold back things that are vital to view openly or the whole relationship might implode."

Keanan nodded. "I can see that."

"It's kind of like a dance. And hey, I'll be the first to admit I'm a lousy dancer. But you hold onto each other and move one way and then the other. Meanwhile, you try to keep from stomping on each other's toes while you learn how to do this thing together."

He'd bet anything Chelsea could dance. On second thought, maybe her upbringing would've been too conservative for that. He wanted to find out. Tuck her close against his chest and sway to the music in his head.

Even though she held back vital information?

Yeah, even then. The first flash of anger had passed, and Gabe made a lot of sense. "Thanks, man."

Gabe glanced over. "That easy? I should hire myself out as a counselor."

A chuckle burst past the slowly-dissolving knot in Keanan's throat. "I'm not certain I'd go that far. But you did draw my attention to a point or two I'd pushed aside."

"Good to know. Sierra rather fancies you as a brother-in-law, you know. She worries about Chelsea."

Keanan stopped at the end of the Green Acres driveway. The lights in Chelsea's windows winked out as he watched.

Gabe nudged him. "She's dropping you off at the airport on Monday on her way to Portland?"

"Yes. Unless she refuses to talk to me again."

"And force someone else to take the extra trip? We won't let that happen."

What would be worse than spending three hours in a car with Chelsea if she refused to talk to him? And he'd brought it all on himself. "I don't know whether to try to speak with her again tonight or not."

"I don't know what went on." Gabe turned toward him, back to the wind. "But maybe it's best to let things simmer down overnight. You've got tomorrow and Monday. Pray. Sleep. Get perspective. Sierra and I will be praying for both of you."

Keanan nodded slowly. Reluctantly. "You're probably right. I'm not sure I can trust myself not to make things worse at the moment." As for the sleep part, he doubted that would come easily.

"You'll get through this." Gabe smacked him on the back.

If he could get through *that* without hitting the ice, he could get through anything.

Chapter 29 --

*T*orture.

Plain and simple. Chelsea had managed to avoid Keanan before church by fixing herself tea and toast in the duplex instead of going up to the house for breakfast. Now she'd made sure she was wedged in the middle of the pew between Claire and Sierra.

Not that Keanan would want to sit beside her anyway, as they'd sometimes done the past few weeks. But she wasn't going to give him another chance to reject her.

He sat on the other side of Gabe. She could feel his presence even through her sister and brother-in-law. This affinity for him was crazy. More than two people separated them. Africa did, too.

Her mind had spun all night. Yes, she'd been wrong to withhold the information. She should've corrected his assumption. She'd gotten good at maneuvering through life by focusing on the things she wanted and avoiding the things she didn't. She'd worn her rose-colored glasses and played God by creating her own reality.

Now she was in love, and her reality was a disaster she'd brought on herself. But no matter what she said to Keanan and he said to her, Africa would still be between them. If he went, he'd... well, he'd be gone. If he didn't, he'd resent her for not going, and she'd feel guilty. But he'd go. No question.

Chelsea stood at the right times but found no joy in singing. Even though Keanan wasn't part of today's worship team, each song seemed to be one he'd sung to her as he tried to share God's love with her.

She sat when told and passed the offering plate and dropped in her tithe check. Never had Pastor Ron sounded so much like he was delivering a monologue. Nothing registered in her frozen brain.

If that didn't panic her, nothing would. She'd spent years of her life listening to sermons that never pierced her armor. Since coming to Galena Landing and finding God's deep love for her, the words had penetrated.

Today? Not so much. Not only had she lost Keanan, but she'd lost God. Both had been new. Tenuous. Breathtaking.

Chelsea swallowed the lump in her throat for the millionth time. If God had deserted her along with Keanan, there was nothing to hold her in Idaho. Portland didn't hold the memories of broken dreams. It was a place she could pour herself into her business. She'd only been gone a few months. She could rebuild her company there.

The pain of the break-up with Robert had been nothing compared to this.

Life would resume as it had before, except without the goal of joining the team at the farm someday. Well, she'd find new goals. She was good at them. Detail-oriented.

Keanan's voice came through the microphone.

She jerked, her eyes focused on the platform. He stood beside Pastor Ron as the minister asked a few questions about the upcoming mission. Keanan glanced over the congregation as he replied, his gaze never coming anywhere near Chelsea.

"I want to pray for our brother." Pastor Ron placed his hand on Keanan's shoulder. "If the church elders would please come forward, and anyone else who would like to join us where two or three are gathered together in Jesus' name."

Ed Graysen marched down the aisle, followed by Tracy Grindle, Wesley, Rosemary and Steve. Others.

Around Chelsea, the entire Green Acres team stood and filed out of the pew on either side of her. Panic surged. Worse to sit here alone? Everyone in the whole sanctuary would notice. Worse to go to the front? Everyone would think she supported Keanan.

She kind of did, right? She rose and followed Claire down the side aisle, gaze on the floor. If Keanan noticed her there, she didn't want to know about it.

Ed Graysen prayed. Noel prayed. Steve prayed. A few others prayed. Pastor Ron prayed.

Chelsea fled to her seat as Pastor Ron called the worship team for the closing hymn.

Take my life and let it be consecrated, Lord, to Thee. Take my moments and my days. Let them flow in endless praise.

Keanan was consecrated to God. She wanted to be. She'd made some steps in that direction. But how could her days flow in endless praise when she was so confused?

Take my voice and let me sing always, only, for my King. Take my lips and let them be filled with messages from Thee.

This was Keanan, too. His whole life was turned toward God.

Take my will and make it Thine. It shall be no longer mine.

Chelsea whispered the words past a clogged throat. Her prayer.

Take my heart; it is Thine own. It shall be Thy royal throne. Take my love, my Lord; I pour at Thy feet its treasure store. Take myself and I will be ever, only, all for Thee.

If only. If only life could really be like that.

oOo

As from a distance, Keanan heard the other guys laughing and talking as they chopped vegetables in the farmhouse kitchen. His mind was still on when Chelsea had slipped from the pew and come to the front to join the prayer circle around him.

A sharp elbow to his ribs made him jump.

Gabe peered at the cutting board. "Welsh. It'd be faster to run those through the blender."

Keanan forced his focus back on his task. Gabe was right. He'd chopped the carrots so finely they might as well have been shredded.

"Those won't take long to cook." Noel reached for the board. "We don't usually let guys off the hook when it's our day in the kitchen, but you're less use than Zach."

Less use than Zach? The man had an infant strapped to his chest while he lifted plates from the shelf above the sink.

"You cause me pain," Keanan said to Noel.

"Not as much as you're going to cause yourself with that knife." Noel's eyes twinkled. "Seriously. Go talk to that woman already."

Keanan nodded slowly. He knew he had to, but what could he say? Would she even step aside with him, or would she stay in the midst of the group of women and protect herself from him? There wasn't much time before the meal was ready, judging from the sounds of the sizzling wok and the aroma of sautéed beef.

He rounded the peninsula and into the dining area then scanned the great room. Jo, Sierra, and Claire had stacks of fabric pieces out. He had heard rumors of a quilt for Claire and Noel's baby.

His gaze swung toward the big windows. Chelsea sat on the floor with Finnley and Madelynn, snapping together pieces of the wooden train track both children loved. Her curls hid her face.

Take my will and make it Thine. It shall be no longer mine.

The prayer of his heart. That and a plea to God for restoration of his relationship with Chelsea.

"Food's up!" called Noel.

That hadn't been long enough to talk to Chelsea, anyway. The children rushed past him to the table. But Chelsea's eyes found his as she clambered to her feet. He was too far away to offer his hand as an assist. He took a step closer as the other women brushed past.

"Chelsea? Can we talk after lunch?"

She tensed, her jaw flexing slightly. Her chest rose with a long intake of breath. Then she nodded slightly and looked away.

Keanan was surprised to find he had an appetite. Just that small nod from his beloved, and his world had tilted right-side up.

Everyone lingered over Sunday lunch. They always did. He usually liked the chance to catch up without the pressure of the farm work looming over them. Today it took John wailing to pull anyone away from the table. Zach left to change the baby's diaper while Jo returned to the great room, preparing to feed him.

Noel and Gabe gathered dishes, each giving him a headshake when they caught his eye. He was free to go. Free to pursue Chelsea.

"Want to walk?" he asked quietly.

She glanced toward the window. "It's nasty out."

Keanan groaned inwardly. She was correct. The wind flung pellets of snow all but sideways. Not a day for a romantic walk. If romance were in the air at all.

"My place?" Sure, the grain bin was much further from the house, but he couldn't assume she'd want to let him into her home after last night.

She pursed her lips and nodded.

Keanan helped her into her coat before reaching for his own. As he opened the door for her, his gaze caught on Gabe's. The other man grinned and pointed heavenward. The reminder that Gabe was praying for him lifted some of the fearful anticipation from Keanan's heart.

Dear Lord, please give me words. May Your will be done.

A few minutes later he hung Chelsea's coat on the rack beneath his staircase. He crossed to toss another log into the small wood-burning stove then turned on the kettle. He fixed two mugs of chamomile tea and returned to the sitting area, where she'd curled up in his armchair, knees to her chest.

Well, that signal came as no surprise. He'd keep his distance until she changed her body language. Panic shot through him. What if she didn't? *God, please.*

"There's a story Jesus told." Keanan set down both cups and reached for his Bible. "It's a parable about forgiveness. It's the one where a man was brought before a judge because he owed a lot of money and couldn't repay it."

Chelsea lifted her cup to her lips, watching him.

"The judge forgave the man. Then he went out, found someone who owed him far less and demanded instant payment. He gave no grace."

No response.

"Chelsea, I am that man. God has forgiven me so much." He thumbed through his Bible and read from Psalm 103. "God takes all our crimes — our seemingly inexhaustible sins — and removes them. As far as the east is from the west, He removes them from us."

The reference to the distance from east to west might not have come at the best time.

"Please forgive me, Chelsea. I don't have the right to hold that passport against you. I did not act in love last night. I didn't keep in mind God's ability to completely forget our sins when we repent." Was her gaze softening any? "I've asked God to forgive me for the hurtful things I said to you. Now I'm asking you. Please."

She lowered her cup to the side table, a little tea sloshing over the rim. "I forgive you."

The words were so quiet his ears barely heard them, but his heart leaped in response.

"I was wrong, too. I should've told you I had a passport instead of letting you believe that's why I couldn't go with you." She took a deep breath and looked toward the flickering flames. "The real truth is that I don't want to go. With all this mess between us, I've tried to come up with a desire but the fact is, I still really don't want to. I know sometimes it is necessary to simply do something even when one's heart isn't in it, but..." She lifted her hands in a helpless gesture.

How could he reply? His invitation for her to join him had been ill thought-out. "I should never have asked you to drop everything at a moment's notice and spend three months halfway around the world. Can you forgive me?"

"I think I can." Her blue eyes looked troubled. "But all this points to a deeper issue. I can forgive you. You can forgive me, I hope, though you haven't said so."

A deeper issue? Hadn't they gotten past the deepest issue when she'd found her joy in Jesus? "Yes, I forgive you." The words dragged past the sense of foreboding that wedged in his throat at what she'd say next.

"Will you want to go on more missions trips?"

The reply was a no-brainer, and it wasn't the answer she wanted. He nodded slowly, trying to catch her eyes, but her gaze flicked away in an instant.

"I thought so."

What did she really mean? That a relationship between them couldn't work out unless he gave up his other calling? That she'd never wish to join him? What kind of a team — what kind of a marriage — would that be?

An impossible one. "Chelsea, to whom much has been given, much has been required. So many people around the world have so little. We have the technology to improve their lives. Solar power is a big one. We also have the words of life they need to hear, and I don't think it's a coincidence that my tutor spoke four languages fluently and taught me as well. I go to put hands and feet and voice to Jesus' commission in Matthew to go out and make disciples in all the nations."

Her expression did not change.

"I can't *not* go. Don't you see?"

"I understand the words. I even believe them. But it's not for me."

"He didn't say some people should do this, Chelsea. If we believe, if we've accepted Him as Savior and Lord, then we need to do what He tells us. And He's told me to go."

She surged to her feet and crossed to the tall narrow window beside the wood stove. "The people in Africa are more important than I am."

"No, Chelsea. Obeying God is more important than you are. More important than Africa." With those words, he felt the finality in his soul. It was over. Really over.

Chelsea turned to face him. "I've come a long way in the past few months."

It was true. He nodded.

"But I'm not there yet. I don't know if I ever will be." She bit her lip. "I want to say what you want to hear. I want to say, yay, everything's good, I'll go with you. But that would be wrong."

How many more times could his hopes swing up, only to be dashed? "Wrong?" he croaked out.

"I'll tell you one thing I'm committed to." She held his gaze. "To being honest. To not letting you believe a lie about me. I won't pretend for you anymore, Keanan. Nor for anyone else."

He nodded, oh so unwillingly. She had him trapped. He didn't want a lie. He wanted her to come freely. In obedience to Jesus, not to him. A thought blasted him as though he'd opened the door to the December wind. What if God was *not* asking her to go overseas? What if it had been his idea all along, not God's?

"Thank you." Did he really mean those words? "If we are to move forward together, it has to be based on honesty all the way around. I don't want to force you. This is something between you and God, and either answer might be correct."

The wariness slid from her eyes. "I appreciate you saying that."

He rose, took the few steps to the window, and clasped both her hands. "Chelsea, can we back up a few steps and try this again? I was so looking forward to sharing my days with you via email and Skype. Can we still do that, or..." He couldn't bring himself to complete the sentence. *Let there not be an or.*

Chelsea looked up into his eyes. "I'd like that."

His heart hiccupped. "Really?"

She nodded, a tremulous smile on her lips.

Keanan wanted to kiss that smile, but no. Too much, too soon. Instead he tugged her into his arms, and she came willingly. He rested his cheek against her soft curls and held her for a long moment, savoring the touch of her arms around him and her body pressed against his.

Chapter 30 --

*D*ear Chelsea,
    I'd forgotten how long a trans-Atlantic flight could be. It gave me so many hours to think of you, to remember every nuance of your smile, every curl on your head, every touch of your fingers. I already miss you with every cell of my being.

I give you to God. I give myself to God. That way, we are both in His hands and close together. The plane is over the Mediterranean now, approaching Dubai, then the next flight to Johannesburg. I'll spend a few days there orienting to the time change, meeting my team, and getting acclimatized to summer again. There will be many planning meetings. You'd like those (grin).

All my love,
Keanan

Dear Keanan,
My drive to Portland was uneventful other than near blizzard conditions north of Kennewick. The highway was fine. It was the visibility that was so bad. Sort of like my life. My prayer is that God will teach me to see clearly.

I had a call from your mom. She said she'd be in the city in a few days and will bring me the pieces she's donating to the fundraiser.

Mom and Dad and Jacob send their love. Okay, Jake didn't exactly say that, but he asked about you. Sort of the same thing.

Love,
Chelsea

Dear Chelsea,

My flight into Johannesburg was interesting. I sat beside Dr. van Leeuwen, a South African doctor who's spent the past decade working in Portland as an infectious disease specialist. Ever heard of one of those? Me, either. Apparently he's teaching a clinic at Steve Biko Academic Hospital in nearby Pretoria for the next two weeks. He had some fascinating stories to tell. He'll be back in Portland by Christmas and said he'd be happy to bring back a gift from me to you.

Say hi to my mother for me. I guess I could email her myself. I will when I have time.

All my love,
Keanan

Dear Keanan,

I hit the ground running to finalize the details for the church event. Via email, it sounded like everything was under control. In person, not so much. Trying to set up an event this size from a distance was a bad idea. If I don't move back to Portland permanently, I'll have to tell them to find someone else next year.

I wonder if that's the same doctor who's married to Greta van Leeuwen from our church. She's been my liaison and doing her best to set up the fundraiser with me via email. I'll ask her when I see her.

I miss you. I've got my phone weather app set for Johannesburg. Or did you say Pretoria? Temperatures of eighty degrees sound terrific. Even in Portland it's nearly freezing.

I set your time zone up in my phone's clock, too. It's almost bedtime here, and you're probably already in tomorrow's meetings. It seems strange.

Love,

Chelsea

Dear Chelsea,

Being in the same place to plan an upcoming event isn't always enough. The man who set this up forgot to hire a translator for the Mozambique part of the trip, if you can believe it. It may wind up on my shoulders, as Ivan taught me some Portuguese. I hope I won't make any crucial mistakes, as it's been a while.

Pretoria is beautiful as it swings into summer. The Jacaranda trees are nearly done blooming. Streets are paved with a purple carpet from the fragrant flowers. You'd love it. I've attached a photo.

Can we set up a time for Skype? I'll get up in the middle of the night if that's what it takes to connect. I want to see your face, even if I can't touch you through the computer.

All my love,

Keanan

Dear Keanan,

Your mother is something else! She brought an absolutely stunning set of jewelry for the auction. She urged me to try it all on: necklace, earrings, bracelet, and ring. It's no wonder her designs are in such high demand. Some wealthy woman is going to be very happy when her husband outbids everyone else, and the church will collect a tidy sum.

We had lunch together and she told me stories of when you were a little kid. Sounds like you were quite a handful! Some things never change. She'll be back the day before the event.

Having her here made me feel closer to you. I'd love to Skype. I've got it on now and will keep it on whenever I'm home.

Love,

Chelsea

Dear Chelsea,

It was wonderful to talk to you last night. I miss you so much it's painful. I hope I can do my job well when every thought is filled with you.

I found out this morning that we're leaving for a tour of several villages in Limpopo province in a few hours. (Remember what I said about disorganized??) Don't worry if you don't hear from me for a while. I'll email as soon as I can.

All my love,

Keanan

Dear Keanan.

It seems strange to write you and not know when you'll read this. I went out for lunch with several old friends today. It was great to catch up. I'm not sure if you can believe it, but their last few months were *not* full of pitting plums, canning tomatoes, and cutting up meat for the freezer! I feel like I learned new skills and actually accomplished something of value this fall, while their lives continued on the way they have for years.

That could have been me. And then I'd have missed meeting you and getting to know God's love in a deeper way. It will seem strange going to church tomorrow in such a big building. Once it was normal, but I have to say Galena Gospel Church has grown on me.

Waiting to hear from you. I hope your trip to the villages went well.

Love,

Chelsea

Dear Chelsea,

Thank you for the emails waiting for me in Pretoria. I miss you with every breath I take.

The trip went well. You should have seen the joy as the team raised the solar panels to light their church and school. And then we handed out dozens of solar cookers and had our first lesson. This will free so many women from seeking out wood and dung for cooking fires. By the next evening the lights were on full in the meeting hall and we had a church service of rejoicing. I've attached a few photos of the happy faces to this email.

I know this is where I need to be right now, and it sounds like God is meeting you where you are at. I pray for you constantly with Ephesians chapter two.

All my love,

Keanan

Dear Keanan,

Countdown to the fundraiser: five days. I hope everything comes together. I'll be utterly exhausted when this is over. They didn't used to take so much out of me.

I've decided to stay in Portland for Christmas. Green Acres would only make it harder to be so far from you. Here, I have my parents, brother, and friends. Mom asked if I wanted to invite your mom for Christmas dinner. I'll ask her when she comes for the event on Friday.

Love,

Chelsea

Dear Chelsea,

I'm sorry to hear you're feeling so tired. Me, too. I've also got a sore throat, perhaps from all the talking I've been doing.

Actually, my neck and shoulders are sore, too. I didn't expect to feel so out of shape after all the farm work this past year. Please pray I'm not coming down with the flu or something. There is much to do, and I need to keep functioning. We leave for Mozambique in a few days but expect to be back in Pretoria by Christmas. We'll do another trip in January.

Mother will likely be delighted to join your family for Christmas. Thanks to you and your mother for thinking of her.

I'll look up Dr. van Leeuwen tomorrow as I've got a small gift to send back with him for you.

All my love,

Keanan

Dear Keanan,

I'm sorry to hear you're not feeling well, and I'm praying whatever it is will quickly go away.

Greta stopped by last night to talk about the fundraiser. Can you believe I've been emailing with your doctor friend's wife for months? I hadn't met her before, but she told me a bit about what her husband is doing in South Africa. She says he teaches this type of clinic in various countries annually. Small world, right?

Love,

Chelsea

Dear Chelsea,

I don't want to worry you, but please pray. My temperature has spiked so high I've had the shakes. I even threw up. Vince called Dr. van Leeuwen. He said he'd swing by Vince's apartment at the mission home, pick up your gift, and have a quick look at me.

Love,

Keanan

Dear Keanan,

I'm glad Dr. van Leeuwen is there, but he sounds over-qualified to look at a guy with the flu! Praying.

Love,

Chelsea

Dear Chelsea,

This is Vince from Keanan's team. He asked me to send a quick message to let you know we're at the clinic. His temp is over 104° so Dr. van Leeuwen wanted to run a few tests. I'm sitting in the waiting room with Keanan's laptop while we wait for results.

Vince

Dear Keanan or Vince,

What's going on? If it's the flu, won't it just pass?

Love,

Chelsea

Dear Chelsea,

I'm feeling a bit better and have gone to the mission house to sleep. Will be in touch.

All my love,

Keanan

Dear Keanan,

I'm glad you're feeling better. Hopefully losing a day like this won't make too much difference to your schedule. I'm on countdown here for the fundraiser event. Two more days.

It's hard to concentrate when I'm worried about you.

Love,

Chelsea

Dear Chelsea,

Vince here. Keanan's fever went back up and he started vomiting so I phoned Dr. van Leeuwen. He's meeting us at Steve Biko Academic Hospital where he's been teaching. He doesn't think it is the flu. Not sure what, though.

Vince

Dear Vince,

If anyone can figure it out, it's Dr. van Leeuwen. What does he think it might be?

Chelsea

Dear Chelsea,

Dr. vL ordered some tests and seems concerned about Keanan's kidney functions. Also something about blood platelets. I don't know much about medicine, so I hope I'm remembering that correctly. At any rate, he had Keanan admitted and has him on a fluid IV to rehydrate him. Hopefully we'll know more later.

Vince

Dear Vince,

I'm checking emails on my phone constantly. Please tell Keanan I love him and we are all praying for him. I've let our friends at Green Acres Farm know. Email me as soon as you hear results.

Chelsea

Dear Chelsea,

Dr. vL said the test results were perplexing. Keanan isn't doing very well, and the team of doctors can't figure out what he has. It's definitely not the flu but something more serious. His breathing seems really shallow, like he can't get air, and his pulse is wild. The doctor put him on oxygen.

I can't believe the difference in him from a few days ago. Unofficially, I'm really worried.

Vince

Dear Vince,

What do you mean, he's not doing very well???? Update me every hour.

Chelsea

Dear Chelsea,

The doctors are concerned about Keanan's chest x-rays. Something about his lungs. I speak English and Afrikaans just fine, it's medical I don't speak. I'll try and find someone else to email you the technical stuff.

Vince

Dear Vince,

I don't speak medical either. Keep writing what you understand.

Chelsea

Dear Chelsea,

Dr. vL asked Keanan's permission to intubate him. Keanan signed for it. He's getting worse, not better, and putting him on machines will keep everything functioning while they continue to search for answers. The specialist is now using Keanan as an example for his clinic instead of teaching directly.

Praying for a good outcome.

Vince

Dear Vince,

What are you not telling me? Keanan is on life support? He might die? Tell me the truth!!!

Chelsea

Dear Chelsea,

Keanan is on life support. He's being sedated so he won't fight the machines that are breathing for him. If God wills it, he will live.

Vince

Dear Vince,

What do you mean, if God wills it? Keanan has given everything to follow what he thinks is God's will for his life. And God took him to Africa to let him die there?

Not so fond of God at the moment. <- That's an understatement.

Chelsea

Dear Chelsea,

I sure can't pretend to know what God wants. He's not human, and He thinks in terms of eternal value. Not like us. This might be a time to cling to Isaiah 55:8. "For My thoughts are not your thoughts, nor are your ways My ways." All we can do is trust God.

Vince

Dear Vince,

Keanan tried to show me how much God loves me. Not seeing it right now. When God heals him, I'll take another look at it.

Chelsea

Dear Chelsea,

Saying we trust God is worthless if we can't trust Him when things are tough. We can't just believe when life is sunny and nice. That's not even trust.

Believe me, my faith is getting a workout, too. I'm not blaming you for faltering. But I'm also not exaggerating when I say only God can save Keanan's life right now. You'll handle everything much better if you can pray and trust God.

Keanan is in isolation in ICU. They're worried he might be contagious.

Vince

Dear Vince,

I'm trying to pray. It's agony being so far away when he needs me. Send an email every hour. Please.

Chelsea

Dear Chelsea,

Things got a bit dicey earlier. A CT scan showed a pocket of fluid behind his lungs. He now has a tube in his chest to drain it. Please pray his fever will break. It's 105° and Dr. vL is still trying to figure out exactly what he's got.

Vince

Dear Vince,

I am pacing the house between emails. Please write oftener. Praying constantly. Trying to trust God, but this is the hardest test in my life.

Chelsea

Dear Chelsea,

Every time they bring Keanan out of sedation to make sure he's doing okay, he tries to talk. I think he's asking for you, but he can't talk around the tube in his throat.

The doctors say more lab results should be back today. Dr. vL has had little sleep in the past three days. Neither have any of us, but he's the one who needs to think critically.

Pray for him. Pray for Keanan. Pray for all of us. I'm praying for you, too.

Vince

Dear Vince,

Tell Keanan I love him and I am on my way.

Chelsea

Chapter 31 --

*C*helsea shoved things in a travel bag.

Clothes. Long skirts. Tops with sleeves. No point in upsetting whatever local customs were with her shorts and tank tops. Hard to even imagine it being summer in Johannesburg. Harder still to imagine she was going there.

To Africa, of all places. So much for saying *never*.

Tickets. Mom was on it. Chelsea shuddered to think of the cost without catching a sale.

The fundraiser tomorrow. She'd have to hope she'd done a good enough job pulling everything together. Better call Greta and see if she could manage the remainder. Greta. Had she heard from her husband?

Chelsea tapped through the call, put her cell on speaker, and tossed it on the bed.

Keanan.

Him going to Africa and *dying* was not on the agenda. She buried her face in her hands as the phone rang over and over. The call went to voice-mail. Chelsea snatched up her phone and asked Greta to call her asap. Threw the phone back at the bed.

She crumpled to her knees. *Oh, God. Please save Keanan. Don't let him die.*

"Chelsea? Sweetie?" Fern.

Chelsea could barely summon the energy to slump the rest of the way to the floor and look up at Keanan's mother, framed in the bedroom doorway.

In a few strides, Fern crossed the room and knelt beside her, gathering her in her arms. "Oh, Chelsea."

She'd kept the tears at bay for several hours, but no more. She grabbed Fern and clung to her while deep sobs wracked them both. As the tears eased, Fern began to pray aloud — fervently and passionately — for her son.

Some of the panic and fear began to ease. Vince had been right. Fighting God on this wasn't worth it. If her faith gave in at the first sign of trouble, it wasn't real faith. First sign of trouble? Keanan might die! No. She'd trust God. She would. She'd be calm and hold on.

Chelsea took a long deep breath and managed to release it without shuddering. Again. Again.

Her phone rang and she swiped it on. "Chelsea here."

"This is Greta. Anders says you are heading to Pretoria." The phone was still on speaker.

"Yes. As soon as I can get a flight."

"Do not worry about the event tomorrow. I will make sure it runs smoothly. It will give me something to concentrate on while I pray for Anders and your Keanan."

Fern leaned toward the phone. "This is Fernanda, Keanan's mother. I'll help you, Greta. I've come over from Salem to help Chelsea."

"Thank you. How are you holding up?"

"Clinging to God for my only son. I pray God will restore his health."

"Where two or three are gathered together in prayer, Jesus promised to be in our midst."

Chelsea's mind shot back to the last Sunday in Idaho, when half the church gathered around Keanan to pray for his mission.

Sierra had been keeping the church in the loop the past few days. Many more than two or three were gathered in Jesus' name in Idaho. The Portland church's prayer team was also on overtime.

"Chelsea? We need to get to the airport. Your flight leaves in three hours." Mom stood in the doorway.

"Keep in touch, Chelsea," came Greta's voice from the phone. "We will not cease praying."

"Thank you. Thank you for everything. And thank God your husband was right there."

"Yes. Through it all, God is good. Hold onto that." The line went dead.

Chelsea stared at her half-packed bag. "What else do I need?"

"Charging cords," said Fern. "A camera so you can send us photos. Your Bible."

Chelsea grabbed her purse and pulled out the pack of index cards Keanan had given her. The precious words of God's love to her. She was going to need those.

Mom folded clothes and put them into the carryon. "I think you've got everything."

"I've forwarded the emails from Vince, so you have his email address. Please get him the details of my flights."

Mom nodded. "I've got it. One last time, Chelsea Marie. Are you sure about this trip?"

Chelsea raised her chin and looked her mother in the eye. "I have to do it."

"You'll be switching planes in JFK. Alone."

"I know. I'm not a child."

"I didn't say you were, but you'll always be my baby girl. I wish I could come with you."

Fern pulled Chelsea and her mom into a hug. "I do, too. If only I hadn't let my passport lapse."

Chelsea took in a deep breath. "I *have* to go. Not just because Keanan needs to know I love him, but because sometimes we have to act our faith. If this is a test for me, and Keanan's life is at stake, I can't *not* obey."

"That's not how God works, sweetie."

"We don't know that. He asked Abraham to sacrifice Isaac. God needs to see that I love Him enough to face my fears and do what I know is right." Her voice faltered. "Without knowing the outcome."

"Then let's head for the airport." Mom turned to Fern. "Would you like to come along for the ride?"

"Please. I appreciate that."

oOo

The red-eye to New York. A few hours to fight her way to the other section of the airport for her flight to Johannesburg. Nearly fifteen hours in the air, trying to sleep, and reading through the index cards over and over every time she was awake. She'd laminated them her first day in Portland, before they wore right out. Thankfully the man next to her had his headphones on the entire trip. She didn't want to talk anyway.

It was morning local time. What was that back in Portland? Late evening Saturday? Somehow the event at home had happened without her while she was somewhere over the Atlantic. It didn't even matter.

Chelsea grabbed her carryon and her huge purse and headed for the inner sanctum of the airport. No checked luggage, so nothing could be lost, and no time would be wasted while Vince waited for her. It still seemed to take forever to clear customs.

Vince. She didn't even know what the man looked like. She scanned the waiting crowd to see a balding Caucasian man starting toward her.

"Chelsea?"

"Yes. You must be Vince."

"I found photos of you on Keanan's laptop. I hope you don't mind."

There couldn't be anything too incriminating. "No problem. How is he?"

Vince reached for her carryon. "The truck is out this way. Let's go."

She scurried after him, trying to squelch the worry that soared once again.

A few minutes later he tossed her bag into the back of a battered jeep. She jerked open the passenger door only to discover the steering wheel. She backed up a step.

"Other side," said Vince. "South Africans drive on the left."

She'd wasted precious seconds. Chelsea jogged around the vehicle and hopped into the other side. It felt so wrong. Backwards. Upside down, like her entire life.

She hadn't imagined Africa like this. South Africa, she amended. This looked like a regular modern city, at least until they pulled up to a traffic light and young black children ran toward her window, holding out their hands.

Vince flicked her a few coins, and she stared at him, aghast. "You want me to give this to them?"

"Sure, why not? Jesus took care of the poor and needy."

She rolled the window down and distributed the coins as the light turned green. The jeep surged forward, and the children dashed for the curb. At the next intersection a black man held up a sign: *I would rather die of hunger than steal.* Was he a drug addict conning, as would likely be the case back home?

Vince handed her money, and she passed it out the window to the man's grateful smile. It wasn't her place to judge here. Guilt smote her. It wasn't her place at home, either.

Chelsea eyed Vince. "Tell me about Keanan. I've been out of touch for almost two days getting here." Surely if things were worse, he'd have said so. Wouldn't he?

"He's mostly stable. He's been up and down all week. That's all I know. Dr. van Leeuwen will be able to tell you more. They think Keanan has some mutated superbug."

She latched onto the word *stable*. That was good. Up, talking, and laughing about the scare he'd given them would be even better. Rubbing it in that he'd gotten her to Africa after all. "They're closer to a diagnosis," she ventured.

Vince nodded curtly. "We can only pray that is true."

Why was the man so pessimistic? Maybe it was just his personality. "Is there something else you should tell me before I see him?"

"You'll have to talk to Dr. van Leeuwen about seeing Keanan."

She swiveled in the seat to see him more clearly. "But I've come all this way. Of course he will let me in."

Vince bit his lip and shot her a glance. "That'll be up to him, I guess. He'll do what's best for his patient."

How could this man possibly think that she might not be able to see her beloved? Hold his hand? Whisper *I love you* in his ear? Thankfully it was the doctor who would decide, not Vince.

Less than an hour later the vehicle jolted to a stop in a parking lot near a gigantic red overhang in front of two square buildings.

"Come on." Vince jumped out of the truck and threw her carryon into the cab.

As soon as she'd shut the passenger door, he locked it down and led the way across the lot, Chelsea all but jogging at his heels. "Vince! Tell me what the panic is. Please."

He paused in the shadow by the door. "Very few people survive superbugs, Chelsea. Keanan is not out of the woods yet. Let's go find Dr. van Leeuwen."

oOo

An hour later Chelsea entered the isolation room, scrubbed and swathed in a mask and gown. She was braced for anything.

At least, that's what she thought until she saw Keanan reduced to a long thin lump on a white bed. The bit of his bloated face she could see held little more color than the sheets. Hoses and lines connected him to gadgets and pumps from various parts of his body.

If it hadn't been for Dr. van Leeuwen beside her, she might have wobbled right off her sensible shoes.

"Please remember the sedation is for his own good. He's not in a natural coma," the doctor said. "It's much easier for him to rest and get well if he isn't fighting the tubes and lines. We're hoping and praying there will be no additional infection. So far so good."

Sounded like something she should be glad about, but it was hard to muster up happy thoughts when he truly looked a mere breath away from eternity.

"The tube you see in his mouth is to help him breathe. Vince says he explained that to you?"

She nodded.

He pointed at Keanan's chest. "This tube is draining excess fluid from behind his lungs. He's looking a bit less bloated now."

Less? Hard to imagine what more would've looked like. She took another unsteady step toward the bed.

"Right now we're running a broad spectrum antibiotic through the IV. As soon as we get a diagnosis, we can zero in more accurately, but it's too dangerous to experiment." Dr. van Leeuwen shook his head, lost in thought. "We'll reduce one of the sedatives today and see how he does. You might be able to talk to him, but even then he won't be able to reply beyond a hand squeeze or gesture. We can't risk removing the ventilator. He's not strong enough to breathe for himself."

"Okay." She sucked in air. The room tilted slightly, as though she wasn't strong enough to breathe, either. No. She had this. God had this.

The doctor spoke to one of the nurses in the room, who adjusted a machine.

"You may sit here for a time." He indicated a chair on Keanan's right. "Don't touch anything but his hand. If there are any changes, we'll know and be at his side in just a split second. Trust me. We are not leaving him unattended, ever. If one nurse needs to use the washroom, another sits in."

That was more worrisome than comforting. Chelsea sagged onto the chair. She must be a sight, having been in the same clothes for two days and nights with only a few snatches of sleep. She reached for Keanan's hand.

"I'm here, sweetheart. It's Chelsea."

No response, but then she'd been told not to expect one.

"You got your way. I'm here in Africa. Good thing I had a passport, right?"

Yeah. That was so not funny.

"I need to tell you how much I appreciate the note cards you made me. I've read them a hundred times. Maybe a thousand. I needed that many reminders this week of God's love." She let out a shaky laugh. "Good thing I laminated them, or we couldn't have disinfected them to bring them in your room. I don't mind telling you I've had my doubts about God's love, but hey, I'm here. I'm hanging on. I believe."

She stroked his limp hand. Would she ever feel those fingers running through her hair again? Be clasped tightly in his arms? Would those puffy lips ever caress her own?

Please God. Restore Keanan. You know he has so much more to do for You.

"Here, let me read some of them to you. Maybe they'll give you strength now as they've done for me." She fumbled in her pocket for the pack and focused on the one on top. "Here's Zephaniah 3:17. Remember writing this one out for me? The Eternal your God is standing right here among you, and He is the champion who will rescue you." She paused to swallow the lump in her throat. Keanan needed that champion. Desperately. She blinked back the tears so she could read the rest of the words. "He will joyfully celebrate over you. He will rest in His love for you. He will joyfully sing because of you like a new husband."

The kind of husband she'd dreamed Keanan could be for her. That's what God was to both of them. A champion for both. Celebrating over both. Resting in His love for both.

She took another wavering breath and focused on his closed eyes. "Keanan, I love you, but God loves you so much more. I need you to know that I'm here. That people are praying for you. That God is your champion."

Man, she was bad at this kind of talk. If only he'd open his eyes and acknowledge her presence. She could pour out her heart even if he couldn't talk past that vent in his mouth, if only he could hear her. Understand. Love her with his eyes. His fingers.

Had he shifted slightly? Were those eyelids trying to open?

The doctor had mentioned lowering the sedation. Would that have an immediate effect?

The door behind her opened and the nurse reappeared. Whatever he said was lost in the heavy accent.

Chelsea shook her head.

The nurse pointed at Keanan, whose eyelids were definitely fluttering.

She surged to her feet and leaned a little closer, careful not to touch any of the tubes and lines connecting him to the machines.

"Keanan? It's me, Chelsea. I'm here for you."

His eyes latched onto hers for a split second before they closed again.

For now, it was enough.

Chapter 32 --

*D*r. van Leeuwen rested his hand on Chelsea's shoulder, and she jerked upright in the waiting room. They'd sent her out while they bathed Keanan's fevered skin. "Do you have a place you can go and rest? Vince said the team is staying at the mission home not too far from here."

Vince. Where was he? Chelsea tried to pull her thoughts into some sort of coherency. She glanced at her watch, but with all the time zones she'd covered, it didn't tell her anything helpful.

"We'll be taking Keanan down for another CT scan in about half an hour." Dr. van Leeuwen pulled a chair close to Chelsea and sat down. His dark gray eyes looked at her with compassion. "I admit I am concerned about his progress. In my field I'm considered something of an expert. I am also a Christian and do not believe in coincidences. I believe that God put me here, at this time, to save Keanan's life. You need to know this could have happened to him anywhere. In Galena Landing, you may not have been able to get him to a larger hospital in time."

Chelsea rubbed her hands up and down her suddenly chilled arms. "This isn't some African disease?"

"Unlikely. We know now it is a gram-negative bug — a superbug — but the treatment isn't the same for all. We don't dare give him the wrong medications." The doctor looked away then back to Chelsea. "His chances are much better if we simply let the machines do their work while we await results. At least we know now that he isn't contagious. That's something."

"Why is it taking so long?" Chelsea couldn't help the words. Didn't doctors know everything?

"We've sent samples to several labs for analysis. Some of the tests take time to incubate for conclusive results. Some have already come back negative and we've gathered other samples."

Tears welled up in Chelsea's eyes. She'd been so strong. At least it felt like it to her.

"Sitting here with your young man, it may seem like nothing is being done other than monitoring. Nothing is farther from the truth, Chelsea. In his room, the important thing is to keep him alive and as comfortable as possible. Outside ICU, doctors and lab technologists and researchers around the world are analyzing results, discussing options via Skype, and working as an extensive team to win this battle."

The magnitude staggered her. "For Keanan."

"Yes. For Keanan. But every time we win a battle like this, we learn more how to win it faster the next time. More conclusively. Medicine has made great strides in the last century, but there is still much we do not know. Whatever Keanan contracted is extremely rare, but he is in God's hands. I hope that is as much comfort to you as it is to me."

She stared at him dully. "You're saying he still might not survive this." How could she fly back to the US if he died? She'd have to arrange for his body to be taken home. She might have once planned Allison's parents' funeral, but she couldn't do it for Keanan. She couldn't.

"There are never guarantees." The doctor ran his hands through thinning salt-and-pepper hair. "In the six days since Keanan arrived in ICU, they've lost four patients. An elderly woman from kidney failure, a young man from a lion mauling, and two men from a vehicle accident. None of us knows when our days on Earth will be done." He smiled wanly at Chelsea. "It's my job to make sure people like Keanan don't go before their time."

The words made sense in one way. Chelsea remembered her Aunt Pam, who'd died too young of uterine cancer. The friends from high school who'd been killed in an avalanche on a ski trip. But... Keanan. Not him. *Please, Lord.*

Dr. van Leeuwen rose. "As your attending physician, I order you to get several hours of sleep. I will call Vince myself to take you from this hospital. I will have someone phone you immediately if you are needed here. At any rate, it will be over an hour before he's back from the scan. His fever is still high — worrisomely so — and we've increased the level of sedation."

Chelsea sucked in air. If only her world would stop spinning. She blinked, trying to focus.

Dr. van Leeuwen tapped into his phone. As from a great distance, she heard him ask Vince to send someone for her. "Chelsea, don't come back for at least five hours if I don't call you, okay? Get rest. A shower. Food. You'll be no good to Keanan when he begins his recovery if you are too exhausted to cope."

A shower? Chelsea touched her tangled curls. She must look a sight for the distracted doctor to notice. She wanted to argue — desperately — but he was right. She was too tired to fight his orders.

"I'll ask Ross to take you to where you'll meet Vince." Dr. van Leeuwen rested his hand on her arm. "Prayers for Keanan fill my thoughts."

Chelsea took off her glasses — man, those things needed

cleaning — and swiped her sleeve across her eyes to catch the tears. Her makeup was probably a disaster, too. "Thank you." A sudden thought hit her. "Are *you* getting any sleep?"

The doctor gave her a tired smile. "Not a lot. There is a bed here where I can retreat for an hour or two as the situation allows. People who can't function on irregular sleep rarely make it through medical school." He glanced at a young black man dressed in navy standing nearby. "Here's Ross. Off you go. I'll talk to you again in a few hours."

Chelsea allowed herself to be led away, the pain of separation from her beloved deepening with every step. Everything in her screamed to disobey the orders for rest, but she didn't have the energy to fight back.

oOo

Keanan blinked and slowly opened his eyes. Where was he? Why was he lying in a semi-darkened room he couldn't remember seeing before? Chelsea! Where was she? Had he dreamed her nearness?

He tried to get to his elbows and couldn't even raise his shoulders off the bed. Couldn't lift his hands. He tried to see why not, but it was too much effort.

"Easy now, young man. Relax."

Simple for that deep voice to say. He wasn't the one with not even a trickle of energy in his veins. He heard a beep and then footsteps.

A second face loomed beside the first. Both unfamiliar. He should really stop reading crime novels. He didn't have any secrets that interrogation could reveal. They had the wrong guy.

"Keanan? Dr. van Leeuwen will be here in a minute. How are you feeling?"

Keanan tried to make a sound but something clogged his mouth. His hands refused to lift and remove whatever it was.

"Relax. I know you can't answer with the ventilator hose. Can you hear me? Understand me? Blink twice."

That he could do. The voice was in heavily-accented English. Like... something he couldn't remember.

"Good, good. Vital signs are positive. And here is Dr. van Leeuwen." The black man stepped aside as another took his place.

"You've been a very sick man, Keanan Welsh. Remember meeting me on the plane into Joburg? Two blinks."

Keanan stared at him. Was this familiar? He shook his head slightly.

The doctor nodded. "I'm not surprised with all that's happened. Many of us are thanking God that I was here in Pretoria when you became ill. It's enabled the top infection specialists in the world immediate access to your test results. We're working hard to make you well."

"Chelsea?" Only the word couldn't come out past the tubes. Why were there tubes?

"The ventilator is to help you breathe. I know you have questions for me, young man. I'll try to answer them, but you won't likely recall the answers. That's okay."

Keanan tried to pour question marks from his eyes even while his lids drooped.

"Maybe it will be a comfort to know that your fiancée is here. I sent her to get a bit of rest. I'm sure she didn't get much on the flight and she's been here twenty-four hours already. She'll be back."

Chelsea? In Africa? Impossible. He shook his head slightly.

The doctor grinned. "She will. You'll see. But for now, you need to get more rest yourself. You've got a big battle going on, but we're going to win this one. Trust in God, Keanan. Hold the faith."

Hold the faith. The room began to slide back into oblivion. Chelsea. God. Yes.

oOo

Chelsea paced the corridor outside ICU. "Why didn't you call me? I needed to see him. Talk to him. Know he knew I was here."

"There wasn't time. He was only alert for a few minutes." The doctor ran his hands through his hair. "We have a name for the bug he caught."

She stopped so suddenly she nearly stumbled. "What is it?"

"Nothing you've ever heard of, I'm sure. It's extremely rare."

"You already said it was."

"Fusobacterium Necroforum."

He was right. She'd never heard it before.

"I know you'll want to run a search." He pressed a paper with the long words scrawled on it into her hands. "The results will terrify you. I guarantee it. You need to remember he's already beat the odds by staying alive for over a week."

Chelsea drooped against the wall. "He still might d-die?"

"Now that we know how to treat it, we should soon see marked improvement, but the odds are still stacked against him. His fever is still high. He's fighting both the bacteria and pneumonia. We've added a central line to speed the targeted antibiotics straight to his heart, so don't be alarmed to see another tube in his body." The doctor rested his hand on her arm. "Keep praying, Chelsea. Let your people know back home that we expect him to turn a corner very soon."

From what he'd said, it could be either corner. To health, or... no, she wouldn't go there. "Thank you for everything you're doing. I can't even begin to tell you—" She choked back a sob.

"Read Psalm 27, Chelsea. Claim it. Read Scripture to Keanan as well, if you haven't been. We don't know how much he can

279

absorb while under sedation, but we must always assume a patient's understanding is higher than it seems. That's why we're never talking about the tough stuff in his room."

"Psalm 27?" She had a bunch of Bible versions on her phone app. Which was Keanan's favorite again? The Voice.

She took her place beside Keanan's bed and ran her fingers down his arm and hand. Unresponsive. She couldn't get close enough to his face to kiss him without disturbing wires and hoses and gadgets. Definitely not an option.

"Keanan, love? It's Chelsea. Dr. van Leeuwen said he'd talked to you a couple of hours ago. That you were awake for a bit. Did he tell you I'm here? I came because I love you." No discussing the terror, the trauma, or the fact that he still might not survive.

"I'm going to read to you. The doctor suggested Psalm 27, so here goes. Ready?"

Had she expected a response? No, but one would certainly be welcome.

"The Eternal is my light amidst my darkness and my rescue in times of trouble, so whom shall I fear? He surrounds me with a fortress of protection, so nothing should cause me alarm."

Her eyes skipped forward over a few verses. "His house is my shelter and secret retreat. It is there I find peace in the midst of storm and turmoil. Safety sits with me in the hiding place of God. He will set me on a rock, high above the fray."

Chelsea didn't feel like she was above the battle but in the thick of it. She took a deep breath. No. God was a shelter. He was giving her the ability to see Keanan like this without dissolving into a full-on mess.

"God lifts me high above those with thoughts of death and deceit that call for my life. I will enter His presence, offering sacrifices and praise. In His house, I am overcome with joy as I sing, yes, and play music for the Eternal alone."

Memories of the night baby John was born slammed into her sideways. Of the times since then when Keanan had allowed her to listen in while he worshiped the Eternal.

She read the next verse to herself. *I cannot shout any louder. Eternal One — hear my cry and respond with Your grace.* She kept scanning. Surely the doctor hadn't meant to read all of this to Keanan, not after his admonition to keep the talk positive.

Chelsea thumbed off the phone and pulled out the index cards. She turned the laminated edges and read aloud all the promises of God's love that Keanan had written out for her in his bold handwriting.

She ran her fingers over the veins in his hand. "I love you so much, Keanan. I need you to know that. To believe it. But what I'm most thankful for is how you led me back to Jesus. Knowing you has changed my life completely. Forever."

Had she imagined it? Had his fingers really moved? She focused on his face. On his green eyes peering back at her.

Should she tell someone he was awake? Too late. A nurse swished past her. "Ah, there you are, young man. Remember the tubes are there to help you breathe, so you mustn't touch them."

How could he? Chelsea hadn't missed the restraints on his wrists.

Keanan's eyes tracked the nurse and blinked twice. Then he turned his head a fraction of an inch and focused on her again.

"I love you, Keanan." She tangled her fingers with his and felt him try to turn his hand to grasp hers. "It's okay, my love. Everything is going to be all right."

Chapter 33 --

Not too much longer in this cubicle, then." The male nurse wheeled Keanan back after removing the ventilator. "Look at you, breathing for yourself and all that."

"When can I go home?" The words coming through Keanan's throat were raw and hoarse.

"That might be a bit yet. You're from America, right? First, let's think about getting you to a bed on the general ward."

He'd gotten the idea that he'd been very sick. So much of the past few days seemed hazy, but one thing Keanan knew for sure. The angel with the golden curls and blue eyes at his bedside nearly every time he awoke was his Chelsea.

She'd come all the way to South Africa. Nothing was wrong with his memory of the autumn months in Idaho. Africa was the last place she wanted to go yet she was here. Because of his illness, whatever that was.

"Your young lady will be here in a few minutes, so let's get you cleaned up before she arrives."

Keanan nodded and allowed Ross to care for him, as helpless as baby John who could only lie there and accept the ministrations of others. Zach and Jo's infant had loving parents to meet his every need. Keanan had God, several skilled doctors and nurses…

and an angel.

So much to be thankful for. His eyelids drooped by the time the nurse finished. It seemed like he'd put in a full day's work at Green Acres rather than lying like a lump on a log while someone washed him and changed his sheets.

"Keanan? You're off the vent!"

His eyes sprang open and he turned his hand palm up on the sheets. "Chelsea," he croaked.

Her gaze took in the machines and lines that still connected him then she threaded through them and leaned over him, clutching his hand, nuzzling her lips against his cheek.

He lay very still — not that he had much choice — and absorbed her presence. Her touch. What had the psalmist said? He'd heard it somewhere recently. *I will move past my enemies with this one, sure hope: that with my own eyes I will see the goodness of the Eternal in the land of the living.*

This was the goodness of God at work. He was alive and the woman he loved was pressed against him.

He turned his face toward hers, feeling her tears on his cheeks. "Chelsea," he whispered. "Don't cry. God is good."

"He's amazing." Her voice caught. "Oh, Keanan. It's so good to see you without that tube. To see you awake."

He couldn't overcome the grip of her hand to squeeze back. But there was no need. Just this once, he'd accept all her love and kisses and tears, and simply revel in the brush of her curls against his face.

After a moment she pulled back enough to wrap his cheeks between her hands and look deeply with all the intensity of her blue eyes.

His emotions swirled and tears prickled his eyes. He'd never seen her like this. Had he? The guardedness was gone. The Chelsea here in this room was fully present. No reserve.

She brushed her lips against his then wiped his eyes with her thumbs. "Don't cry, Keanan. I'm here. Everything is going to be all right."

"But how? Why?" If only he could remember what had happened. But everyone — Dr. van Leeuwen, the nurse, and now Chelsea — seemed happy. Said things were better.

"You've been very sick, my love. Vince sent for me, and I came. I've been right here as many hours a day as they would let me."

A memory simmered. "Reading the Bible."

She nodded. "Reading the cards you made me. Reading the Psalms." Her fingers combed through his hair, still damp from the sponge bath. "God loves you, Keanan. He loves me."

He rolled his head to one side, capturing her hand beneath his cheek. "I know. He really does." With supreme effort, he lifted one hand and touched her. "I love you, too."

o0o

Keanan drifted back to sleep with a slight smile on his face and his fingers still tangled with hers. She tucked her toe around the chair's leg to scoot it at an angle so she didn't have to relinquish that touch.

He was off the ventilator. He was breathing on his own. Other machines still took care of assorted life-sustaining needs, but that fact didn't negate this huge victory.

Chelsea closed her own eyes. Easier to pray without the distraction of the beautiful man in the bed beside her. To allow herself to wonder, for the first time, about things at home. Home in Oregon, home in Idaho. She needed to send an email and let everyone know this first huge sign of Keanan's recovery. It could wait a few more minutes.

How long had she been here? The days and nights were likely as jumbled in her mind as they were in Keanan's. She'd

284

experienced nothing of Africa beyond the traffic between the mission headquarters and the hospital.

Keanan wouldn't be up for crossing the Atlantic for a while yet. Dr. van Leeuwen hadn't said that, but Chelsea wasn't born yesterday. Keanan would have to be well enough to sit for hours and navigate airports.

Christmas!

She bolted upright in her chair and let go of Keanan's hand. What day *was* it, anyway? She thumbed on her phone. December 24.

Christmas Eve.

She was going to be in South Africa for Christmas. Sitting in a hospital still, no doubt. She couldn't stop the giggle that erupted. Who could have known this was exactly where she wanted most to be?

oOo

Keanan shuffled down the hospital corridor, pushing a wheeled pole with his intravenous bag on it. His other hand was caught in Chelsea's strong grip.

"Merry Christmas!" called a nurse.

"Is it really Christmas?" Keanan leaned closer to Chelsea. "I don't have a gift for you." He frowned, searching his memory. "I was going to send something back to Portland with Dr. van Leeuwen but I don't remember if I bought it yet."

"Seeing you up and walking with only one line stuck in your body is all the gift I need." Chelsea's blue eyes, looking up at him, glistened with tears. "I didn't bring anything for you, either. I was on my way to the airport less than an hour after I knew I had to come."

"You brought yourself. That's so far beyond a gift that it's a treasure." Keanan draped his arm over her shoulders. How he wished he had more strength, though this was a far cry from when he awakened a couple of days ago. Patience. He'd get stronger every day until he could twirl Chelsea right off her feet. He couldn't help the grin spreading across his face.

"We'll pretend it's Christmas when we get back home." The image of his little round house covered with snow beckoned him. Was there any doubt now she'd be his wife, living there with him before Christmas came around again?

He could ask.

But of all the ways he'd dreamed of placing his future — his very soul — at her feet, this wasn't one of them. Who could have planned this?

"Keanan! Chelsea! Good to see you both."

Keanan glanced up to see Vince coming toward them. "Merry Christmas, Vince."

"And a merry Christmas to you, too." Vince gave him a gentle thump on the back. "The team just got back from Mozambique. So many people now can use the sun for power and learn to know the Son of God."

The group had gone on without Keanan. Of course they had. No way would he have wanted them to sit around in Pretoria waiting until he could rejoin them. Good thing, too. Who knew when he'd be able?

They didn't really need him. They'd obviously found a translator after all. The realization hit him like a punch to the gut. Did that mean it had been his own stubborn idea to come on this trip? But no. Look who was here, tucked under his arm. Chelsea.

Romans 8:28 had never come clearer in his mind. *We are confident that God is able to orchestrate everything to work toward something good and beautiful when we love Him and accept His invitation to live according to His plan.*

If all this had been necessary to bring Chelsea into a closer walk with God, it was worth it. Absolutely worth it. Keanan could only be thankful that his own death had not been required. Asked, though, he'd have given it. He loved her that much.

With a start he realized Vince and Chelsea still exchanged words, and he scrambled to catch up to the conversation.

"That would be great." Chelsea hugged Vince. "I'm sure Keanan would like some home cooking by now himself."

Keanan shook his head to clear his thoughts. "Pardon me?"

"Vince offered to bring Christmas dinner up for us later." A funny look crossed her face. "I'm guessing that won't be roast turkey."

Vince chuckled. "Sure it will. Our colonialist roots will show, after all. I can't guarantee all the side dishes will be what you are used to, but there's the fun of it, right?"

Keanan held his breath as he watched his beloved.

"I can't wait to see what you come up with. Thanks, Vince."

Whew. She really had changed. Keanan hugged her against his side. "Yes, thank you. I only hope it is not you who is cooking."

His team leader grinned. "I will be doing my share for sure. If you want only food others have prepared, you will miss the best parts."

"Then bring it on."

Vince nodded at them both then turned away, disappearing a moment later through the doors at the end of the ward.

Chelsea's arm tightened around him. "You're looking tired." She steered him toward the row of metal chairs lining the hallway.

He'd like to argue with her, but couldn't.

oOo

Nurses arrived for shift change at the nearby nursing station. Nurses Chelsea now knew by name, mostly black women wearing navy uniforms and genuine smiles. A low hum began from behind the desk and, in seconds, the women began to sing *Rise Up Shepherd and Follow*. No one seemed to be leading the music.

Chelsea's spine tingled as they continued their tasks and the sweet words harmonized. From there the nurses launched into *Sweet Little Jesus Boy*.

Sometimes she could imagine she'd step out of this hospital and into a chilly Portland day. The carols — even though not the ones she knew best — reminded her of home, where in a few hours her family would awaken on Christmas morning and exchange gifts. At Green Acres, her sister and friends would gather in the straw bale house and share Noel's famous French toast. Allison and Brent must be back from their honeymoon by now, becoming a true family with young Finnley. It would be baby John's first Christmas, and Maddie would ricochet off of everything in her excitement.

In Africa? Keanan. Her love. Her life. She couldn't regret her rash decision to hop a plane and fly around the world for even half of a second.

"I have come to a strange realization," Keanan mused.

She tilted her head to look up at him. "Oh? What's that?"

"That carol said we should rise up and follow, and we should. But God doesn't need me to serve Him."

Chelsea frowned. "That doesn't sound quite right."

"Hear me out. He's perfectly capable of doing His work without Keanan Welsh. Look how sure I was the team needed me, yet they are doing the work of God without me."

He must be going somewhere with this, if she only sat tight and listened.

"The need is on my side. I obey, not because He needs me, but because I need Him. He has His own plans, if I'm willing."

She had to know. "Would you have come if you'd known you'd wind up in the hospital here fighting for your life?"

"It could have happened at home, too. This wasn't an African bug, but something that could happen to anyone, anywhere. Praise be to God, it very rarely does."

Chelsea nodded. "But would you?"

He drew her closer, if that were even possible. "Yes, my sweetheart. I would have."

"Why?"

Keanan brushed his lips across her forehead, causing a tingle that swept her body. "Two reasons. One, I had to obey."

"And the second?"

"For your sake." He sucked in his lower lip. "Tell me why you came. How did it happen?"

"Vince kept emailing me as you got worse. Being so far from you tore at me. I could think of little else but being at your side." She lowered her gaze and whispered, "Where I belong."

His cheek rested against her head, and she took a deep breath. "I felt as though God was asking me how much I loved Him. Enough to trust Him with you? Enough to go to Africa if He wanted me to?" She swallowed hard. "How could I say no when He said *go*?"

"Sweetheart."

She closed her eyes to gather strength then looked up at him. "Yes?"

"I love you, Chelsea Marie Riehl. You are the treasure God has brought into my life. You provided strength these past days, reading Scripture to me, praying with me, holding on for me." His fingers flexed against her side. "I don't remember much of the time I spent in ICU. In fact, that's about all I do recall. You gave everything for me."

His green eyes, alive again. Alive with love. His lips, once bloated and unmoving, smiling at her as he kissed her gently. Somehow she knew he had more to say, that she shouldn't keep those lips too occupied for a few minutes yet.

"Will you marry me, Chelsea? I know I'm not much good yet—"

"Yes."

"Dr. van Leeuwen says it may be months before I recov—"

She put her finger across his lips. "I said *yes*," she whispered and kissed him. "When doesn't matter. Where doesn't matter. I love you."

Epilogue ---

Chelsea turned the car into the driveway at Green Acres on a gray evening in late February. The team poured toward them, waving and yelling.

Keanan reached across the console and squeezed her hand. "Welcome home, my sweetheart."

This *was* home. The little grain-bin house she'd spurned would be her home soon, where she could lie in Keanan's king-size bed and look out the windows at the treetops in every direction. Unless she was too busy with her husband to look out windows.

Her face warmed as she parked in front of the duplex, still her home for a few more months.

Sierra yanked her car door open and pulled her out. "Chelsea! I've missed you so much. Welcome home."

On the other side of the car, the guys hauled Keanan to his feet in the late winter air. Thankfully, a bit gentler, though much of his strength had returned in the six weeks they'd been in Portland. Her parents had taken him in, hiring a part-time nurse to care for him and arranging for his physical therapy.

"Let me see that ring!" Allison tugged Chelsea's left hand into the open and whistled. "Wow, look at that! It's gorgeous."

"Keanan's mom made it for me." She still couldn't believe the amazing jewelry that had awaited her when Fern had met them at the airport along with Chelsea's parents. The beauty and craftsmanship of this engagement set was a league above the fundraiser donation, stunning as that had been.

"I'm so happy for you." Sierra squished her again.

"That's beautiful." Claire ran her fingers over the ring then grinned at Chelsea. "Too bad you had to chase it halfway around the world."

Chelsea glanced over at Keanan in the midst of the Green Acres men, with Finnley gazing up in adoration. "No chasing," she said. "Just — finally — putting myself and Keanan in God's hands."

Claire laughed and pulled her close. At least as close as they could get with that baby bump in the way. It wouldn't be long until Green Acres Farm would welcome its next addition.

"Uncle Keanan! Uncle Keanan!" yelled Maddie.

Chelsea glanced over to see him lift the toddler. Could she still call the child that? Madelynn had celebrated her third birthday while they'd been away. How time had flown.

"C'mere, you." Jo tugged Chelsea into a hug. "I've missed you. I'm so glad you are home where you belong." She pushed a well-wrapped bundle into Chelsea's arms. John wiggled and smiled at her with a toothless grin.

Chelsea gazed down at the baby's alert brown eyes. "He's gotten so big!"

The guys rounded the car and joined the women. Keanan plucked the baby out of Chelsea's arms and made faces at the little guy who chortled with glee.

Sierra hip-checked Jo away from Chelsea's other side. "So when's the big day? You must have set a date by now."

Now or never. She glanced up at Keanan. "We eloped."

"You *what?*"

"No way!"

"You can't do that!"

"I don't believe you."

Keanan slid his free arm around her and winked. "And why not?"

Sierra crossed both arms and tapped her foot. "You wouldn't do that to us. We are your wedding-planning team." She thumbed toward the other women. "I know what kind of celebration you've always wanted. Just because you got all brave and gallivanted halfway around the world doesn't mean you'd toss aside everything else you've ever wanted." Sierra narrowed her eyes. "Would you? I'll need to see that wedding certificate before I believe a word you say."

How much longer would they let Sierra spout? Chelsea raised her eyebrows at Keanan, and he leaned over to kiss her while Zach rescued the baby.

"Besides, Mom and Dad would have said something. You've been living with them, so there's no way they wouldn't know."

Chelsea wrapped both arms around Keanan's neck, tangled her fingers in the hair that tumbled to his shoulders once again, and kissed him back. Yeah, brazen, but at least her friends had someone to go home with and kiss. They'd all done it in front of her in the past when she had no one. That'd just been mean.

"Chels, joke's over. Did you or did you not elope?"

Keanan kissed Chelsea's nose. "No, we didn't." He kissed her lips, his gorgeous eyes twinkling as he focused on her.

"Did you — *what?* You brat!" Sierra smacked Chelsea's backside.

Keanan twirled Chelsea to his other side. "Hey now. No hitting my bride-to-be."

"Trust me, we certainly considered it." Chelsea laughed. "We knew what you'd be like."

Her sister's hands plunked to her hips as Gabe came up

behind her and slid his arms around her. He smirked and whispered something in Sierra's ear. She shook her head and leaned back, a little grin showing at last. "Okay, you had me for a minute there."

"Let's head on into the house," said Noel. "We've got a turkey dinner waiting. No one would let me keep the tree up for an extra two months, so it's not quite like Christmas, but we'll give it a try."

Chelsea kept her arm around Keanan as they joined the troop toward the steps. Not because he needed her support anymore, but because staying close to him was the best place in the world to be.

"I even made a pan of plum upside-down cake for dessert." Sierra bumped her hip against Chelsea's. "If I remember correctly, it was plums that brought you two together."

And Chelsea's entire world had been topsy-turvy for months afterward. Only in South Africa had it flipped right side up. Whichever direction she faced now didn't matter. Not with Keanan at her side as they both walked in God's abundant love.

The End

Recipe for Plum Upside-Down Cake ----

I may have given Aunt Pam Riehl credit for this delicious dessert in the novel but, in reality, it is my own concoction. I hope you enjoy!

Plum Upside-Down Cake

Fruit Layer:
3 tablespoons butter
1/3 cup brown sugar
1/2 teaspoon cinnamon
1/4 teaspoon cloves
dash nutmeg
Fresh or frozen Italian plums, pitted and halved (enough for one layer)

In a ten-inch oven-proof cast iron skillet, melt the butter and remove from heat. Swirl the butter up the sides so the cake won't stick. Mix the sugar and spices together, then stir into the melted butter and smooth the sauce. Arrange the halved plums cut-side down in the pan.

Alternatively, if you don't have a cast iron skillet, pour the melted butter into a 10" cake pan and proceed.

Cake Layer:

1/2 cup butter

1/2 cup organic white sugar

1/2 cup organic brown sugar

2 free-range eggs

1/2 teaspoon vanilla

1/2 teaspoon cinnamon

1/2 teaspoon salt

1/2 teaspoon baking powder

1/2 teaspoon baking soda

1/2 cup buttermilk OR 1/4 cup plain yogurt + 1/4 cup milk

1 1/2 cups organic white flour (up to 1/2 cup whole-wheat flour)

Preheat oven to 350 degrees.

Beat sugar and butter then add eggs and beat at medium until smooth. Add all but flour and beat 2-3 minutes. Add flour. Mix until well blended. This will be a fairly thick batter. Spoon it over the fruit in the skillet and level it.

Place in preheated oven and bake until a toothpick inserted in center comes out clean, about 45 minutes. Let sit off heat for 30 minutes before attempting to invert. Serve warm with vanilla ice cream, if you like.

Dear Reader ----------------------------

Do you share my passion for locally grown real food? No, I'm not as fanatical or fixated as our friends from Green Acres, but farming, gardening, and food processing comprise a large part of my non-writing life.

Whether you're new to the concept or a long-time advocate, I invite you to my website and blog at www.valeriecomer.com to explore God's thoughts on the junction of food and faith.

Please sign up for my monthly newsletter while you're there! My gift to all subscribers is *Peppermint Kisses: A (short) Farm Fresh Romance* that follows Wild Mint Tea in chronology. Joining my list is the best way to keep tabs on my food/farm life as well as contests, cover reveals, deals, and news about upcoming books. I welcome you!

Enjoy this Book? --------------------

Please leave a review at any online retailer or reader site. Letting other readers know what you think about *Plum Upside Down: A Farm Fresh Romance* helps them make a decision and means a lot to me. Thank you!

If you haven't read *Raspberries and Vinegar,* the first book in the series, with the story of Jo and Zach's romance, *Wild Mint Tea,* the second book, containing Claire and Noel's story, *Sweetened with Honey,* the third book with Sierra and Gabe's story, or Allison and Brent's story in the fourth book, *Dandelions for Dinner,* I hope you'll pick them up.

Keep reading for the first chapter of Liz and Mason's story, *Berry on Top,* the final book in the Farm Fresh Romance series.

Also, please join my email list to read *Peppermint Kisses,* a short story that takes place at Claire and Noel's wedding.

Berry on Top

A Farm Fresh Romance
Book 6

Valerie Comer

GreenWords Media

Chapter 1 --

*Y*ou have arrived at your destination."

"Come on, GPS," Liz Nemesek muttered. "At least pretend you're as nervous as I am."

She angled her rented car to the curb and stared at the small trim house with a neatly shoveled sidewalk holding back the snow. Number 74. This was her parents' new home? Even the street hadn't existed when she left Galena Landing.

She switched off the ignition and took a deep breath. The curtain beside the wrought-iron numbers twitched then fell. An instant later the front door swung open and a gray-haired woman ran out, arms outstretched.

Liz surged from the car. "Mom?"

She barely got the word out before she was rocked from side to side and squeezed breathless. Who knew Mom had so much strength in her?

"Liz. Oh, Lizzie, you've come home."

Liz's face was damp from either kisses or tears. Was Mom crying or was she? She hadn't planned on getting emotional. Hadn't expected to be treated like a prodigal daughter. Would a reunion feast in her honor be next?

"Come inside, Liz. Your daddy can't wait to see you. How long are you staying? Please say you're home for good." Mom looped an arm around Liz's waist and tugged her up the sidewalk. "Let me call your brother. Maybe he and Jo and the kids can come for dinner."

Third millennium version of the fatted calf. Check.

Liz took a deep breath and allowed Mom to tow her into the house. She blinked, adjusting to the dimness after the bright December sun. Her vision narrowed to her father as he struggled to rise from a leather recliner across the room.

"Lizzie Rose?"

Her heart hiccuped. Sure, news of the illness that devastated him had reached her in Thailand over six years before. Six years. How could she... No. She wouldn't let the guilt get her.

Would. Not. Let it. She was here now, and it had to be soon enough.

Liz blinked back tears. "Hi, Daddy." She closed the distance and wrapped her arms around him. That horrid disease—Guillain-Barré—had done a number on him. He seemed frail. Much older than his sixty years. She should've...

No guilt, Liz. No guilt. She just couldn't go there.

He hugged her close. "Good to see you, Lizzie Rose. How long are you staying?"

That question again. She kissed his cheek. "Not sure, Dad. We'll see."

His brown eyes searched hers. "You're welcome as long as you can. We have room. Always for you."

Liz pushed out a smile. "Thanks." Where that space might be, she couldn't guess. If her parents extended the dining room table — about the only piece of furniture she recognized from her childhood — it would take up half the living room. A tiny hallway revealed three doorways and no stairs.

Yeah, she wouldn't be able to stay with them more than a day or two. Certainly not long enough to figure out her life. Oh, who was she kidding? She'd been trying for the last decade and more. Why think she might nail it this week... or next?

"Zachary is stopping in on his way home from work. He says Madelynn was up all night sick, and he doesn't want to give us all her germs, so they won't be coming for supper today."

Maddie. A niece Liz hadn't met yet. How old was she? Three? Four? "I'm sorry she's not feeling well." But it would be easier seeing her brother alone than with his happy little family around him. She'd never have guessed Zach would get his degree in veterinary medicine and return to northern Idaho to buy out the old vet clinic. He'd wanted out of Galena Landing as badly as she had.

Who else had come back? Hopefully no one from her high school class.

"Would you like a cup of coffee? Or do you prefer tea?"

"Whichever you'd like. Really. I drink both."

"Or maybe hot apple cider. I know you used to like that."

Oh, man. Mom was fluttering. "It honestly doesn't matter."

"Or hot chocolate?"

"Mom..."

Mom dabbed her eyes. "I'm just so happy you're home. I can't believe you're really here. You look so nice. So tanned. Thailand must have agreed with you."

At times it had. Other times, not so much. Liz managed a smile. "It was a good place. A good job."

Dad shuffled over to the table and lowered himself into a seat. "Was? Are you home for good, then?"

Keep the smile on, Liz. "I'm moving back to the States permanently, yes, but I'm not sure exactly where I'll make my home. I've got some leads in California."

Biting her lip, Mom stared at her a moment before turning to put the kettle on.

"Galena Landing has really grown in the past twelve years." Dad folded his hands on the table. "You might find a good opportunity right here."

Trust Dad to have kept track of the exact amount of time. "I'll see." She might have to. The opportunity she'd returned to interview for in the Bay area had been offered to someone else. Life wasn't fair. It never had been and apparently wasn't starting now.

The kettle whistled, and Mom poured hot water into the teapot. At least that was still the same one Liz remembered from her childhood. Why couldn't her parents have kept the old Formica kitchen table and padded vinyl chairs instead of the formal dining table and wooden chairs? It seemed her parents had ditched everything when they moved to town.

Of course, she'd ditched everything when she moved to Thailand.

Not going there. She'd had good reasons, and one of them was her high school boyfriend. She'd managed to block him out of her mind — sometimes for weeks at a time — but not since driving north to Galena Landing. Being back in Idaho brought too many memories surging to the surface.

She didn't need a better reason to look for a job elsewhere. Mason would return to visit his parents, at least occasionally. Because everybody did that, except her. She'd poke around a bit, find out where he lived now, and find herself a new job somewhere across the country. The USA was big enough for both of them.

"Here you go, Liz. Cream? Sugar? Or maybe honey. We get buckets of it from Green Acres."

"Green Acres?"

"Where Grandma used to live. We sold the farm to three young ladies back before your dad got sick. Then your brother married one of the girls, and we've all been one big happy family ever since."

Right. One daughter had run away, but no big deal. Three

306

random strangers could take her place. *Way to go, Mom. How to make me feel valuable.*

"That's nice. I can't wait to meet everyone." It might not be exactly true, but it was appropriate. At least meeting her niece and nephew would be a good thing. She liked kids.

Picturing her big brother as a husband and father, though? That took a ton of imagination.

Mom removed a package of meat from the freezer and put it in the microwave.

"What kind of work are you looking for?" asked Dad.

The million-dollar question. How did a one-month course on how to teach English and more than a decade of experience in a foreign culture translate into a job back home? "I'm not entirely sure."

Dad nodded. "The feed store is looking for someone, or there's always Super One. Or you might be able to find a spot at Green Acres."

Her brother's commune? Not likely. Besides, what part of *not sure* did her parents not get? "I'll see what's available." Somewhere else. Liz rose. "If you're certain you have room for me for a few nights, I'll get my bags in from the car."

Mom turned, flapping her hands. "Oh, leave them. Zachary will be here in a few minutes. I know he won't mind getting them for you."

Liz opened her mouth, shut it again, and sat back down. Honestly, how long could she live like this? She'd once been able to talk to Dad, at least about everyday things. Mom, not so much.

A truck rumbled to a stop outside the house and a couple of doors slammed.

Mom rushed over to the door and opened it. The winter wind whistled in. "There's your brother now!"

Liz took a deep breath. She could do this. She stood and

took two steps closer before Zach stomped in wearing a down parka, knit cap, and mitts. He was followed by another man, equally bundled up, who shut the door behind him.

Liz reached for Zach, and he wrapped her against his cold coat. "Lizzie! Good to see you." He released her and smiled into her eyes for a second before turning. "You remember Mason Waterman?"

No. Couldn't be.

The other man pulled off his knit cap, revealing the blond hair and square jaw of someone she used to know far too well. His blue eyes warmed. "Hi, Liz. Welcome back to Galena Landing."

Not Mason. Anyone but him. Reports had him several states away. The room swam, and she grabbed Zach to stay upright.

oOo

Mason Waterman glanced at Steve, Rosemary, and Zach. They were all staring at Liz, who looked about to faint dead away.

Not the response he'd been going for, but perhaps not unexpected. He reached for the doorknob behind him. "I, uh, I'll just wait out in the truck."

That snapped Rosemary out of it. "No, Mason. It's too cold out there."

It wasn't all that cozy in here, either. At least not when Liz's narrowed eyes met his again. Her set jaw told him she remembered every minute that had passed between them in high school. He had plenty of regrets, but maybe this wasn't the right moment for apologies. After all, what did her family know about their past? By everyone's current confused response, he'd bet the answer was *nothing*.

"I just put on a pot of tea." Rosemary pointed back at the

kitchen. "And I baked chocolate chip cookies. Please don't rush off."

Zach shrugged out of his parka and kicked off his boots while Liz backed away. "We can stay a few minutes. Can't turn down homemade cookies, can we, Mason?"

At this moment, he'd have no trouble doing so.

Liz gripped the back of a dining chair with enough intensity to turn her knuckles white. There were no rings on her left hand. That was good, right? Or, no. It might have been better if she'd found some other guy. Gotten married. Had a few kids. That would've proven he hadn't hurt her too deeply.

Mason had skipped the wedding part and gone directly to having kids. A family hadn't been enough to keep him and Erin together, though. Man. Where would he even start explaining — let alone apologizing — to Liz? Erin certainly hadn't been open to hearing any of it.

Please, God. You've forgiven me for all the messes I've made. Is it too much to hope that Liz might, too?

By the look on her face, he'd better not hold his breath.

Mason slowly peeled off his coat and hung it in the nearby closet before removing his boots. Zach had already taken a seat at the table with a mug of tea in front of him. Liz still stood, her hands on the chair between her father and brother.

Keeping a buffer. He couldn't blame her. How could she have guessed he'd follow Zach in the door? She couldn't. Likely no one had even thought to tell her he and the kids had moved back to Galena landing. Their old crowd had dispersed long ago. No one knew or cared anymore about what had happened way back then.

Except Liz.

And him.

Mason took the chair on the other side of Zach and smiled at Rosemary. "Thanks for the tea."

"You're very welcome. What brings you along with Zach?"

He shrugged. "I dropped my car off at the shop to get a new transmission installed this morning. He offered me a ride for the next couple of days until it's ready."

"Handy you live so close then." Steve reached for a cookie then nudged the plate closer to Mason.

Liz's head came up and she glanced sharply from one to the other. She knew as well as he did that the Waterman farm was across the valley from her childhood home.

Steve turned toward Liz. "Mason's renting our old farmhouse from Green Acres. Did your mother tell you your brother and his group bought the home place?"

Her nod seemed a bit jerky, but her gaze flicked back to him. "That's nice." Not at all what her eyes said.

"Come out to the farm tomorrow for supper?" Zach asked Liz.

"Mom said your daughter was sick."

Zach chuckled. "Nothing keeps Maddie down for long. We do, however, try to remember that Dad has a compromised immune system, so we give him a buffer of a few days to make sure."

"You'll want to meet Jo and the children," said Rosemary.

Liz hadn't been home in how long? She'd taken her retreat to the Far East more seriously than Mason had realized.

She took a deep breath. "I, um, I could probably do that."

"And the rest of the gang," Steve put in. "Busy place they have out there."

"Th-the gang?" Liz's eyes flicked to Mason's then away.

"The other members of their community," Rosemary said.

"Um..."

Liz probably wanted to know if he'd be there for dinner. If he was part of the gang. Then she could find a way out. He wasn't going to make it that easy. Not until he'd found ten minutes of privacy to let her know how sorry he was.

He hadn't received an invite for tomorrow's meal yet, but it wouldn't be hard to wrangle one. He nudged the plate closer to her. "Want a cookie? Your mom hasn't lost her touch."

She shook her head. "No, thanks."

Rosemary jumped to her feet. "So sweet of you to say that, Mason. Let me send a few home for the twins."

Once again Liz's eyes snapped to meet his. "Twins?" The word came out more a breath than audible.

Mason tried to hold her gaze with sheer force of will. "Avery and Christopher. They're not quite seven."

A smile that didn't reach her eyes pushed at the corners of her mouth. "Well, congratulations to you and the missus."

Not what he wanted to get into in front of her family. "There is no Mrs. Waterman, Liz. Besides my mother."

"I'm sorry for your loss."

He was sorry, too, but the loss likely wasn't what Liz expected. "I've never been married."

"Then—" She clamped her mouth closed.

Mason took a deep breath. "My life didn't exactly turn out the way I'd intended when I was a teenager. Did yours?"

Twin red dots rose high in her cheeks. "That is none of your business, Mason Waterman. Excuse me, please. I need to get my things in from the car before it turns pitch dark."

"Let me do that." Zach pushed back his chair, glancing from one to the other as he snagged another cookie. "Staying in town long, Liz?"

Her eyes shot fiery darts at Mason. "Two or three days. Tops."

She wasn't going to make this easy, was she? But he'd do what it took to grab a few minutes. She had to hear him out.

Berry on Top releases in early 2016.
Join my email list to stay up to-date!

Author Biography

Valerie Comer lives where food meets faith in her real life, her fiction, and on her blog and website. She and her husband of over 30 years farm, garden, and keep bees on a small farm in Western Canada, where they grow and preserve much of their own food.

Valerie has always been interested in real food from scratch, but her conviction has increased dramatically since God blessed her with three delightful granddaughters. In this world of rampant disease and pollution, she is compelled to do what she can to make these little girls' lives the best she can. She helps supply healthy food — local food, organic food, seasonal food — to grow strong bodies and minds.

Her experience has planted seeds for many stories rooted in the local-food movement. The six-book Farm Fresh Romance series will close in 2016, but there will be many more tales to delight fans.

To keep up with what's happening next, visit her website at www.valeriecomer.com, where you can read her blog, explore her many links, and sign up for her email newsletter.